The Chronicles of Henry Roach-Dairier:
New South Dairy Colony 50
by
Deborah K. Frontiera

ISBN: 0-9753410-2-2
Library of Congress Control Number:
2004093108
Key words: 1. fiction 2. fantasy 3. insects 4. future worlds 5. young adult
6.adult
The Chronicles of Henry Roach-Dairier:
To Build a Tunnel
Second Edition
Published by Jade Enterprises
11807 S. Fairhollow Ln., Suite 106
Houston, Tx. 77043-1033
713-690-7626
Printed in the United States of America

Acknowledgements

Sincere thanks to all those who believed in the author and helped bring this work to its second edition.

Special thanks to these professionals:

Cover art by Korey Scott, Denton, TX
Cover design by Ira VanScoyoc, Emerald Phoenix Media, Manvel, TX

Looking Back:

In *To Build a Tunnel*, the first book of the trilogy, Henry narrates the story of his great-grandfather, an ant who, along with two other ants, was tricked by roaches into building better tunnels in Roacherian plastic mines. The ant colony realized too late that its members had been forced into slavery. The ants managed to solve the issue diplomatically, but were prepared for war.
ISBN 0-9753410-1-4

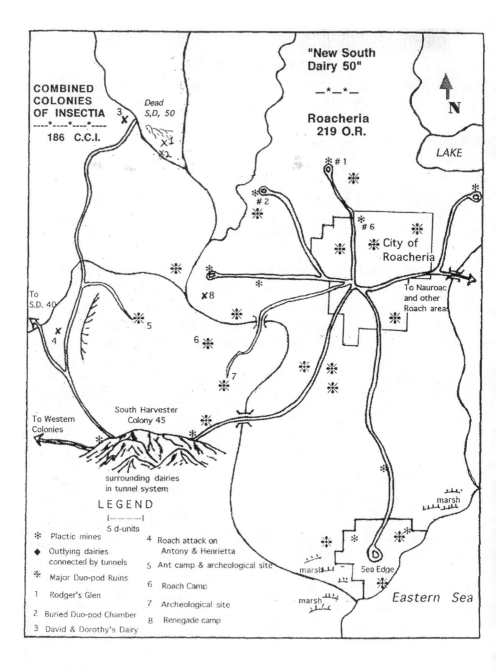

"New South
Dairy 50"

—*—*—

Roacheria
219 O.R.

N

LAKE

COMBINED
COLONIES
OF INSECTIA   *Dead*
—*—*—*—   3   *S,D, 50*
186 C.C.I.

* #1

* #2

* #6

* City of
Roacheria

To
S.D. 40

8

* 5

6 *

7

To Nauroac
and other
Roach areas

To Western
Colonies

South Harvester
Colony 45

surrounding dairies
in tunnel system

LEGEND

|———|
5 d-units

* Plactic mines
◆ Outlying dairies
  connected by tunnels
* Major Duo-pod Ruins
1 Rodger's Glen
2 Buried Duo-pod Chamber
3 David & Dorothy's Dairy

4 Roach attack on
   Antony & Henrietta
5 Ant camp & archeological site
6 Roach Camp
7 Archeological site
8 Renegade camp

marsh

marsh   Sea Edge

marsh

marsh   *Eastern Sea*

The Beginning:
as revealed to Daeira Dairier in dreams and meditation

In the beginning, Essence roamed the skies looking for the right place to start a world. She saw that our planet already had cycles of day and night, water and air. It had a set path around its sun so its cycles could be numbered, but it had no life.

I will see what can live and grow here," she said, and joined herself with it. The Creative Life Force of Essence endowed the waters with miniscule plants and creatures and the cycle of life began.

Essence cherished this new life, but was tired from her journey across the cosmos, so she entered the earth and went to sleep.

Eons later, when she awoke, the planet was filled with life forms. The water and land and air teemed with a great variety of plants and creatures. Some were tiny and frail, others huge and fierce. There was great variety even in their coverings—smooth, hard, scaly, furry. The large, scaly ones dominated at that time.

Essence watched her world. The sun fed the plants, which fed the moving creatures, who then were eaten by larger ones, and on and on. They grew, propagated, and returned to feed the earth when their time was over. Some creatures failed and disappeared, but new ones evolved to take their place.

And ants were there.

Essence, satisfied with the balance and cycles, cradled her world, and went to sleep again.

The pain of many shocks woke Essence. Chunks of matter hurled through the cosmos and struck the planet, killing millions of life forms and knocking the planet in its cosmic path. The dust from their impact screened the sun's light, denying life-giving energy to plants. Essence watched in dismay as thousands of species disappeared from her cherished world. In her grief, she shook. Hills tumbled. Mountains sent forth liquid fire from within.

But even in grief, Essence's Creative Life Force found its way again. An infinite variety of flowering plants came to be. A few species of the scaly creatures and the small ones with fur and feathers survived.

And ants were still there.

Essence watched for many eons as the fur creatures increased in size and began to dominate. "What would happen," Essence said, "if I interfered and gave one life form an advantage? If I gave a tad of my intelligence to a creature, could it create something original, as I have?"

Essence looked closely at each species and finally chose one that seemed different from others. This species was not entirely covered with fur, stood on only two appendages, and had a well developed nervous system. She infused them with more intelligence and waited to see what would happen.

Season cycles passed. Generations of Duo Pods came and went. Essence saw that they made tools, built things, and developed the planet. Their machines grew ever more complex. Satisfied, Essence took a nap.

Essence awoke with a fever. The planet's surface was a shambles. The air and the water were fouled. All the Duo Pods, all of the feathered creatures, and most of the furry ones were dead forever.

"What has happened to my world?" Essence cried.

Grief for her failed experiment and illness consumed Essence. The earth shook. Storms raged. Her tears covered many lands. Then slowly, the earth healed itself. Although it would take many more eons for all of the Duo Pod creations to return to the earth, the world looked new and fresh once more. Essence found that one substance the Duo Pods had made would not break itself down and feed the earth. They had indeed created something original. Her experiment had not been a total failure.

She looked around hopefully and found that ants, roaches and other insects were not only still there, but had to grown greatly in size and changed in other ways.

"Ah, my faithful ants," she said. "You have been with me from the earliest days and have always been civilized. Perhaps the intelligence I gave the Duo Pods was not enough. I will try again. I will give you not only the gift of knowledge, but my compassion as well. And this time, I will not sleep, but will watch over my world. I will be available to my creatures, speaking to their minds when they seek me. When each one's time on earth is done, the part of me that is in them will return to me in unity forever. Eat then, my ants, of the lasting creation of the Duo Pods—

plastic—and receive my gifts. Cherish my world and seek to understand its mysteries."

And so we are.

While Essence was speaking, a group of roaches approached. They took the gift of intelligence, but ran away before the second, more important gift of compassion and inner essence was given. Thus they received no more of Essence than had the extinct Duo Pods.

Bemused, Essence observed the roaches as they ran from her. "I must watch and see what comes of this development."

Prologue:
Henry Roach-Dairier

*M*y grandfather, Antony Dairier, was no ordinary ant. I had always known that, but I came to understand it in a very special way during my thirteenth summer when I made my final molt into an adult roach body.

I was the youngest of five, hatching after a space of six season cycles, while my brothers and sister had but a season cycle or two between them. I was not an easy creature to raise. I could be sly and deceitful, clever and conniving, and I enjoyed manipulating my parents to get exactly what I thought I wanted. I was very good at talking my way out of trouble, until that summer.

Only a creature who has been through it can fully understand the pain of molting. Ant larvae, who undergo complete metamorphosis, have no idea what it is to be trapped inside an exoskeleton that has become too small for one's body. They get a bit uncomfortable, whine for a few time frames, sleep seven season cycles, and wake up as adults. The crickets and other wild insects that grow up as nymphs, and the grasshoppers we raise for food at New South Dairy Colony 50, do not seem to be bothered as they molt. Maybe their nervous systems are not like that of a roach. We must endure molting four times between hatching and our twelfth or thirteenth season cycle.

I remember my father, the physician in our colony, giving me a potion to drink during my other molts. He was rarely around as I approached my final molt. In my usual impatient way, I decided to get it myself. I had often watched Allie when she assisted my father. I thought I could do better. During the late spring and early summer of that season cycle, I slipped into the dispensary at night several times and tried some interesting combinations of herbs that made me feel pretty good. One night, I was in so much pain I didn't look at what I grabbed. I simply dumped several things into a mug of honey dew and drank it.

It certainly took care of the pain. I wanted to laugh and float away on an imaginary cloud. I must have climbed the cupboards, because suddenly I fell, breaking several shelves and glass containers. I hit the floor like a rock. I couldn't move, and when I tried to scream, no sound came. Then there was only blackness.

When awareness returned, I felt a breathing mask over my face and a tube in my mouth. The pain was back. I could hear my father and my grandfather talking.

"Will he be all right?" my grandfather asked.

"I hope so. It was hard to know what antidote to give. I'm not sure what he actually took. Dad, he frightens me. This isn't the first time I've caught him in the dispensary. Why is he so persistent about getting into trouble? The others didn't have problems like this."

"No two young are the same. Give him time. He'll molt out of this stage. He's grown up with the same values you did. He's good at heart, really; I know it."

"I'm not so sure. All he talks about, when he does talk to me, is how he wants to go to Roacheria for training."

"So, let him go."

"You can't be serious! If he went there and did even one of the things he's done here, he'd find himself on a one-way trip to the mantis compound without his mandibles. I won't expose him to that."

"Calm down. I didn't mean now. Forgive me, but I find it rather ironic that I argued with my father because I didn't want to leave here for training, and I argued with you because you didn't want to leave, and now you argue with your son because he does want to."

I kept listening and was surprised to hear my father crying. My grandfather moved closer to him, the brace on his mid-right appendage made a soft clip-clapping sound as he moved.

"I don't know what to do. The others were so easy. Henry has always been different. He reminds me of old Rex."

It was silent while my grandfather comforted my father. He stroked my father's antennae, not an easy thing to do since my grandfather was quite a bit shorter and about one third as wide as his adopted son. A small wave of guilt rolled over me, but at the same time I felt angry. I needed comfort, too. I couldn't remember the last time my father had even touched me.

Grandfather spoke gently. "Henrietta always said that a good cuddle, a cup of floral herb tea and a good night's sleep would solve anything. Most of the time, she was right. When was the last time you really talked to Henry, stroked him, told him how special he is and how much you care about him?"

"It's times like this I really miss Mum the most."

"I know, but when have you attended to Henry's needs?"

"When have I had time?"

"That's what I thought. Rodger, first of all you are working much too hard. You've got time for everybody in this colony except those who need you the most. You had your problems too. Never forget them. That's what helps us achieve wisdom, and the ability to help others through their times of trial. You took each of your other young out to the glen, like I took you once, and told them parts of your own life so they could understand theirs."

"It'll take more than an afternoon on seventhday to get through to Henry."

"I know. That's why I'm going to take him. How long do you think it will be before he molts?"

"About a quarter time frame."

"You stay with him now. Keep talking to him. I'm going to gather supplies. I'll take him out there when he's recovered, just the two of us, and we'll stay as long as it takes. Tell everybody to leave us alone. Don't worry, I'll stay clear when he starts thrashing around."

"Are you sure about this? Your health . . ."

"Don't worry about me. Give me the herbs that I need and tell me how much to mix for Henry. I will tell him everything, including the things you'd prefer to forget. When he does go to Roacheria, he should be fully informed about the possible consequences of his choices there."

My father was silent for a moment. "Everything?"

"Everything."

I felt torn. The prospect of seven days alone with my grandfather did not excite me, but the idea of learning about my father was tempting. I wanted to open my eyes but couldn't.

Later, I heard my father's voice echoing through my brain. "Why didn't I see it? Why didn't you come to me and tell me you were hurting, Henry? Why wasn't I listening? I'm sorry I left you alone for so long . . ." on and on.

I awoke to the touch of his pods softly stroking me and I cried for the first time in many time frames. I really felt glad to see him, for once.

He sighed with relief, caressed me again and began to remove the breathing mask and the tube. I noticed that I was in one of the clinic chambers, not at home. I felt genuinely confused, and, for the first time, frightened.

"Please, don't scare your mother and me like this again. We've been out of our minds. You nearly ended your life. You've been in a coma for four days."

"I'm sorry," I stammered. It sounded so insufficient.

*   *   *   *

The following morning, a little before dawn, knowing I was in more trouble than I could possibly talk my way out of, I followed my grandfather and carried a large basket filled with supplies. Later I carried him, too, when he was too tired to walk.

We headed eastward across the stream that ran beside the tiny mound he had first known as home, and into the meadows beyond. When I asked where we were going, he said only that it was a place we both knew and that it had special memories for him.

An h-unit later, with early morning sun in our faces and long shadows behind us, we arrived at a small grove of wood plants whose foliage touched the ground, leaving a protected place within. I did know it well. It was one of my favorite places to hide when I didn't feel like going to training, or wanted to get away from adults. It was also a place I had wondered about because there were two carefully made memorial markers there. One said, "Sir Rodger, my mentor;" the other, "Geree', she wanted something better."

One rule I'd never broken was asking personal questions about someone else's past. I'd always waited to be told. I had a feeling I was about to find out a lot of things and resigned myself to hearing my grandfather's version of the Antstory of New South Dairy 50.

$\underline{1.}$

*A*ntony Dairier awoke from his long pupate sleep and found himself in total darkness. He reached up instinctively and pulled a feeding tube from his mouth, discovered he had legs, and rolled over onto them. He kicked something that went clattering about.

He stretched and said, "That's better," and was surprised by the sound of his own voice. He turned his head from side to side, let his antennae find a way out of the chamber, moved toward the portal, fumbled with the latch and finally pushed it open.

Before him was a large, softly lit chamber. It seemed familiar though he could remember nothing certain. He sensed that there should be other creatures around, but the chamber was empty.

"I'm here," he shouted. No answer. His confusion increased. He froze, shaking, unable to think of what he was supposed to do. He had no idea how long he stood there. It seemed like an eternity. His anxiety increased with every moment.

With a click and a scraping noise, a portal on the opposite side of the chamber opened and someone entered. She was carrying a wiggling white thing. A blast of light blinded Antony. He raised his pods to his face and cried out, "Aggh!"

He heard a voice. "Antony! You've emerged. And I wasn't here. How awful." She put the white thing in an oval basket. Caring pods surrounded him, stroked him, held him. The voice, which now seemed familiar, continued. "I'm so sorry. I'm your mother. We hadn't expected you to emerge for another half a time frame. I would never have left the mound if I thought you were ready. It must have been dreadful to find no one here to greet you."

Gradually he relaxed as she continued to stroke and reassure him. Things began to make sense. This was home. This was his mother, Dorothy. He began to remember the names of things. He leaned against his mother. "I'm all right now."

She stood back and looked at him. "You are so fine looking, and larger than we thought you would be. You're at least half an f-unit longer than your father. He'll be so surprised to see you. You hadn't been moving around. I listened this morning and couldn't hear anything. Are you hungry? I've been out gathering wild fruit."

She walked on her back four appendages to a table and picked up a basket with her front two pods. Antony noticed he was a little longer than she but her abdomen was larger. Like his, her exoskeleton was black.

He ate several berries and she continued to explain. The white wiggling thing she had been carrying was his sister, Arlene, a three season cycle old larva. He had a brother, Drew, and another sister, Deedra, both pupating. Drew would not emerge as an adult for another five season cycles. Deedra had just begun to pupate. It would be nearly seven season cycles before he would see her. She showed him several images on parchment. His mind cleared. He didn't remember things exactly, but as she continued, he found himself thinking that he knew what she meant.

Late in the day, his father, David, came in and embraced him. They talked as they cleared all the equipment from his pupation chamber and turned it into a sleep chamber. They placed a wooden frame around the thistledown mattress he had used as a larva and pupa, brought in a lightning bug lamp, a small work surface, and a chair.

For the next few days, Antony followed his parents everywhere. He heard explanations about everything around him and absorbed it all like parched soil soaks up the sky's water. He climbed the wood plants with his father and tended the aphids, extracted their juice and processed it into honey dew. He helped gather honey from the bee hives. Together, they cut the tall grassfronds, stacked the poles and gathered the unusually large seeds into baskets.

"The grassfronds are a recently evolved plant," his father said. "As near as our experts can figure, this type of grass used to be short. It suddenly increased in height, even as we did."

Antony made a game of climbing the twenty to thirty f-unit stems of the graceful plants. The stems would arc with his weight, until he nearly touched the ground. Then he would jump off and watch the stem spring back and forth, scattering seed everywhere.

"We won't have to plant any next spring if you keep doing that, Antony," his father called. "Please, no more. The rest of the seed must be gathered."

"Why?"

His father laughed. "One for wild creatures, one just to be, three for the colony, and one for me. Well, for us, really, but it doesn't rhyme that way."

"What creatures? What colony?"

"The little creatures deserve their food. We are all part of the interdependent chain of life, and each creature is important, so I always leave some seed on the ground for them. You've planted the ones 'to be,' the seed for next season cycle. Most of what we produce goes to South Harvester Colony 45. Soon, carriers will arrive, bringing supplies we need and taking our harvest. We depend on each other, even though our family is alone right now, and, of course, we need our own food for the next season cycle. This is a busy time for us. I'm glad you are able to help."

David embraced him and held him close. "Soon you will understand exactly how special you are, and know our dream."

*   *   *   *

The next day, when Antony returned for lunch from gathering seed, he was greeted by a wonderfully delicious aroma. The main chamber of the mound was decorated with fall blossoms and foliage.

"This is the fourteenth anniversary of the day you hatched," his father said.

The aroma came from a honey cake on the dining surface and from freshly roasted grasshopper. The meal was fabulous, down to the last drop of warm honeydew and scrap of plastic salad. They laughed, talked, meditated together, played with and cuddled Arlene.

His father looked at him more seriously. "Antony, come with me. There are things I must explain to you now."

Antony followed his father out of the mound, across the small stream that flowed near it, up its further bank, and into the meadows. He had not been on this side of the stream before.

"Why isn't mother coming?"

David Dairier's voice was sober. "This day and the short journey we are making are still difficult for her to talk about. She will need my comfort when we get back."

Antony was confused. Some instinct told him not to ask, but to wait patiently for an explanation. He could see ahead of them a large, obviously unnatural hill. They continued toward it until they stood before an oval metal plate in its side, four times as wide and five times as tall as the two of them. It was covered with strange markings.

His father spoke at last. "Soon you will be trained to decode and understand our written language, but until then I'll read it for you: 'In memory of over 40,000 ants who perished on the eighteenth day of the tenth time frame, 165th season cycle of the Combined Colonies of Insectia. Let all who come here lift up their thoughts and meditate upon all those who are no longer a part of this world.'"

David took Antony's front pod in his and lifted it up. "For my family, Dorothy's family, for our Arthur, and all the others, I offer these thoughts. Help me find joy and peace in Antony. For you we live, we grow, and build again."

He led Antony up the side of the mound, stopping about one third of the way up at a small wooden marker that said, "Arthur, our first." He motioned to Antony to sit down.

"Our domicile used to be straight down from this spot. Almost everyone perished the day you hatched. I have you and your mother only because you happened to be ready to hatch at that time.

"Many season cycles ago, underground explorers found salt dome caverns to the northeast of here. They were filled with many containers left by the extinct, intelligent creatures who came before us on this planet. Our scientists call these creatures 'Duo Pod Erectus'. The containers were filled with many substances, most of them highly toxic. The first one our chemists studied proved to be beneficial. It's called tunnel liquid and has revolutionized the way we build tunnels. Your mother's mentor worked on that project in his younger days.

"A time frame before you hatched, all our chemists were involved in a project to study a different substance, a powder. Your mother was in charge of it. They found it produced a heavy toxic gas when mixed with water. Though still wondering if it had any useful purpose, your mother had recommended that it be left alone and permanently labeled 'too dangerous for study.'"

He stopped a moment and took a few deep breaths before he could go on. "Arthur was your older brother by almost seven season cycles. He was about to enter pupation and you were about to hatch, so your mother took a quarter-time-frame's holiday. We prepared Arthur's pupation chamber and he began his sleep that sixthday, the sixteenth.

"Firstday, I went out to the surface with two others to mind the grasshopper herd. Sky water was falling again, so no one else was out. About midmorning the whole mound shook. We felt it three d-units away. Your mother knew that something terribly wrong had occurred in the lab. She grabbed your egg and ran into the main tunnel to set off the alarm system. Unfortunately, alarms almost always mean there could be tunnel flooding from too much sky water. It usually means to stay in, or enter the nearest emergency chamber. Since it had been a very wet fall, everyone supposed that was the emergency. No one attempted to leave. Your mother could sense the poison and began banging on domicile doors, begging ants to get out. She finally roused her brother but by then the poison was choking them both. He pushed her ahead of him and told her to leave and get you out.

"We found her at the main entrance crying hysterically, and you squeaking away in her pods. Donald and Cassie, a newly mated pair who were working with me that day, went to check the other mound entrances to see if anyone else had escaped. They returned with two others, a young male, Cort, and a female, Alexa. The toxic gas was heavier than air and stayed within the mound. We sat, huddled, cold and wet, in shock and disbelief, while you squealed in hunger.

"You pulled us back to practical concerns. Donald and Cassie headed down the trail for South Harvester 45 to get help. Your mother leaned over you, cradling you and trying to keep you warm and dry. The rest of us began to dig a shelter and searched for something to wrap around you. No larvae had ever been out of a mound before then.

"Donald and Cassie returned with carriers, doctors, and other scientists from South Harvester Colony 45. They had collapsed the intercolonial tunnel so that the poison couldn't spread further underground. There was nothing they could do for the colony. The entrances were sealed. They took us to South Harvester 45.

"We stayed there through the winter. Donald and Cassie, Alexa and Cort decided to go to South Dairy 40, where they had other family members. Your mother tried to work in South Harvester 45's lab, but she found she couldn't work with chemicals anymore, in spite of the caring help and support she received. We were miserable. Finally, we convinced the Intercolonial Council to allow us to return and rebuild. Several workers volunteered to go along for the first time frame. They built our mound, helped round up some of the herds and got us started."

David took Antony up to the very top of the mound. Antony looked out onto d-unit after d-unit of lush meadows, small streams and ponds, the cut patches where they had harvested the grassfronds, and small groves of wood plants. He could see the glen where their mound was and the low slope on western side.

"This is perfect surface for dairying. This colony will live again through you, your brother and your sisters, if you choose to be a part of my dream. You are the living memorial, the only young who survived. Your mother chose your name because it means 'all ants.' With us, you live for all of them. That is why this day holds both joy and sorrow for your mother and me."

The two of them remained there a short time, meditating silently, before going home.

*   *   *   *

Half a time frame later a group of carrier ants arrived from South Harvester 45. The tiny mound was quite crowded, but jubilant as they celebrated Antony's emergence. They brought his parents several written communications, the latest Colonial Bulletins, manuscripts and training materials that his father had requested, some new tools, and enough plastic to last for two time frames until they returned again. They said not to be concerned about credit. The Council knew how hard they worked and would never let a family go in need of anything.

*   *   *   *

Life settled into a more peaceful routine once the harvest was completed. Antony became very good at handling the grasshoppers and aphids. His father had more time, so the surface became Antony's training center. He learned the names of every plant and creature and how each depended on some other, an intricate chain of life. He learned to interpret sky signs, the feelings that indicated a change in the weather, how to know the h-unit, and to find his way at night by the stars. David trained him carefully to avoid the lairs of spiders, and to defend himself against the mantis and other predators. He learned to respect every form of life for its own sake.

Each evening for an h-unit or two, and all day during the cold, damp winter, his mother became the trainer while his father took charge of

Arlene. She taught him to decode, comprehend, and write their language, compute and solve problems, understand his culture and the Antstory of the Combined Colonies of Insectia. He learned it easily enough but disliked being cooped up inside the mound.

Antony's first strategy for avoiding his studies was to get through them quickly. He found this only resulted in more and more complex lessons. Then he tried dawdling and daydreaming.

"Is something wrong?" his mother asked.

Antony stared at the problem he was supposed to be doing. Dorothy turned to David. "This is the fourth time in as many days he hasn't been able to do the problems. Could his mind have been damaged by the fumes, making him unable to learn more complex things?"

"I don't think so. He caught on quickly to everything I taught him about the surface."

Antony sighed. "There's nothing wrong with me. I don't like being stuck inside with all these books and problems. I'd rather be outside with the herd."

"Formal training is important, Antony. No matter what your life's work, there are certain things all of us must know. You're too inexperienced to make decisions about your training. Finish the problems and don't worry your mother."

Antony signed and finished his assignment. He accepted studying as a necessary but distasteful part of his life and longed for spring to come.

Formal training was set aside when the weather grew warm again. The aphid and grasshopper eggs hatched and it took all of them to corral and protect the tiny nymphs. At first he was an observer, holding Arlene, learning from both his parents.

On the fourth day, Dorothy said, "Antony knows what to do now. I'm going back to the mound with Arlene. I don't like having her out of the mound more than absolutely necessary."

"I know. Go on," his father replied.

Through his parents' respect for each other, Antony learned basic ant philosophy: every ant should seek a life's work that suited his or her talents and interests.

When the grasshopper nymphs had grown enough to molt the first time, Antony and his father moved the herd to the eastern side of the stream. He had grazed them on the western side for two season cycles and the meadows there needed time to rejuvenate. The herd settled itself immediately, grazing on the lush grass of late spring. They left them for a while so that David could show Antony the agreed upon limits of their surface area. Coming over a low slope, they saw a crowd of flies hovering and buzzing around a dead creature.

"It's another banished roach," said David as they came close. "I find a few every season cycle. Help me dig a hollow. He still deserves to be decently covered."

Antony looked at the roach as his father drove off the flies. "Did the flies do that to his face?" he asked.

"No. When roaches commit some violent crime, their outer mandibles are cut off so they can no longer harm any other creature or defend themselves. They're either banished or simply fed to mantises they keep penned up for that purpose. Some of the banished ones wander around here and steal from us. Most starve to death because they don't know what wild foods to eat. Others eat something poisonous or some predator gets them."

"What do you mean by steal and violent crime?"

"To steal is to take something without asking. If one creature intentionally hurts or kills another, that's a violent crime."

"Why would one creature want to hurt another?"

David sighed. "You have so much to learn. Our isolation here makes it difficult for us to instill a real sense of colony life in you. I wish I could send you to a training center in South Harvester 45, but I need your help too much. The roaches are intelligent, as we are, but their ways are very different. While we work together, they have little regard for each other. They care only about plastic and owning more than they need. They don't take care of each other, so some steal what they have no credit to buy. Often, they intentionally hurt one another."

They finished digging the hollow, dragged the dead roach into it and covered him.

"What was that mark on his back?"

"It's the mark of the banished, burned in with a hot iron. It warns all other roaches not to help in any way, or they could be banished themselves."

David led Antony a little further, and pointed to a line of wood plants about a d-unit away.

"That line of wood plants and the stream that flows out of it are the agreed upon limits of our surface area. Promise me you will never go there."

"I promise. Dad, I'm confused. You told me last fall that our part is to be in harmony with everything, take no more than we need, replace what we take, and respect the natural cycles of the planet. If the roaches don't care for each other, why did we cover that dead one? Why not leave him for the flies for all the wrong I studied about last winter?"

David sat down. "Yes, there have been many violent conflicts. Yes, the roaches and their leaders on the South East Roach Control Board constantly cheat all the colonies. They keep increasing the cost of plastic by demanding more of the food we produce. They would enslave us if they could. We have taught them our language, but they refuse to teach us theirs. Some time ago, a few in South Harvester 45 learned to read it. I've come to know a fair amount through bargaining with the traders who come here in the summer, but not enough to be helpful to the colonies. By all rights, we should hate them, but our creed demands more of us. We can't set an example of good by lowering ourselves to their level. Their ways remind us of the consequences of choosing greed and selfishness."

"Why don't we fight back?"

"The fire ants in all the colonies are for defense only. We are not aggressors like our ancient antcestors. War only makes bitter feelings worse. We must win by showing them our ways are better. As for our family, we are safe as long as they think this surface is worthless. All the plastic was mined from here long ago and the Duo Pod ruins around here aren't important. The only thing I fear is that someday they might think that we have something of value and attack us. We have no defense here."

Antony thought about everything his father had taught him and what he had seen that day. He chose to embrace his father's dream.

2.

*T*he more skillful Antony became at handling the grasshopper herd, the more his father left him alone with them. With Antony's full time care, they lost fewer nymphs to predators. Antony liked the peacefulness of the herd and the time to think and observe the world around him. It seemed as though his father always arrived with more food and water when he began to feel truly lonely. Sometimes he didn't even mind taking along a manuscript to study.

It was around summer solstice when Antony looked up to see a roach near the far side of the herd. He jumped up, waved his front pods and shouted, "What do you want?"

The startled roach turned and scurried off. As he did so, Antony saw the mark of banishment on his back and noticed that, although it still had speed, the roach moved with the awkward stiffness of old age. It disappeared into a grove of wood plants in a low area near a small pond. Antony sat at the edge of the herd, tense and alert, wishing his father would arrive with lunch.

He sighed with relief as his father approached him. "Dad, there is another one of those banished roaches. I yelled and he ran into those wood plants, but he had his outer mandibles, and he moved as if he were old."

"He had his mandibles?"

"Yes. Should we move the herd?"

"No, but I'll stay out here with you at night. If he were violent, he would not have his mandibles, but I've never seen a banished one with them."

That night Antony had trouble staying awake during his watch. He stirred up the fire, stretched and tried not to nod off. Suddenly he heard a scuffling noise behind him and turned to see a mantis poised to pounce on a half-grown hopper. Before it could leap, the roach swept out of the darkness, jumped on the mantis and closed its mandibles around the mantis' neck. Antony screamed. The mantis dropped. The roach disappeared into the night.

Antony's father jumped up at the noise. He stared at the mantis and at Antony, who stammered to explain. "The roach... he did it. . . I don't think we need to be afraid of him. He helped us. Suppose we left some food somewhere. He wouldn't need to steal from us then. He's old. What harm could it do?"

"None, unless we are seen by others, or the traders learn of it somehow. If they found out, we could be viewed as enemies for helping a banished one."

"What would they do to us?"

"I don't know."

After a sleepless night and much discussion, David told Antony, "Leave a small bundle with food, a coverlet, and some cooking tools near the wood plants. Be very careful no other creature is around. Watch to see if the old roach finds it."

Holding the bundle, Antony did look carefully around. Curiosity drove him beyond leaving it near the wood plants. He lifted the foliage and found a shaded shelter within, a natural chamber. Heart pounding, he stepped in and saw the roach asleep, not ten f-units from him. He dropped the bundle and ran, then sat in the distance near the grasshopper herd and watched.

The roach appeared later, stooped low and said, "Thank you."

Antony was surprised. "You speak Ant?"

"Not much. Not to fear me."

"I am Antony."

"Rodger," he said, pointing to himself. Then he turned and left.

They didn't see much of him for a while. Antony left a small bundle of food every quarter time frame.

     *   *   *   *

The roach traders arrived in the middle of the eighth time frame. Before trading, they asked David if he had seen any banished roaches lately. He replied that he had covered a dead one in the spring. They wanted to know if he had seen any with mandibles.

David laughed. "When did you creatures start doing that? Do you want to trade or not?"

Antony smiled when his father told him about it. He liked the way his father had avoided answering their question.

David had given them two large measures of honey and three hopper nymphs in exchange for what he later discovered was very poor quality shredded plastic. The bottom of the container had been packed with shredded parchment and gravel. He stormed out of the mound and vented his anger pulling weeds from a patch of ground where Dorothy was trying to cultivate some wild berries. Antony looked toward his mother for an explanation.

"It's not the first time," she said. "Every time he thinks he's ahead of their tricks, they have a new one."

Antony stood silently for a few moments and then left, saying he should get back to the herd. He did check on them but then went on, straight to the grove of wood plants that Old Rodger now called home. Antony felt less sure of himself when he got there. Some of his anger and resolve had evaporated.

He hesitated, then called, "Rodger?"

The old roach came out and looked at him.

"Please, will you teach me your language?"

"Why?"

"The traders cheat my father."

"Not easy."

"I don't care."

"Take long time."

"That's all right," Antony replied. "Please, will you teach me?"

The old roach studied him a moment, twitched his antennae, and then nodded. "Keep secret. Never seen with me." Through gestures, he indicated that he would come to Antony when he was alone with the herd.

*   *   *   *

Two days later, Antony looked up from his manuscript. Rodger approached and stood in front of him at his fullest height. Antony rose to greet him as he would another ant.

Rodger shook his antennae in disapproval. "I high. You low. I teach. You learn. This is way you greet me."

He stooped low and swept his front pods out to the sides. From that time on, he never said another word in Ant.

Antony mimicked the gesture. Old Rodger acknowledged it by tipping his antennae. He reached for Antony's book. "Kolootie suc ac," he said, pointing to it.

Antony responded. "This is a book. Kolutie suc ac."

"Moc." Rodger shook his head. "Kolootie."

Antony tried again. Rodger corrected him again. After the fifth try at pronouncing the strange sound, Old Rodger examined Antony's mouth parts, to see if he could produce the sound. Gently, he corrected the way Antony moved his inner mandibles, so that he pronounced the word exactly as Old Rodger said it.

Old Rodger smiled. "Com." He opened the book and began to name things in the images. Antony repeated each, over and over until he had it perfect.

When the first lesson ended, Antony could name each item in the first three images.

In the days that followed, Antony learned more and more. He slipped some of the first manuscripts he'd used to learn to read into his satchel, because they had more images than the ones he was currently studying. His vocabulary quadrupled. Days turned into time frames.

"Mi saygay!" Old Rodger often said. It meant, "Very good."

By winter, Antony understood why Rodger was so particular about pronunciation. One slightly different sound changed the meaning of a word. Furthermore, a gesture, even a small one, changed the overall context. It was indeed a difficult and complex language.

"Tat sa eetu cu," Antony replied to a question one day, trying to apply the pattern he'd learned the day before to a new situation.

"Moc. Tat sa ee tuu cu," corrected Old Rodger.

Antony sighed. Every pattern had an exception.

Old Rodger smiled patiently and put one front pod on Antony's thorax. Antony smiled back, determined to get it right.

*   *   *   *

The following summer when the roach traders arrived, Antony listened carefully. Without letting his father or the traders know he understood what was going on, he guided his father into a very fair trade. He was pleased with himself and felt he had accomplished his main goal, but he wanted more. He had become fascinated by the roach language and culture. He craved learning, but not in the traditional ant sense.

"I caught their trick," he told Old Rodger in Roach the following day. "One of them signaled the other to change the placement point on the parchment. I told my father to check the numbers. He did and they corrected it. My father got all the plastic he bargained for."

"Good. I told you they would respect his power to that degree. They see him as a surface owner, and they have less. So to them, he has more power."

Why didn't they respect him before?"

"The powerless will always try to take from others as long as they think they can get away with it. In Roacheria, the more one owns, the more power one has to control others. In the colonies, the one with the best ideas and leadership is the Council Chief, correct?"

"Yes."

"On our Boards, the one with the most power rules. We have a Supreme Executor on our Board, but these days, another dictates from behind. He controls with credit and treachery. Beware of him."

"How would I ever meet him? Who is he?"

"Even here, it is not safe for me to speak his name. I hope that one day you do meet him. You will know when the time comes, and if you learn well, you can beat him at his own game."

*   *   *   *

In Antony's third season cycle of adulthood, his mother laid another egg. It came as a bit of a surprise to his parents, since most females his mother's age would have laid a lifeless egg by that time, signaling the end of the fertile stage of their lives. The larva was a male and they named him Allen.

"Antony, I need you in the mound today," his mother said as he started to leave.

"Again? I was inside all last quarter time frame while you experimented with preserving all that wild fruit."

"I haven't finished that job. I can't do that and care for Arlene and Allen."

Antony turned to his father. "Why don't you stay here? I'll do all the surface work. I'd rather be outside. If I'm supposed to choose my life's work by what I like, why am I always stuck in here? I hate it inside. Mom, you stay in here because you like it. Why can't I work outside where I like it?"

"How many times do we have to go through this? Larva care and family obligations come before your own desires. I won't argue about it with you again. How can you learn to care for the young you'll have one day, if you don't learn with your brother and sister? You know what you need to do today," his father said.

Antony gave in, thinking that Arlene would pupate soon, and he would be free to spend more time with Old Rodger. He began to enjoy caring for Allen in spite of himself. This little brother loved to cuddle and wanted the affection Antony found himself willing to give. Somewhere deep inside, he remembered the good feelings of being stroked and wanted to give those feelings to Allen.

Arlene, on the other hand, was no longer cuddly. Close to seven season cycles, she was whiny and irritable most of the time. It was a relief when she slept, but her increased sleeping concerned his parents. Dorothy worried that she would enter her pupate sleep before the carriers brought a pupate plastic supply kit. If she entered pupation without plastic nourishment, she could reach adulthood deformed, unable to learn, or even die.

"The carriers always arrive on time," David reassured her. "Remember how we kept Drew awake for five days?"

*   *   *   *

When they arrived, the carriers stayed two extra days. They helped prepare Arlene's pupation chamber. Antony watched them hook up the tubes and machinery and thought about the day he emerged and kicked away the same things. The second day was spent waiting for Antony to complete his basic training exam, so that they could return it for evaluation on the same trip.

Antony's father explained about the exam. "This will show what you have learned studying with us and on your own. You must pass it to be eligible for job exploration training in South Harvester 45."

"Do you mean that if I do well on this, I won't have to study any more?"

"If you do well on it, you will have learned all you can here," his father replied. "For any other advanced studies, you would have to go to South Harvester Colony 45."

Antony rejoiced. Arlene was out of the way, no more books; he could get back to learning from Old Rodger. He settled down to do his very best on the exam. They left him alone in his sleep chamber, all manuscripts and study helps removed, for four h-units. He finished it with a quarter h-unit to spare. David sealed it, and the carriers took it with them when they left in the morning.

*   *   *   *

Life settled back into what Antony considered normal. He spent much more time with Old Rodger. They no longer needed manuscripts, but simply conversed for h-units at a time in Roach, or wrote in the mud at the edge of the pond. Antony listened eagerly when Old Rodger explained the politics and government of Roacheria. He learned about their social life, economic system, values, or lack of them. He found out how they schemed to get information from the ants or plotted unnecessary increases in the price of plastic. He learned their side of the various political agreements, wars and confrontations that had taken place since the inception of the Combined Colonies. All these things Old Rodger explained with an open mind. Antony learned to see both sides, think both ways, and he kept all of it to himself.

*   *   *   *

"I thought you said I wouldn't have any more training if I showed how much I'd learned," Antony said when the carriers arrived the next time with a letter about his exam.

"That's not what I said," David replied. "I said that was all you could learn here. I'm so proud. Imagine, the top training center in South Harvester 45, specializing in the sciences and technical fields, hopes you will choose to go there."

David picked up Antony's mother and twirled her around. Both of them laughed. The carriers patted Antony's thorax, congratulating him. Dorothy started to fix a honey cake. Antony cursed himself for trying so hard.

"What's the matter? Here we are celebrating your achievement, and you seem so disappointed," Antony's mother asked him.

"I'm all right."

"I can see in your face that something's wrong."

"It's just that . . . well . . . nobody ever asked me what I wanted to do. Maybe I don't want to go there."

The group fell silent.

"What do you mean, maybe you don't want to?" his father said. "With your talents and intelligence, you could get any mentorship you wanted and bring some vital skills back here."

Antony changed his tone and smiled. "That didn't come out the way I meant it. I'm sorry, Dad."

The others relaxed and counted off the possibilities: medicine, chemistry (like his mother) power development, tunnel engineering. Antony stopped listening, and seethed on the inside. Here they were planning his life for him, and he seemed to have no say in the matter at all. Their voices dimmed as they realized that since they had expanded the herds, David could not manage without Antony's help. He wouldn't be able to leave for training until his brother, Drew, emerged from pupation. Then Drew could help out and Antony could leave. Antony sighed in relief.

*   *   *   *

Antony waited two time frames before he brought up the subject of training again, choosing a seventhday, when his parents were calm and relaxed after meditating.

"Mom, Dad, about this job exploration training, I don't understand why I need it. I've been working here with you for almost four and a half season cycles. Why should I change? I'm content with what I'm doing." He tried to stay calm and logical in his approach.

His father said, "It's not a matter of need or contentment. You've never had a chance to try anything else. If we were in a regular colony, your training would have been very different. You would have spent three season cycles full time on your basics. As we grow here, many new skills will be needed. It's the exposure to other things your mother and I want you to have."

"I can understand that, but if my experiences have been so unusual, why change it now? If we have to wait for Drew to emerge, why not let him go instead? Then he would have his training in a traditional way. I don't mind giving it up for him."

"That's very generous of you," his mother said. "But we want all our young to have a full range of experiences. We can handle the basics here. You've shown us that." His parents brought out other points: he would meet many others, perhaps find a mate, learn advanced group and cooperative problem solving, and other things they couldn't do with the limitations of their small family.

"I don't understand why you reject this," his father said. "I want you to be the best that you can be. Seek many ways you can serve everyone."

Antony sighed and left it at that. He could not find the words to express his fear of leaving everything he knew and cared about to be among so many strangers. The mere thought of it sent him into a panic, like the day he emerged from pupation and found himself alone. He gave up, spent more and more time with the herds and Old Rodger, dreading the day that Drew would emerge.

*   *   *   *

Antony happened to be in the mound with Allen the day Drew awakened from his pupate sleep. He heard the noise, remembered his own confusion, and stood near the portal waiting, so he could be the first to greet his brother. He was glad when David had him start training Drew to handle the grasshoppers.

A few days before Antony's scheduled departure, Antony faced his father. "Dad, I can't! I just can't leave. I ..."

"You can't? What nonsense is this now? It's been decided. You've been accepted and you were expected by the first of the tenth time frame, even though that was after the term began, and then I gave you another half a time frame. Your lodging has been arranged and a small service. You promised you would not start this again. This whole thing is a sham for you. You only want to stay here so you can keep sneaking off with that old banished roach. Yes. I've seen you, so don't deny it. Now I realize more than ever how much I need to get you away from here. He's poisoned your mind!"

"That's not true!" Antony shouted. "He has a name. It's Rodger. It's not what you think at all. You never listened. I'm tired of you planning my life for me. I've always ended up doing what you wanted. No one ever asked me how I felt!"

Drew stared at both of them in confusion. Dorothy dropped her basket of wild fruit. Allen whined.

"You don't even realize why their traders haven't been cheating you the last few season cycles," Antony continued yelling. "I got him to teach me the language and guided the deals. So don't you accuse him of poisoning my mind."

His father stared at him. "Then what is the matter?"

"I don't know anyone there. When I say who I am, everyone will want to know why it took me five season cycles to start job exploration. They'll think I kept failing the exam."

"Won't know anyone? Honestly, is that all? You got to know the carriers, didn't you? Other trainees will understand when you tell them that your help was needed here." David started laughing with relief, which only made Antony angrier.

Antony stalked out of the mound, off to the eastern meadows, in search of understanding from Old Rodger.

"You really did that well on your exam? That's wonderful. I wish one of my young, or their young, had even half your talent. Why are you not proud of yourself?"

"I suppose I am, but I've never liked training."

"You don't like training, yet you spent thousands of h-units with me over the last four season cycles mastering my language."

"That was different. I wanted to do it."

"Why are you so afraid of going to South Harvester 45?"

"I told you. I don't know anyone and I don't want to be alone."

"In a colony of over 75,000 ants, how can you ever be alone? You creatures nearly trip over one another in a colony. That makes no sense. It's here that you are alone."

"But I don't know them."

"What did you know of me when we first met? Was I not a stranger? We barely understood each other then."

"You're starting to sound like my father. Whose side are you on, anyway?"

"You forget what I am, Antony. I'm on no one's side but my own. Do you consider me a friend?"

"Yes, of course I do."

"Then listen to me. I owe your family a lot. I would not have lived long at all without your gifts of food, or your showing me which wild plants were edible and which were poisonous. Your company has made my situation much more bearable. That is part of why I kept teaching you, but I had my own reasons as well. Tell me again why you first asked to learn to speak Roach."

"Because the traders cheated my father."

"Exactly. Your world is too limited here. Your talents wasted. Stop and think. Aren't all the colonies constantly cheated in their dealings with Roacheria?"

"Yes."

"I would wager all of what I once owned that you are the only ant in all the Combined Colonies who knows as much as you do about our language and ways. I know that because any roach who trained an ant as I have trained you would be found guilty of treason, de-mandibled, and condemned to the mantis compound. They can do nothing more to me, so I don't give a fat fly larva. But think what you could do with this knowledge! You could be directing the plastic trade and end all the cheating. Beat the one who sent me here. Ah, sweet revenge." He sighed.

"Antony, things must begin to change between our kinds. I had not the power, but you could make it happen. That was my reason for training you. How can that be accomplished if you do nothing with what I taught you but sit with your herds?"

"You mean you want me to go, too?"

"I want you to go so much that if you do not, I swear I will never speak to you again."

Antony stared at him, dumfounded. Old Rodger turned his back. Antony left the glen and wandered in the meadows for a long time. He went up to the top of the old mound and meditated until sundown, then he slowly returned home. His father tried to speak to him, but Antony went straight to his sleep chamber and closed the portal.

*   *   *   *

In the morning, Antony came out with his satchel packed and said, "Where are the letters I'm supposed to take?"

His father pointed toward a shelf near the portal. Antony stuffed them in his satchel, filled a water flask and dumped several grassfrond seeds in with everything else.

"I'm going. I hope you're satisfied," he said and stalked out before anyone could say anything, afraid he would lose his nerve.

About three d-units down the trail, Old Rodger appeared as if from nowhere. "Good luck, Antony. Whenever you meditate, or whatever it is you do, think of me sometimes. I'll be thinking about you. When you come back to visit, if I still live, you'll know where to find me."

Antony didn't trust his voice. He nodded and headed down the trail.

3.

*M*aster Adriana, the assistant director of the science and technology training facility in South Harvester Colony 45, greeted Henrietta Harvester. "It's good to see you again, Henrietta. I hope you don't mind a short wait. Your problem solving trainer would like to join us. Would you like a mug of warm honey dew?"

"Yes, please. I don't mind waiting," replied Henrietta.

Henrietta sipped the honey dew and thought about some of the events of her first season cycle of adulthood. She remembered her father's fond greeting when she opened the portal of her pupate chamber. He told her she was the oldest of four. Her next younger sister, Hilda, was three season cycles younger and pupating. Annie and Andrew were still larvae, five season cycles and one season cycle old.

A time frame later, it had been discovered that she could only bear five times her own weight, compared to the normal fifty to seventy-five times one's weight for a normal ant. Her parents were quite concerned, but the doctors found her healthy and intelligent and recommended only that she not participate in tasks requiring strength. What she lacked in strength, she more than made up for in intelligence, whizzing through manuscript decoding, and finishing all her basics in one season cycle. Now, here she was on the first day of the ninth time frame, waiting to see if she would be accepted into job exploration training when the new term began.

"Tell me, how do you feel you did on the exam?" asked Master Adriana when trainer Albert had arrived.

Henrietta hesitated. "I know I did well on the literature and essay portions, but that has always been easy for me."

"And the problem solving?"

Henrietta sighed. She might as well be honest. "I don't think I passed it."

"Why not?"

"Problem solving is harder for me. Even when I think I'm right, my father finds errors in my work. I haven't done very well on regular tests lately, and I didn't even finish that portion of the exam."

"What do you think you should do now?"

"I suppose I should stay at the third level of training for another term, but I don't really want to. I don't mean to be disrespectful, but the other third level work is boring. Is there any way I could take some advanced level units while I repeat problem solving?"

"A good suggestion, but it would be a scheduling nightmare."

"Could I at least do some research projects independently?"

Trainer Albert looked into her eyes. "Suppose we allowed you to go on. How well do you think you could keep up in advanced group problem solving, since you don't feel you are strong in the basics? What elective units would you choose?"

She began to feel more hopeful. "I would like to take more literature and Antstory. They are easy for me, so I would have more time to spend on the problem solving. Maybe I could work back through the third level materials with my father."

Albert and Master Adriana exchanged glances. Then Master Adriana said, "You have very good ideas, and you are skilled in self evaluation. I wish we had more trainees with your abilities. We both agree that you need the challenge of job exploration. The truth is, you did pass all portions of the exam. I'm sure your father has enough to do without tutoring you. Albert will continue working with you one h-unit earlier than the beginning of the usual morning schedule every first, third, and fifthday, until you feel you are truly competent. Will you be able to do that on top of a full advanced level load?"

Henrietta's eyes lit up. "Oh, yes! I'm sure I can."

      *   *   *   *

Henrietta spent the first quarter time frame of job exploration with her father, a tunnel engineer. He gave her a long manuscript to read beforehand so she would have some idea about what was happening. She had to get up extra early to make it to her session with trainer Albert and then hurry home to leave with him.

"I'm glad you start work after the rest of the colony. I'd never have made it," she said.

He smiled. "It would be pretty hard to repair or widen a tunnel with everyone trying to get to their own jobs. It's important for you to observe carefully but not participate. You lack the physical strength. It's my responsibility to keep you and my whole crew safe from injury."

"I know. I'll watch from a safe distance as you test the soil and rock ahead of them and calculate how much tunnel liquid is used."

"Tell me what you remember reading in that manuscript I gave you," Henry said as they headed down a long, slanting tunnel toward a new section of the colony.

"After master chemists learned tunnel liquid could dissolve rock, tunnels became much easier to build. It must be used carefully because of its caustic nature. For reasons not clearly understood, after it is left for a time, it changes the rock or soil around it into a hard, strong surface, making tunnel collapse much less likely. Through further research, our chemists learned to produce it, even though the supplies originally found are gone."

"Good job. You did your homework," he said, directing her to a side area. He also had her put on protective breathing gear.

Henrietta was fascinated. Her father seemed to be everywhere at once. First the tunnel liquid was sprayed by diggers wearing masks like hers. The sprayed area was cleared of loose gravel and rock. Diggers filled large, metal baskets with amazing speed and the strongest carriers carted it off. Finally, the diggers used large, curved rollers to press the new wall smooth, so it could harden. During their brief lunch break, her father explained some of what she had seen.

"Sometimes we forget that manual labor such as this is impossible for other creatures. Even before we evolved and grew nearly to the length of the extinct Duo Pods, no living thing on the planet matched our strength in proportion to our size."

"But I don't have it. Am I a mutation? What if we all lost it?"

"Your condition is not genetic. While there are some jobs you will not be able to explore, there are many more you can. You are very gifted. Don't limit yourself more than necessary."

By mid-afternoon they had finished that day's section, and Henrietta was once again scurrying as fast as she could to keep up with her father. He quizzed her all the way home about what she had observed, took her straight back to his home work chamber, pulled up an extra stool, and began to explain what would take place the next day. He took out a chart and began his calculations. They didn't take a break until it was time for him to go and help her mother, Adeline, carry Andrew and Annie home. Henrietta headed for the kitchen to start supper.

The second evening he let her try some of the calculations. When she handed the parchment back to him, he shook his head, put his pod on her thorax and said, "You've done in the entire roof and collapsed two tunnels above that."

Thirdday she sat in silence and listened to the day-long conference of all the engineers who were working on that particular tunnel. She beamed with pride when she heard the others address her father as "Master Henry," but they might as well have been speaking another language for all she understood.

By fifthday she was totally frustrated. For the first time, Henry ambled slowly along their way home. "Henrietta, I haven't been intentionally hard on you these past few days." He put one front pod around her as they moved along. "You'll find many jobs are more difficult than you expected."

"I've been totally lost since secondday."

"Don't be too concerned," he reassured her. "I spent three and a half season cycles with my mentor. I want you to promise me something."

"What?"

"Promise me that you'll take your full three season cycles of job exploration. Try many things until you find just the right one. Don't take it right away. Keep trying other things after that. Only then will you be sure you are making the right choice."

"I will."

                    *   *   *   *

Henrietta spent the next quarter time frame in the larva nursery with her mother. Although Adeline did not quiz her constantly, or hand her manuscripts to read, Henrietta went home every evening exhausted. It seemed like some larva was always begging to be picked up and stroked, while the older ones whined if you so much as touched them. She was truly fond of Annie and Andrew, and supposed that someday she would find a mate and have larvae of her own—though that was not very high on her list of priorities—but a whole chamber full of them was too much.

"Mother, how can you stand it every day?" she asked as they carried Annie and Andrew home on fifthday.

Her mother chuckled. "It's not so bad. All larvae really need is the touch of caring pods. You can't blame the older ones for being irritable. They are very uncomfortable as they near their time to pupate. When I think I really can't take any more from one of them, he or she pupates, and that ends the problem."

"Was I that awful?"

"Not like some, but you had your moments. I wouldn't worry if I were you. I think you've learned your lesson this quarter time frame with me. My job requires different talents."

"How will I know when I've found the right thing? How did you know?"

"I took my time. I tried many things. I meditated about it. Deep inside, I knew. You will, too."

When Henrietta met with her base group, she found that she was not alone in feeling frustrated and inadequate. Some trainees' experiences with their parents had been even more disastrous than hers.

The base group leader reassured all of them. "What might be a disaster for one of you, might be exactly right for someone else. The whole point of job exploration is to learn to appreciate the work of others while you find what is best for you."

*   *   *   *

Antony stopped about one-eighth of a d-unit from South Harvester 45's main entrance. The size of the mound frightened him. Ants were everywhere, carrying in baskets of grassfrond seeds, thistledown, herbs and other surface products, and plastic from South Harvester 45's mine. Yet another stream of ants bore loads of soil and rock from new tunneling to the top of the mound. Antony had not the least idea what to do or where to go. The Ant language did not contain many expletives. He cursed himself in Roach for not waiting to travel with the carriers.

A familiar voice came from behind. "Antony?"

He turned and recognized Denton, one of the carriers who regularly came to his parents' dairy.

"What are you doing here?" asked Denton. "I thought you were supposed to come with us the day after tomorrow."

"I decided not to wait." Antony shifted, his antennae twitching. "I have no idea which way . . . I have these letters." He reached into his satchel and handed them to Denton.

Denton looked at the letters. "Andy's work place. That's easy. I'll show you the way."

"Thanks."

Antony followed him through a maze of tunnels and down three or four levels. He feared he would never find his way out. Denton pointed out a large tunnel to the right.

"Take this tunnel a little farther, and you'll see the main portal to the Council Chambers on your right. Someone there will show you where Andy's work chamber is. Good luck. Maybe I'll run into you again sometime."

Looking around, Antony doubted it, but he expressed his thanks, took a deep breath and went on. Finding the portals just as Denton had said, he relaxed a little, went in and found himself facing a receiving ant who directed him to Andy's work chamber.

Andy greeted him cheerfully, asked about his family, said how much he looked like his mother, went on and on, as though he knew Antony very well, and all the while Antony squirmed inside.

Antony finally broke in. "Excuse me, Andy, I really appreciate all this, but I don't know my way to the training center. Have you got a colony location chart I could borrow?"

"Of course. I'm sorry. I've been rambling."

Andy opened a storage compartment beneath his work surface and found a location chart, marked the training facility, and pointed out several small dots near it.

"The dots are emergency chambers. Your father asked me to find some service you could perform that wouldn't interfere with your studies. There are about fifty of them in the lower, western quadrant. Once each season cycle, they need to be cleaned and checked for supplies. Here's a complete list and instructions. It shouldn't take you more than half a day to do one, so you'll have plenty of time to study and some leisure to enjoy yourself. Keep the location chart. We've got a chamber all ready for you at our domicile."

Antony shifted. "I don't want to seem ungrateful, but I'm used to being by myself. Couldn't I live in one of these chambers that I'm to keep up? I'd be closer to the training facility."

"You want to live alone?"

"Yes. Is that a problem?"

"No. But it's unusual."

"Do the directors at this training facility have to know that I'm not from any colony, or that I'm already nineteen season cycles old?"

"I would think you'd want to share your experiences, but I'll respect your choice. Are you sure?"

"Yes."

Antony gave his father's introduction letter to the director of the training facility to Andy. Andy dropped it in the re-use bin and wrote a simple one. It stated Antony's name, vouched for the fact that he had passed his basic training exam, and asked that he be admitted. Antony thanked him, took all the materials and left.

Getting around in a colony was very different from the surface. Antony had to think in three dimensions when using the location chart. He got lost twice on his way to the training facility, but he was determined not to ask directions again. He would prove that he could handle things on his own.

By the time he had met with the director of the training facility, been assigned to a base group, received a schedule, manuscripts and supplies, it was quite late in the day. He had managed to appear calm and confident during his interview, but now felt exhausted. He found his way to the nearest emergency chamber, entered and went right to sleep.

For the first time frame Antony remained quiet and aloof. He spoke when questioned, but did not volunteer any responses. He sat back, observing how the other trainees interacted with each other, soaking up information about how he was supposed to act in a group. He lived on sheer determination to make it alone.

*   *   *   *

Several time frames later, Antony's base group leader asked to see him.

"Antony, your work on the last group project was excellent. I'd like you to take the leader's role on the surface survival research project. Next time frame, when we look at the work of our council, would you be willing to be an aid to a council member for two quarter time frames?"

"I'll be glad to lead the research project, but I've got family obligations. I don't think I'll have the time required to be a council aid," he replied.

"I see. I'll find someone else for the aid position."

*   *   *   *

The members of the surface survival research group were amazed at how much Antony knew.

"Have you spent time on the surface?" asked one. "I have yet to see the light of day and you must have lived there."

Antony's careful response was, "My uncle is a dairier. I wrote and asked him for information."

"Then, he sure knows a lot. We're headed for the Leisure Center later. Why not join us?"

"I can't. I'm way behind on some reading assignments. Maybe next time."

On the way to the emergency shelter he called home, he stopped in the message center. Disappointed that he had no letter from his father, he pulled out another invitation from Andy to have dinner on seventhday. He wrote a quick reply. "Thank you, but I have a major project due on firstday."

"I don't need anybody," he muttered, crumpled the invitation and tossed it in the re-use bin.

*   *   *   *

Totally immersed in job exploration, Henrietta became increasingly interested in the research of scientists who worked on the planet's surface and Ancient Antstory. It seemed as though all the really exciting discoveries and advancements in technology in the Combined Colonies of Insectia came from the surface.

In earlier times, ants had been enriched as they expanded their tunnels and combined their talents with other varieties of ants. There were tunnels between all the colonies. The many secrets of the underground were open to all. Each ant variety shared its particular specialty. Harvesters had taught seed gathering and growing. Dairying ants had brought them aphid care, honey dew and many other varieties of food. Carpenters knew more about the wood plants than anybody, and those were only a few. The use of thistledown and other plant products had made their lives more comfortable. Lightning bug power had brightened their tunnels and domiciles and led to imaging equipment and video walls, which brought instant knowledge of events throughout the colonies.

Although she had never seen it, Henrietta knew the surface had its dangers, too. She was confused by what little she knew of roaches. The facts in manuscripts left something out. Whenever she brought up the subject at home, her parents lapsed into silence.

Once, her father had said, "I don't want to deal with something personal right now."

She wondered what could be personal about roaches, but politely let the matter drop. She had a feeling that the answers to many of the ants' problems lay somewhere on the surface, and began to dream of being the one to discover them.

*   *   *   *

Antony's first season cycle went well. He wrote home frequently and received caring replies from his mother. He longed for some word from his father, but none came.

"I know you didn't mean it," one letter said, "but your arguments with your father hurt him deeply. Even though you obeyed his request in leaving for training, he won't write. I meditate each day that the anger between you will heal."

The resentment he'd felt for so long ebbed, and with it, his determination. An empty loneliness crept inside Antony.

"Are you ill?" his base group leader asked. "You don't seem yourself lately, Antony."

"I'm fine," he said. "Just tired."

His only contentment came from going to the surface each seventhday. He would rise before dawn and climb to the top of a very tall cone-bearing wood plant near the colony's main entrance. There, he meditated and watched the arrival of the day, gaining strength from a feeling of oneness with the natural world. No matter what the weather, he was there. But as the second winter wore on, not even that helped.

He wrote to his father. "I appreciate the opportunity I've had in coming here. You were right about learning new skills. I could design a lot of new equipment that would make our work a lot easier. I still haven't found anything I like better than what I was doing with you. Could I come home at the end of the next time frame?"

The reply, which came as soon as the carriers returned, was brief:

"Dear Antony, I'm proud of your training reports. We agreed on two season cycles of training. Please, honor my request and finish it. Your cherishing father, David."

His academic progress came to a halt. He no longer cared about unfinished assignments, or unread manuscripts. Only his excellent auditory memory kept him from failing altogether. Master Alex, the director of the facility, summoned him for a conference.

"Antony, your performance the last five time frames is not in agreement with your abilities or your work last season cycle. It's apparent that something is very wrong. There is not a trainer here, including myself, who wouldn't turn inside out to help you, but we can't unless we know what kind of help you need."

Antony was almost desperate enough to let it all out, but his pride got in the way. He had been asked about illness before, and used it as an excuse. "I know I haven't done well lately. I've had a low-grade infection for some time, but now I think I'm over it. I'll do better from now on."

"Why didn't you tell someone? Have you been to the medical facility?"

"Yes," he lied. "They gave me something. It seems to be working."

"I hope so. I have many trainees waiting to enter this facility. If you do not make a concentrated effort to catch up on your work, or if you miss any more major reports, I'm afraid I'll have to ask you to leave. Perhaps another training center with a less rigorous program would help your recovery."

Master Alex put a pod on Antony's thorax. He realized later it was meant to encourage him. But at that moment, it only reminded him how long it had been since he had felt an affectionate touch. He left quickly, afraid he would break down.

The following morning there was a special announcement. All base groups would spend the next time frame investigating the work of archaeologists in preparation for a visiting master archaeologist, who would give a special lecture. Everyone in the second or third season cycle of job exploration was to prepare a research report. Master Diandra planned to select a trainee for a mentorship with her on the basis of the reports and personal interviews.

Antony went to his base group leader to ask for an extension of time. Hopelessly behind, the thought of another major project overwhelmed him.

"Could I form a group?"

"No, but partnerships are acceptable."

He decided to find a partner.

Antony started cleaning two emergency chambers each sixthday and began to dig his way out of a pile of late assignments. He listened closely in his Ancient Antstory training unit, while he looked around the group for a partner.

"When did the Duo Pods first appear?" the trainer asked.

Henrietta's antennae twitched.

"Henrietta?"

"The earliest evidence we have dates from the last time sheets of ice covered much of the planet. Many think there may have been some before that, but archaeologists have not found definite evidence. The making and intelligent use of tools indicates that they had developed true intelligence at that time."

"You certainly have done your research."

"This is my favorite area of study."

Antony looked at her with interest. He remembered her from the surface survival project. She had worked hard, hung on every word he'd said.

He approached her at the end of the noon break.

"Hello, Henrietta. Where are you headed?"

"To my base group."

"I was wondering if..."

"Yes?"

"Never mind. I don't want to make you late."

   *   *   *   *

Henrietta devoted more time than ever to studying surface exploration and preantstoric times. She was fascinated by the process of evolution. She wondered why insects had always been around, but had never cognitively developed until the last twenty thousand cycles. What had caused the rapid change from numerous, but tiny and insignificant creatures to the much larger, civilized Insecta Sapiens they were now? Although all insects had evolved in size, why had only ants and roaches become intelligent? Why had their development come right after the Duo Pods disappeared?

Parchment after parchment of research notes lay in organized piles on her home work surface. She wanted her report to be impressive enough to gain the mentorship with Master Diandra. It wouldn't be easy. Master Diandra had plenty of bright young ants from which to choose. Henrietta had to show special knowledge and extra desire to learn more and work harder than any other.

She paced her sleep chamber, thinking out loud. "A different angle. That's what I need. Background information first? No. Everybody knows that. Trace Duo Pod development? It's been done. Master Diandra knows what she's already published. What doesn't she know? Notes . . . notes."

She looked at the piles of notes. "Social structure . . . Disappearance at the height of development . . . Climate changes . . . Theories of extinction . . . Writings . . . There's nothing here on the writings! I've got to go back to the research center."

   *   *   *   *

The next day, when Henrietta came out of the research center, Antony approached her again. She looked at him curiously. Of all the males she knew at the training center, he was the hardest to figure out. The others were open about themselves. He wasn't. He seldom talked to anyone.

He nodded politely.

"Your antennae are drooping. Are you all right?" she asked.

"I'm fine," he said. "You sure have a pile of manuscripts there."

"More research," she smiled.

"Have you thought of . . . "

"What?" Henrietta coaxed.

"Of . . . Never mind. It was a foolish idea. I didn't mean to take your time."

He walked away before she could respond.

   *   *   *   *

For several days, Henrietta did nothing but stare at the images of Duo Pod writings found in stone and metal. She looked at the way the symbols were grouped, made a chart listing each symbol, counted how frequently each was used, looked again. Then she went back through all her notes detailing the theories of extinction and the changes in climate that had occurred around the same time. She dipped the tip of her pod in the ink and began to write.

On The Importance of Duo Pod Writings
by Henrietta Harvester

Two important unknowns remain concerning the Duo Pods. We must find the reason for their disappearance and we must learn to decode the written symbols. Such an advanced life form should have been able to survive all but the most cataclysmic of natural disasters. Such things had happened many times during the eons that they dominated the planet. Why would one more destroy them all? They were well adapted to extremes of climate. Why, with all the evidence of their technology that we find, were they not able to overcome further environmental change?

Evidence shows that the entire interdependent chain of life was disrupted when they disappeared. Could it happen again? There were other mass extinctions in the planet's past.

We could bring ourselves into closer harmony with the planet's natural cycles by studying what happened to them. We might benefit from learning more about their technology, as we did with tunnel liquid; perhaps even find the secret of plastic.

The key is in their writings. Such an advanced group must have left clues. Somewhere, if we devote much time and energy to the search, we will find the way to read the symbols.

I have noted some patterns and consistencies in the inscriptions we have already found. The number of different symbols in the images I examined is limited. Some are used only after several groupings of the others, not unlike our own punctuation marks. Others are probably numerical. Five of the smaller ones are used most frequently, at least one in every group. This could be a phonetic system similar to our own, but also very different. If given enough images of writings, the best minds of all the colonies could learn to read it. This would open a whole new world for us.

Henrietta stopped. Then she felt a sudden urge to add a more personal appeal.

Dear Master Diandra,

Pardon my forwardness. I truly desire to devote myself to the study of Duo Pod Erectus writings. Please, consider allowing me to study with you as my mentor.

Most humbly, your trainee,
Henrietta Harvester

4.

*H*enrietta arose elated. Her entire body radiated a confident glow. Henry paused after turning a grain cake on the griddle. "My, but you're cheerful this morning. Have you met someone?" He handed her a plate of hot grain cakes and a container of honey.

"No, Dad, sorry. I finished an important training report last night. I think it's the best manuscript I've ever written." She cut herself short, remembering her father's dislike of the surface and her promise to spend three season cycles in job exploration.

"What is it about?"

Henrietta altered her voice and said, "Ancient life forms. An archaeologist will visit next quarter time frame. We all had to prepare something."

"That certainly is a dull answer for such a glowing face," replied Henry.

Henrietta gobbled up her grain cakes and started toward the portal. Then she stopped. "Do you have anything complicated planned for supper tonight? I have to return a lot of manuscripts to the research center. I might be late getting home after training."

"No. There are some things left from last sixthday that we could warm up."

*　　　　　*　　　　　*　　　　　*

With only a quarter time frame remaining, and the pressure mounting, Antony grew more desperate. He spotted Henrietta leaving the training facility at the end of the day, not going in her usual direction. Her satchel looked heavy. He took a deep breath, put up his best front and called out to her. "Henrietta, is that you?"

She stopped and turned. "Hello, Antony."

"Are you headed for the research center?"

"Yes, I have to return some manuscripts."

"May I join you?"

She smiled and nodded.

"May I carry your satchel for you? It looks heavy."

"Thank you," she replied and handed it to him.

"How many manuscripts have you got in here? Maybe I should check them back out."

"You haven't started your archeology report yet?"

"Well, yes and no. I've thought about it." He paused. "Have you finished yours?"

"I finished it last night."

"Have you got a few minutes?" he asked as they reached the research center. "I really would like to check out some of these. Which ones did you find were the most helpful? I only have a few days to get mine done."

"Maybe you should've started sooner." She sat down with him at one of the work surfaces and took out the manuscripts.

They began to talk and she found herself eager to share her ideas. He seemed so genuinely interested, and she was anxious to tell someone. He questioned her critically, and it helped her refine her ability to explain her theory. Before they realized it, the research center was closing. She hurriedly checked in the materials and he checked them out again.

"I'm sorry I kept you so long. May I take you home?" he asked.

"Thank you. I'd like that."

It was quite late when they reached her domicile. She opened the portal. "Henrietta, it's more than a little late," her father said. "I've been worried."

"Dad, this is Antony. Antony, this is my father, Henry. I ran into him on the way to the research center, Dad. I'm sorry. We started talking and I forgot the time."

"It's really my fault. I asked Henrietta a lot of questions about her report," Antony apologized. "Henrietta, would you like to go to the Leisure Center with me for a while after training tomorrow?"

"Yes, I would."

Henry smiled. "Be sure to come home in time to help with supper." He wished Antony a pleasant evening and Antony left.

The next day was a blur for Henrietta. She was still excited about her report and glowing from Antony's warm invitation. She found it very difficult to concentrate on anything. When she reached their appointed meeting place, Antony was already there. He took her front pods in a cheerful greeting and led her down a quiet side tunnel to one of the colony's Leisure Centers.

Within the huge open chamber, many young adults of training age lounged about at tables while others interacted with a variety of games, laughing and talking. Several were lined up at the vending booth waiting for honey sodas. Antony led Henrietta to a quiet, padded bench near an edge curve.

"Wait here. I'll get something for both of us."

Henrietta looked around. Although many of her friends came here often, Henrietta had never come herself. Her parents had always needed her help with Annie and Andrew. Then she had been too wrapped up in her report.

Antony returned with two honey sodas and crisp fried fungus strips. They talked about training and family, but Antony kept returning the conversation to the ideas in her report. She began to relate them in even greater detail. He listened and questioned her critically, as he had the day before. When he left for a moment to get a second honey soda, one of the other females in Henrietta's base group came over.

"Hello, Annette," said Henrietta.

"How did you manage to get Antony down here?" Annette asked.

"What do you mean?"

"Oh, come on. Don't tell me you haven't taken a good look at him. He is so handsome. I've been trying to get him to notice me for half a season cycle. Some ants have all the luck."

Henrietta gave her an odd look. "It's not like that. We've been talking about my report."

"Have a good time," Annette said as she ambled off.

"Was that Annette?" asked Antony when he returned.

"Yes. She wishes you'd ask her to come down here. She wants you to notice her."

"I have noticed her. She wouldn't know an intelligent idea if it bit her."

"What a thing to say."

"I'm sorry. I didn't mean to be insulting."

Henrietta smiled to herself, because she knew he was right, but she would never have said it. They finished their sodas, and then Antony noticed the time.

"I guess we better leave. I said I wouldn't keep you too long today."

When they reached her portal, Antony said, "I really enjoyed being with you today. Could we go again tomorrow?"

"Sure," she said. That was the first time she saw Antony smile.

       *   *   *   *

Antony now had all the information he needed and sat down to write his report. He could remember what Henrietta had said almost word for word. He finished it quickly and was pleased with the result. It had been so easy: a few honey sodas, a couple of compliments. Then it hit him. Not a word of it was his, and it was intentional plagiarism.

He thought about her, so open, so eager to share. She was everything he had been taught to be. The unique shade of her exoskeleton stuck in his mind, the deep reddish black of ripe sand plums. How many varieties of ants had united in her background? She fascinated him. For the first time since he had come to the colony, he did not feel lonesome.

Antony crumpled up the report, threw it aside and picked up one of the manuscripts, trying to get an idea of his own.

He continued to see Henrietta every day after training. The evening of fifthday, he went to her domicile uninvited but found himself welcomed.

They sat in the parlor watching colonial events on the video wall. The announcement stated that the Intercolonial Council had made a new agreement with Roacheria allowing ants to work with roaches in the Duo Pod ruins not far from South Harvester 45.

"Humph," Henry said, "I wonder how long they'll honor this one."

"If we don't give it a chance, we'll never be able to show them we could work together," Antony said, thinking about Old Rodger.

"You wouldn't feel that way, if you'd been through what I've been through."

"Henry," Adeline cut in, "we put that behind us long ago. This isn't the time."

He sighed. "I'm sorry. I don't want it to happen again to anyone else."

Antony tried to smooth things out, although he wasn't sure what Henry was referring to. "My family runs a dairy. I guess we've had different experiences. Would you like to go for a stroll, Henrietta?"

"Yes, if you'll tell me more about the surface."

The two young adults rose and proceeded toward the portal.

"You'll really like the surface," Antony said as they wandered down a side tunnel. "The sun is so warm and there is so much light. You can see for d-units, not just to the next curve of a tunnel with nothing but brown earth, and the sky goes on forever," his voice trailed off.

"If I ever get there."

"Of course you will. You'll get that mentorship."

"What makes you so sure?"

"Because you know so much. I wish I knew half as much. My report is awful. I don't even want to turn it in."

"It can't be that bad. Maybe this subject isn't the right thing for you. I've had plenty of disastrous time frames of job exploration." She told him about what had happened when she went to work with each of her parents and about a time she had passed out at the medical facility. They were quiet a moment. He wanted to tell her how much he hated it underground, and that he wanted to be a part of the surface expedition so he could be with her. He wanted to say how much joy he felt when he was with her, but the words would not come. Instead, he painted her a word picture of the surface: its color, its beauty, the feeling of sky water on his face, the strength of the wind, the graceful curve of a grassfrond heavy with seed.

She sighed as they stopped and rested in a small alcove. He looked into her face and felt something he had never known before. She smiled and stroked his back with one of her middle pods. It felt wonderful, so he stroked hers in return.

"I've never had a friend like you before," he said.

"I've never had a friend like you either," she replied.

They returned slowly to her domicile. He hated to say good night. She went in to her family, and he returned to the emptiness of the emergency chamber he called home.

Working on another chamber the next morning, Antony thought about Henrietta and his still unwritten report. If she got the mentorship, she would be gone and he would still be in training, lonely again. If he did not turn in a report, he would be asked to leave.

He wondered what the chances were of being caught with a plagiarized report. There were over 200 trainees who had to turn in this particular project. Every other time they had had projects like this, the reports had sounded pretty much the same. They probably would this time as well. Who would know? If he put his at the bottom of the pile, maybe this master archaeologist wouldn't even read it.

When he finished the chamber, he returned to his own, picked up the crumpled report, rewrote it neatly and put his name on it.

*　　　　*　　　　*　　　　*

Firstday, Antony sat right in the front with Henrietta, and actually enjoyed Master Diandra's lecture.

"My young trainees," she began, after the usual introductions. "It is with much excitement that I address you today. I'm sure you are all aware of the wonderful news of last fifthday. At long last our Intercolonial Council has helped the South East Roach Control Board understand the importance of a cooperative effort in the formerly contested and now neutral area.

"This area is unique for the study of the ancient, extinct, life form you see before you." She gestured toward a reconstructed Duo Pod. "Your own South Harvester Colony 45 is closest to some of the best Duo Pod ruins. The ruins found in arid climates are better preserved, but this area is much larger. Additionally, because of the warmer climate, we are able to study them all through each season cycle. Our northern colonies, though free of roach interference, can be active on the surface only during the warm time frames.

"The western colonies enjoy our fair temperatures, but most of that region was destroyed by violent earth tremors and fire mountain eruptions around the time Duo Pod Erectus became extinct. What remains is difficult and dangerous to study because of the way the buildings collapsed and fell. More than one life has been lost in attempted excavations over the season cycles. Even plastic mining is difficult there. The conditions do, however, lend credence to the theory of natural disaster in causing their extinction.

"Here, along the southern, curving shore of the eastern sea, their remains were battered by severe summer storms, covered by rising seas, then gently buried in soft, muddy sediments as the seas retreated again. These sediments covered things that might have been destroyed by circulating air and water. To our east, in the roach territories, some areas are still partially submerged in bogs, making access difficult. The sea level is about ten f-units higher than it was 20,000 season cycles ago. If our efforts are successful here, we may be able to convince the roaches to allow us to enter some of the other ruins they control.

"You may wonder how it is we come to know so much from such little evidence. The answers are not easy, and no one can say whether our conclusions are correct. Each thing we find either supports or contradicts previous theories. Oddly enough, some of our best artifacts come from the layers of the plastic mines, rather than the ruins. If I could give you all the answers in this session, you wouldn't need to be here in training."

A ripple of laughter spread across the chamber. When it died, Master Diandra asked, "How many of you are genuinely interested in archaeology as a life's work?"

About ten twitched their antennae, all of whom were seated in front.

"That's about what I usually get. I know many of you have other things you'd prefer to do, so feel free to leave at any time."

Master Diandra continued to tell about an archaeologist's day. How h-unit upon h-unit or days and days of tedious digging often went into a single good find. Then again how a good find might reveal new and exciting things every minute.

She told about how carefully artifacts had to be removed, noting the soil conditions, depth and other surroundings for comparison with others. She told of days spent in collaborative discussions with other scientists, detailing possibilities and theories. Often they found that some locations had been scavenged, the best artifacts destroyed by their own less intelligent antcestors or primitive roaches. The time passed all too quickly, and the session was extended by popular demand. Even the newest trainees began to raise questions and no one left.

"No one has asked about the coded symbols," whispered Henrietta. Her voice faltered when she was called upon to speak. "Master Diandra, has there been any progress in decoding the writings found in stone and metal?"

"No one has studied them enough to find a decoding method. We have often thought that more of their manuscripts may have been written on some type of parchment like our own, which would not have lasted the ages. What is your name?"

"Henrietta Harvester."

"Well, Henrietta, good question."

Henrietta's eyes were shining with excitement when she sat back down. Antony's mandibles opened in astonishment as he realized that her report would not sound like everyone else's, and neither would his.

When they left for lunch, he made an excuse to get away and stumbled into the male lounge in a panic. He was well aware of the consequences of plagiarism as a form of theft. He hated to think about what Henrietta could do to him for his abuse of her trust. His mind was a confused mess of feelings for her that he had never experienced before and hatred of himself.

He decided he could not let anything happen to her. Her ideas were brilliant. She deserved the mentorship.

Running from the facility and the colony crossed his mind, but where would he go? Even Old Rodger would have nothing to do with him under those circumstances. He decided on a desperate move. He would take his report back, even though that meant being suspended from training. Facing his father would be better than being caught for plagiarism.

He left the lounge and made his way to Master Alex's work chamber, where he knew the reports had been taken. He watched until the receiving worker left for lunch. Breathing heavily, he slipped in. The outer chamber was empty. He listened at the portal of the inner chamber. Silence. He turned the latch and entered. The pile of reports lay on Master Alex's work surface. Henrietta's was right on top. He began to look through the pile for his.

A voice came from the outer chamber. The latch clicked and Antony found himself facing Master Alex.

"Antony! What are you doing here? Did we have an appointment?"

Antony gulped. His mind went blank. Master Alex stared at him, waiting for an answer.

"Master Alex," he stammered. "I'm sorry. I know I should have waited for the receiving ant, but I, uh . . ." In his panic he said the first thing that came to mind. "I think I forgot to put my name on my report and

I wanted to check. Remember, you said I couldn't be late with another one and . . ."

"Let me see," Master Alex looked through the pile. "Look, yours is right here. You didn't forget," he said, plopping it on top of the pile with Henrietta's. "Have you been feeling better?"

Antony gulped again. "Yes," until now.

"Lunch is about over. You'd better head on to your next training unit. Have a good day."

"Thank you, Master Alex." Antony backed out, defeated.

For two days Antony lived in agony. Once, he thought he should go to Master Alex and admit the whole thing before he was discovered, and beg for another chance. Another part of him hoped that, against all odds, no one would read his report. He could not face Henrietta and avoided her as much as possible. She kept looking toward him during their Ancient Antstory unit. The confused look in her eyes after all his attention toward her burned through him and tore at his conscience. He did not eat, could not sleep. He vented some of his anxiety cleaning three more emergency chambers.

                    *   *   *   *

After the noon break on thirdday, Henrietta received a message from Master Alex to come to his work chamber to meet with Master Diandra. Her heart skipped a few beats as she scurried down the training facility passageways.

She opened the portal and entered. Seated before her were Master Alex, with a very sour expression on his face, and Master Diandra, looking quite calm. To her complete surprise, Antony was seated to the right.

"It's all right, Miss Harvester," said Master Diandra. "I'm sure we'll get to the bottom of this. Please, sit down."

Henrietta had no time to wonder what she meant. Master Alex was blunt. "Antony and Henrietta, when two trainees collaborate on a manuscript, it is expected that they will put both their names on one copy. What we have here are two amazingly similar, but unique reports to which each of you claim sole authorship. I expect a reasonable explanation."

Henrietta's mind was swimming. "I don't know what you're talking about. I worked alone on my report. I spent several time frames researching and writing it. I didn't . . . I . . ." She clenched her mandibles together for control as she thought of the last quarter time frame—the flattery, the discussions, and how much she had told Antony about her ideas. She looked directly at him. "Antony, why? How could you?"

With all eyes fixed on him, Antony sank lower. His abdomen seemed to shrivel instead of protruding normally from the open back of the chair.

He hung his head. "What's the use? I've ruined everything anyway. Yes, I used Henrietta's ideas. No, I didn't ask her if I could. If you want to banish me from training, fine. I hate it down here. All I ever wanted was to stay on the dairy. I only came because Old Rodger wanted me to. Don't blame Henrietta. She had nothing to do with it. She didn't even know. Look, Henrietta, I'm sorry. I never thought this would happen."

Henrietta stared at him. All her energy was focused on controlling the hurt and anger she felt, so she could continue to be polite in front of two ants she respected very much. She wanted them to think she was mature and responsible enough to enter a mentorship. Bursting into an emotional rage wouldn't help.

Master Alex's voice broke the silence. "That was easier than I expected."

"Wait, Master Alex," interrupted Master Diandra. "Appearances can be deceiving. In my business nothing is ever simple. Antony, if you aren't from here, where did you come from?"

"I'm not from any colony. All I have is my family. We were among the few survivors of South Dairy Colony 50."

Master Diandra looked at him with renewed interest. Master Alex's and Henrietta's mandibles opened wide in shock.

Master Alex asked, "Why wasn't I informed of this when you enrolled?"

"I didn't want any pity or special treatment. I felt awkward enough being so much older than the other trainees."

"Who is Old Rodger?" asked Master Diandra.

"A banished roach who lived near us. He taught me their language."

Master Diandra stared at him. "You speak Roach?"

"Yes, fluently."

"Master Alex," continued Master Diandra, "forgive me if I overstep my bounds and interfere in your role as director of this training facility. I had a higher purpose in choosing to speak here while looking for trainees. You have a reputation for turning out the best, and that's what I sought. I am not disappointed.

"Antony, your actions in this incident are truly deserving of banishment, not only from this facility, but from the colony. You are rash, devious, and unconcerned with the results of your actions, but there are extenuating circumstances here. The truth is I need you. You think like a roach, but you seem to be, at heart, truthful and dutiful. I need an interpreter who will not deceive me. No colony has anyone who can speak Roach. Only a few read it. Master Alex, I would like to have this young male in my custody under a probationary contract."

Under such a contract, Antony would belong to Master Diandra. She would control all his rights under ant law.

"Under the circumstances, I agree," stated Master Alex. "Is that all right with you, Henrietta?"

Afraid she would break down if she spoke, Henrietta twitched her antennae in agreement.

"Antony, gather your things and report here first thing tomorrow morning to sign the parchments. Your family will be informed. Since you confessed this freely, I don't think an escort will be necessary. You're excused."

"Thank you, Master Alex. Thank you, Master Diandra. I will be here tomorrow. I promise. You will not be disappointed in me." He looked toward Henrietta, but she looked away. He bowed respectfully and left the chamber, head down.

Master Diandra turned and smiled. "Now, Henrietta, we may speak more easily. I'm sorry this began with such unpleasantness for you. I was quite sure the report was yours, because of your question and your personal note."

She turned to Master Alex, who handed both of them a cup of warm honey dew. Henrietta sipped, recovering her composure.

"You are a remarkable young female," continued Master Diandra. "If I were you, I might have sunk my mandibles deep into one of Antony's vulnerable areas."

For the first time since she had entered the chamber, Henrietta smiled.

"How did you figure out the patterns you wrote about? What you stated is more than anyone has accomplished to date."

"I looked at them for a long time. It reminded me of learning to read when I began basic training. I decided to count how many different symbols I could find. That was when I noticed the five that are used so often, like our six open-voiced sounds."

"Master Alex, where did you find this young female?"

"Her parents brought her two days after she emerged from pupation. After only two time frames, she was doing so well at basic decoding that she tested out of first season cycle training and went straight into second level. She has always been our top trainee."

Master Diandra set down her mug. "Henrietta, I shall be honored to be your mentor. Your parents must be very proud. What did they say about your report?"

"They haven't seen it yet. I wanted this to be a surprise."

"So it will be. We shall be leaving this coming firstday. Will that give you enough time to prepare and say your farewells? We may be gone as long as two season cycles. With the restraint and maturity you displayed here today, I feel you are more than ready." Master Diandra handed Henrietta a mentorship contract and an ink pot.

Henrietta glanced over the contract and signed it. "I'll make it be enough time. This is my life's dream coming true. Thank you, Master Diandra. Where shall I report on firstday?"

"We'll begin with a ceremony at Colony Council Chambers, seventh h-unit. I hope your parents will be able to attend. Here is a list of things you should plan to take." She handed Henrietta another piece of parchment. "Everything else will be provided. I have one more request. Unless Antony violates his contract with me, it must remain confidential. Do you think you can manage that, Henrietta?"

"I think I can."

Henrietta scurried home and burst through the portal calling, "Mom, Dad! I did it. I got the mentorship." She was met with silence and remembered that it was still early in the afternoon and neither of her parents had returned from work. She tossed her satchel into her sleep chamber, placed the report in the middle of the dining surface and began to bake a honey cake. She was removing it from the heat box when her parents came in. They gave her an odd look as she held out the cake.

She told them everything, except the part about Antony's actions and the contract.

Adeline plopped Andrew into his larva coop and sat down to recover her thoughts.

"Well," Henry stammered, "it certainly is a surprise."

"Aren't you happy? I thought you'd be so pleased."

"We are," Adeline assured her daughter. "But it's quite a shock. You never even mentioned the possibility. I thought you were going to say you had promised yourself to Antony when you held out the cake."

Henrietta cringed at the thought. "No, I'm not ready for anything like that. I have my dreams about how I want to serve our colony."

Over dinner, she told them that Antony would be going as an interpreter. When pressed for details about him, she sat silent a moment, and then related what she had learned about his background. Her parents were surprised at this and seemed sympathetic toward him.

Would they feel that way if they knew?

When Henrietta had retired to her sleep chamber, Henry tapped on her portal, came in and sat down on the edge of her thistledown mattress. He put his front legs around her and embraced her, stroking her antennae in a fatherly way.

"No wonder you were so elated that morning. I'm very proud of your accomplishment, but I'm not thrilled with your choice for your life's work. Perhaps it's just as well you didn't mention it. I would have tried my best to change your mind. Now I can't, as much as I want to."

"I don't understand."

"There are many things you don't understand. I fear for your life."

"Why?"

"It's time you knew why I don't trust anything about the S.E.R.C.B. That Board has about as much control over its members as it has over the weather. Some make an agreement while others plot to break it before it's even signed.

"Many season cycles ago, when I finished my mentorship, and took my first tunnel engineering job, they contracted with our council for three of us to help them learn to build proper tunnels in their plastic mines. They offered huge amounts of credit. I had made my promise to your mother only two days before. I didn't want to go, but they requested me. Your mother and I both felt it was my duty.

"The contract was supposed to be for half a season cycle. We were attacked by renegades and the Board Member with whom we signed the agreement was murdered. His son, whose name we never learned, enslaved us. They kept us under close guard and nearly starved us to death. No communication was allowed with the colony, and they put off our council's request to return us. At times we thought of sabotaging the whole operation, but we knew that would mean our deaths. All we could do was endure it, clinging to hope and to our dignity. Finally, after a season cycle, the roach engineer we were training helped us escape. We returned with only our lives. We asked the colony not to retaliate because we knew the punishment would be severe for the one who saved us. That's why I don't trust them and am afraid for you."

"Why didn't you tell me this before?"

"It's something I've tried hard to forget. But I intend to stress the need for adequate protection for your entire group, even with this neutral zone agreement."

*   *   *   *

After he left the training facility, Antony packed his satchel, took the location chart, the list of emergency chambers and his records of checking them, and went to Andy's work chamber. He knew he was not required to tell anyone about the contract, so he only told Andy that he was to be an interpreter and would no longer be in the colony.

Sick at heart, he decided to spend the night at the top of his favorite wood plant where he could feel the freedom of the wind, but he felt no comfort there. In his dreams he saw the hurt in Henrietta's eyes over and over again. At dawn, he returned to the colony and arrived at Master Alex's work chamber even before the receiving ant. He sat in the outer chamber and waited.

He heard the click of pods on the passage floor. Master Alex and Master Diandra entered.

"Good morning," said Master Diandra.

Master Alex gave him a look that was colder than freezing sky water on some bleak midwinter dawn.

Master Diandra handed him his contract:

"I, Antony Dairier, fully admit my guilt in the matter of my archaeology report. I did no research. With full knowledge that my actions were wrong, I gained the trust of Henrietta Harvester, convinced her to share her ideas with me, and then betrayed her trust, using her ideas as my own. I did not think of her feelings as I betrayed her. I thought only of myself. I have seriously violated the sacred values of honesty, integrity, and care for others.

"To make restitution for this, I now place myself in the service of Master Diandra for a period of two season cycles from this date. I will do whatever she requires of me to the best of my ability.

"I understand that if I betray Master Diandra, or any other member of the surface expedition of which I am to be a part, I will be banished to permanent underground work in North Carpenter Colony 5. I will never be permitted to see the surface, my family, or any other ant I care about, for the rest of my natural life.

"Signed_____ this 20th day of the Third Time Frame, 186th Season Cycle of The Combined Colonies of Insectia."

Antony stared at it. "Permanent! Underground? North Carpenter 5? Why don't you just extinguish me right now?"

Master Diandra looked at him as if she had expected such a reaction. "I spent a long time yesterday visiting with several of your trainers. Extinguishing you would be an incredible waste of talent and intelligence. Look on the bright side. You'll be free in two season cycles."

Antony knew if he did not sign it, she would take that as a violation of trust and enforce banishment immediately. He had made his choice last sixthday. His pods began to shake in rage and despair.
He took several deep breaths. "May I ask one question first?"

"Yes, you may."

"Did you give Henrietta the mentorship?"

She smiled. "I've spent more than half my adult life looking for a trainee with her intense interest and abilities. Of course I did."

"Then I don't care what you do to me," he said and signed the parchment.

"Thank you, Antony. Master Alex, an archaeological project isn't a very good place for a document like this. Would you keep it for me until we return in two season cycles to consume it?"

"Of course."

"Have a good day, Master Alex. Come along, Antony, we have a lot to do, and don't hang your head like some abused roach."

He followed her to the main science facility, past the public viewing area and the work and research portions, where she waved a greeting to several scientists. Behind the work area was a small passageway leading to guest domiciles. Master Diandra opened the portal to one and entered. The parlor was small but inviting. Images of the surface decorated its curving, earthen walls. On the right he saw a small area for food preparation and the farther wall had two more portals. Master Diandra opened one.

"This chamber will be your home for the next four days. It's quite comfortable and you will find everything you need." She paused and looked into his eyes. He turned away to shut out her penetrating gaze. Her voice was calm, yet deadly serious.

"Please, give me your satchel. You won't need it until we leave on first day. I know you aren't ready to talk to me, and you don't like it when I look at you. But don't shut me out, because I'm your only hope right now. What I see is a young male whose problems go far beyond this crisis. I think you are lonely, angry, and afraid, and I know you refused help from all who offered it. I don't know why, but I intend to find out. I'm the one ant who can ask you personal questions and expect an answer. Enter this chamber and do some serious thinking about how you want to spend the rest of your life. You can quit pretending and unload that anger. Tear the place apart if that's what it takes. No one will hear you. I'll be gone most of the day, since I have many arrangements to complete. For your own safety, I will secure the portal."

Antony handed her his satchel, hung his head and entered the chamber. She closed the portal behind him and he heard a second latch click. He looked around in despair, then searched the chamber and its sanitation area for something he could use to extinguish himself. There was nothing. He cursed her in Roach for not leaving him that option. He continued to yell in Roach at his father for sending him for training, at Old Rodger for the words which had finally convinced him to leave home, and then he let loose his anger.

He upset the work surface, threw the chair across the chamber, tore the images of the surface from the walls and ripped them up. He threw the cushions, then tore at them with his mandibles, and threw the fluff. There was little satisfaction in throwing fluff, so he ripped up the mattress. Its woven thistledown cover was strong, but his rage was stronger. He shredded the mattress until there was not one piece larger than the tenth part of an f-unit. When there was nothing left to destroy, he lay amid the fluff, pounded the floor with his pods, let out hot tears of anger, and cursed himself until his voice was nearly gone. Exhausted and miserable, he went to sleep.

Much later, he felt a pod on his back. "Antony?"

He groaned.

"Are you finished? Are you ready to talk to me now?"

His eyes pleaded with her. "Master Diandra, I don't want to spend the rest of my life underground in a chamber like this, but I don't know how I'm going to do this alone." He began to shake with sorrow and loneliness.

The last thing he expected happened. Master Diandra circled him with her front and middle appendages, handed him a cloth and stroked him. He let himself go and leaned against her, desperate for comfort.

"I would like you to tell me everything about yourself," she said when he was calm. "Perhaps we can find the cause of all this anger and a way to avoid it in the future. I'm not here to dangle your contract over your head like a spider web, waiting for some small error on your part. I happen to believe that there is a caring ant under all this, and if we dig deeply enough, we can find him. Please, talk to me. You need not be alone."

The two of them sat amid the mess, as he related the details of his life, from the moment he emerged up until his botched attempt to take back his report.

"You told him you forgot your name?"

He nodded. "I can't believe I was so stupid."

"Not stupid, desperate," she sighed. "It doesn't excuse what you did, but I understand now. You were so depressed, it never occurred to you to write about what you knew and offer your services as an interpreter. Wait here. I'll be right back."

She went to the food preparation area, leaving the portal open. In a few minutes she returned with a steaming mug. "Drink this. It's a tea made from several floral herbs to help you sleep. Did you think you could conquer your fear by forcing yourself to be alone?"

Antony shrugged. "I don't know."

"That's the problem with young adults. You're full of knowledge, but lack wisdom. Unfortunately, your wisdom often comes through crisis and pain. You shouldn't have isolated yourself. We were meant to work together and support each other. Are you ready to rebuild your life?"

"Yes."

"One thing more," she said as he sipped his tea. "Why Henrietta?"

"Because she's so intelligent."

"You didn't expect to begin to care about her in the middle of it, did you?"

"No. She probably hates me now."

"Hate is a strong word. I don't think she hates you. I'm sure she'll be bitter for some time, but she obviously cared about you enough to leave you to me."

The herb tea took effect. Antony lay down in the mess and slept soundly.

"Wake up. It's sixthday morning." Master Diandra shook Antony gently.

He sat up, looked around, and groaned, remembering everything. Master Diandra placed several baskets along one wall and held out some woven thistledown and a small sack.

"Think of this chamber as if it were your life. How you repair it and fill it are up to you. Separate things into the baskets by the type of material. All of it can go to the re-use center. Here is a new cover for the mattress and sewing materials. Do you know how to use them?"

He nodded.

"Refill the mattress and stitch the last edge. Clean up the whole mess and yourself. I'm leaving you some seeds and honeydew if you get hungry. I'm also leaving some parchment and ink. The letter your parents will get from Master Alex will be blunt and factual. I think they deserve an explanation from you. I'll see that yours is sent with his. Can you manage all this?" She rubbed the back of his thorax.

Antony looked around and then up at her. "Yes."

"I've got to meet with the Colony Council and some others. Will you be all right by yourself? Do I need to lock the portal?"

"I really want to do a good job for you. Please, don't lock the portal. I won't leave."

Her eyes searched his again. This time he didn't mind, and looked back at her steadily, hoping she believed him. She nodded her head and left the portal open.

It was late in the evening when he finished. He heard Master Diandra return. She nodded her approval and said good night. The blank parchment was still sitting on the floor, along with the uneaten seeds. Dreading what he must write, Antony picked up the parchment and sat down at the work surface. A dozen beginnings later, his words still sounded lame. Hoping that they would understand, he began once more and simply related the events of the last few time frames. He folded the parchments together and crawled onto the mattress he had refilled and stitched.

When he awoke, the domicile was silent. The portal of his chamber stood open and there was a note attached:

"Dear Antony,

"I tried to wake you, but you were sleeping too soundly.

I have gone to meditation service and will be back soon.
You must be hungry by now. The cold storage unit
is well stocked. Make yourself at home. Master Diandra."

He had eaten next to nothing since firstday. Before long, he was seated at the dining surface—plate piled high with cold roast grasshopper, seeds, fungus muffins and a large mug of warm honeydew. Master Diandra came back in the middle of his second plateful.

"Good morning. It's good to see you have your appetite back."
He smiled and handed her the letter to his parents. She sealed it without reading it. "So, you do know how to smile. How did you usually spend your seventhdays?"

"This probably sounds silly, but I would climb up that tall conifer by the main entrance and watch the sun come up as I meditated."

"It doesn't sound silly at all. You've missed the sunrise, but would you still like to go?"

"Yes, I would."

"Would you mind if I joined you?"

Master Diandra was full of surprises. She was in charge of his life, yet asked to come with him.

"No, I wouldn't mind."

It was a short jaunt from the science facility up the main tunnel to the surface. A warm spring wind blew as they ascended the wood plant. When he reached the top, Antony sat down on a branch, raised his front pods above him and breathed deeply. He felt Master Diandra sit down beside him. He lifted up his thoughts aloud.

"Guiding Force that binds all life together at its source, I am so afraid. I don't know where I'm going, or what I'm doing. I have no strength left to make it on my own. I don't know where to begin, or how to change my life. I only know I want to try." He felt her pod join his.

"Wisdom of the Ages," she said, "greater than all of us, so often we forget that the strength we seek from the Source of All Life comes through each other. May we remember it is as close as the tip of our front pods, reaching out to those near us, for the care and comfort we so desperately need. Through one another, may we find the unity and peace we seek."

In the silence that followed, Master Diandra continued to hold Antony's front pod. He began to feel he could do what she required of him. A tiny seed of confidence he had never felt before began to grow inside him. He lowered his pods, opened his eyes and looked out at the green meadows before him. A giant orange and back butterfly flapped silently toward them, alighted on the topmost branch of the conifer and flew off again.

On the way back, Master Diandra spoke only once. "Whenever you need to talk, I'll be here for you."

5.

*A*fter lunch on seventhday, Master Diandra took out the jug of honeydew and reached for three mugs. "I'm expecting Captain Alexander and we have some things to discuss regarding your duties."

Before she had finished pouring the honeydew, a fire ant of medium length entered. He took both Master Diandra's front pods in his in a greeting of friendship.

"What kind of a project have you gotten me into this time? Last season cycle wasn't enough for you?"

"Captain Alexander, meet Antony, our interpreter."

Captain Alexander took Antony's front pods in greeting. Antony noticed that he was a good f-unit longer than Captain Alexander. But fire ants were known for their strength, fierce fighting ability and the deadly poison in their sting, not for their size.

"You have to watch out when you sign on with this female," Captain Alexander said to Antony. "She doesn't like to let go. She's taken my unit of guards from one end of the southern region to the other, ever since I finished training ten season cycles ago."

"I only request the best," said Master Diandra.

"Actually, the council sends me with her because she's too trusting and I'm too suspicious. We balance each other to make a good team." He turned back to Master Diandra, "Where did you find someone who speaks Roach?"

"At the same facility as my trainee, Henrietta Harvester."

Antony told the captain where he came from and a little about the time he had spent with Old Rodger.

Captain Alexander grinned. "Now there's a roach I'd actually like to meet!" He placed one pod on Antony's back. "Master Diandra, I think you were very lucky when you found this young male."

Master Diandra grew serious. "I want every single word translated, Antony."

"Listen closely to their interpreter," Captain Alexander emphasized. "They've lied to us many times. If you catch even a hint of sabotage or treachery, I want to know about it. But tell me privately. I don't want to alarm the other members of the group unnecessarily."

"I'll do my best."

        *   *   *   *

Henrietta awoke very early on firstday, straightened up her sleep chamber and went to the kitchen. She had just taken a batch of graincakes off the griddle when Henry came in.

"Too excited to sleep, hmmm?"

She smiled.

Henry embraced her affectionately, as he had so often the last few days. "You won't understand our feelings for many season cycles. It's hard for your mother and me to let go of you. It seems like only yesterday that your mother laid your egg."

She snuggled against his thorax. "You act as though I'm never coming back."

        *   *   *   *

In the council chamber, expedition members and their families were directed to the front. With musical fanfare, two ant guards entered, bearing the Intercolonial Banner. The many varieties of ants, partly erect and holding front pods to symbolize their interdependence, stood out against the banner's white background. All present rose to dedicate themselves to their ideals.

"We promise loyalty to the banner of the Combined Colonies of Insectia and to the spirit of cooperation which it represents, one group of beings, in unity with Essence, with care and concern for all."

South Harvester 45's Council Chief stepped up to the podium and addressed them. She spoke about the importance of this project, wished them all the best and introduced some other Council Members who spoke briefly. The ceremony ended with special blessings and uplifted thoughts.

Antony watched Henrietta say good-bye to her parents and wished he had family there. Henrietta's father approached him. Nervousness made Antony's antennae twitch, but Henry extended his front pods.

"Henrietta tells me you speak Roach."

Antony nodded.

"I'd like to ask you a favor, because I think you care a lot for Henrietta. You know I don't trust the roaches. Help the fire ants protect all of you, especially my daughter."

Hope surged through Antony. Henry must not know what had happened. If Henrietta had not told her parents, maybe she cared enough about him to forgive him. Perhaps he might earn her friendship once more.

"I'll do everything I can, Henry."

"Thank you," Henry said, giving Antony a warm embrace.

*   *   *   *

Henrietta and the other expedition members entered an adjoining meeting chamber. A large oval surface sat in the middle, surrounded by padded benches. Expedition members rested their abdomens on the benches, middle and back appendages on the floor in front of them, and placed their front pods on the surface. Master Diandra sat at the head, her abdomen protruding from the open back of her chair. She leaned on one side of the chair and spoke with a fire ant officer.

The chamber portals closed. Master Diandra straightened up and said, "Welcome to each and every one of you. Since many of you are strangers to each other, some introductions are in order. This is Captain Alexander, my co-leader. He will be in charge of the fifty fire ant guards who will be with us for protection. They will also assist us with much of the routine work around the camp so we may concentrate on our own tasks. He must leave us now for a short time to speak to those under his command."

Captain Alexander waved and left by a side portal. Master Diandra continued to introduce the others. There were two chemists, Daniel and Aaron, from South Harvester 45; two geologists, Hanna and Arnold, from West Harvester 30; and two other archaeologists, Carl and Carrie, from North Carpenter 20. They were the largest carpenter ants Henrietta had ever seen. Carrie was also a trainee, but had more experience than Henrietta.

Master Diandra came to Henrietta. "I'm pleased to introduce Henrietta Harvester. I found her four days ago while lecturing at one of the training facilities here and am now her mentor. She has some very interesting ideas about decoding the Duo Pod symbols. If any of you find any etchings in stone or metal, summon her immediately so she can make an image and take notes about the surroundings. She will need many images and notes for season cycles to come."

Henrietta slipped the tip of her pod around a mug of water in front of her and sipped, self-conscious at Master Diandra's praise.

"Finally, a fortunate surprise. This is Antony, our interpreter. Antony's parents are survivors of South Dairy 50. During his early adulthood, he had a lot of contact with a banished roach official and managed to learn the language. I have spent many h-units in serious discussion with him over the last few days. If the roaches approach you in our own language, put them off politely until he can be summoned. The S.E.R.C.B. does not have a reputation for honoring agreements. We must lead by our example, but balance that with good sense."

Captain Alexander re-entered. "I ask your cooperation with a few security measures," he said. "Keep your communications to friends and family on a personal level. Nothing is worse than misunderstood rumors. All announcements of our findings will go through the Science Facility. For your personal safety, always be with a partner. Keep our camp within sight. If you wish to go farther, let me know, so that I can send at least two of our guards with you. I know you will all look out for each other."

Everyone nodded in agreement. They gathered their things and proceeded out of the chamber into the colony's main tunnel. The fire ant guards joined them from a side tunnel, bearing all the expedition's equipment.

Henrietta gasped when she reached the open air. No amount of description or images could have prepared her for the vast openness and brightness that met her. A warm spring wind touched her face and she sighed.

Carrie was beside her. "It's your first time, isn't it?"

"Yes."

"I don't think anyone ever forgets the first time on the surface." She laughed softly in a way that Henrietta found reassuring. They fell into step together, talking about their lives and families.

The group followed the main trail north toward South Dairy Colony 40. After about one and a half h-units, they turned onto a fainter trail leading east.

"How far have we come?" Henrietta asked Carrie.

"Only about ten d-units. Are you tired?"

"Yes, a little. I didn't have to go far for training. I'm afraid I don't exercise much."

An h-unit after that, they arrived at another cross path running north. The group stopped to rest and have their mid-day meal. Henrietta sat with Carrie, rubbed her pods and nibbled on the chunk of bread a guard had handed her. Antony approached uncertainly and sat down.

"Hello, Henrietta. It's good to see you. Are you all right?"

She gave him an icy stare. "I'm fine."

"It's nice to talk to you in a less formal setting, Antony," Carrie said.

"It's good to be here," he said. "This trail leading north goes straight to my family's dairy. It's only about twenty d-units."

"Really?" replied Carrie.

"You two go ahead and visit," said Henrietta in a huff. "I'll see you later." She picked up her bread, seeds and water flask, and her satchels, stalked over to where Master Diandra sat with some of the others, and plopped herself down. She walked with her mentor when the journey resumed.

"The small piles of rubble protruding a little above these grassy fields are all that remain of what must have been many individual family domiciles," Master Diandra explained. "There is little of importance here. It will be another h-unit before we reach our campsite. They let us in this area briefly last season cycle."

Antony came up on the other side of Master Diandra but said nothing. Henrietta ignored him.

Master Diandra continued. "This area has always been part of The Combined Colonies. Roacheria took advantage of our grief after the death of South Dairy 50 and claimed it. We didn't protest, since the area was not in use. It has taken us all these season cycles to regain it. Archaeological research has always been our only goal."

Henrietta was grateful for the conversation, as it eased the tension she felt with Antony present. Putting the hurt behind her to work cooperatively was going to be more difficult than she thought.

They passed more and more piles of rubble and some buildings with parts of walls standing. In the distance, they saw what remained of long, rising arches of synthetic stone and metal, curving over and around each other in multiple layers.

"We find these structures wherever two main transport systems cross each other," said Master Diandra. "We'll be camped in the flat area near them. Henrietta, come with me up the arch. It's quite safe and the view is spectacular. Antony, go on with the others and help set up camp."

Antony nodded and left them. Henrietta followed her mentor up the slope of synthetic stone. When they reached the highest point, she saw stretched out before her d-unit upon d-unit of ruins.

She let out a long drawn out, "OOOOOOOOO!"

The two of them sat down. Master Diandra explained the scene before them. Henrietta, fascinated, forgot how tired and sore she was from the journey.

"We began to excavate an extensive marketing district on that side of the transport system last season cycle," Master Diandra said, pointing to her right. "Over there, lie the remnants of what were probably multifamily domiciles."

In the clear spring air, they could see the remains of numerous tall buildings. Henrietta saw another crossing of arches perhaps five or six d-units away, with more tall buildings a little to the south. Another five or six d-units beyond these, the largest spires at the center of the ruins loomed above the meadow grass. Henrietta knew that they could work here for decades and never uncover all of it. It was nearly sundown before they went down to the camp.

6.

*T*he camp consisted of several dome-shaped structures. The largest was a meeting and dining facility. It stood a few f-units from a water well dug by guards the previous season cycle. On either side of it were two smaller domes for the male and female members of the expedition with sanitation facilities near each. Ten small bunking domes for the guards formed a circle around the other structures.

Each dome's frame consisted of light weight, easily bent grassfrond poles bound together. Tightly woven rush mats covered each frame. Overlapped and bound with hemp lines, they kept out wind and sky water. Only the most severe summer storms could upset the domes. But by that time, the guards would have finished their emergency underground shelter.

Henrietta and Master Diandra entered the female dome. Henrietta set up her folding work surface and a stool, unpacked her manuscripts and writing materials, and rolled out her thistledown sleep sack. Master Diandra hung a portable lightning bug lamp in the center of the dome and turned it on. Carrie and Hanna had already set up their things and gone on to the dining dome.

Supper was delicious: grasshopper steaks, plastic salad, fungus muffins and honey dew. Everyone relished each bite. The camp had no permanent cold storage. They would only have such perishable food once each quarter time frame when the carriers arrived from the colony on sixthdays.

They had a short meeting to set up a schedule for various camp chores and daily routines. Henrietta was grateful for the unusually warm spring evening. She flopped down on top of her sleep sack, too tired to crawl into it.

She awoke as the first rays of sun poured into the dome through its open portal. She turned to gaze at it and found herself terribly stiff and sore. Groaning, she flopped back down.

Master Diandra was at her side immediately. "What's the matter?"

"My legs ache. I can barely move."

Master Diandra examined her carefully. "You've trained your mind well, but neglected you body. Your muscles are a little swelled under your exoskeleton from the journey yesterday. You'll be fine." She reached out a front pod and pulled Henrietta up.

"Your first and daily assignment is to get some exercise. I want you to scurry up to the top of the arches once today before breakfast. That will loosen up your joints. Each day from now on, get up one h-unit earlier and increase the number of trips up and down until you can do it twenty times at top speed with ease."

As Henrietta winced and limped toward the portal, Carrie joined her. "I'll go with you."

*   *   *   *

Antony's antennae twitched as the ants, flanked by ten guards, proceeded three d-units east to their first meeting with the roaches. What if he made mistakes? Would Master Diandra think he was disloyal? She seemed supportive but she still had the right to banish him. He recalled how he had subtly directed his father's trade, and put himself into a roach frame of mind.

"The meadow grass is so short," he heard Henrietta say to Master Diandra. "Why don't grassfronds and wood plants grow here?"

"There's a lot of synthetic stone under a thin layer of soil. Grassfronds and large wood plants need good deep soil to take root. Sometimes, the presence of this type of grass tells us where to dig."

The roach group, smaller in number than theirs, approached. Several solid brown warriors, nearly twice Antony's size, stood on each side. Their leader, standing in the center, was the larger type, like the warriors. Antony couldn't count the number of ornaments hanging about the roach leader's head. He took a deep breath to calm himself.

A smaller roach next to their leader introduced himself. "I am Randal and will interpret for you."

Antony stepped forward and introduced himself in Roach. The one with all the ornaments spoke.

Antony repeated. "This is Sir Rex, representative of the South East Roach Control Board. He is pleased to see us and surprised that we have an interpreter."

Master Diandra said, "Tell him he is welcome."

Randal introduced the other roaches: Master Gerald, a geo-chemist; and Master Roland and Master Gerard, both archaeologists.

Master Diandra pointed to ten small, slender roaches behind them. "And these?" she asked.

"Workers. Their names aren't important," replied Randal.

Sir Rex spoke in a low, gruff voice.

Master Diandra turned to Antony. "What did he say?"

"He referred to their workers with an insult."

"What was it?"

Antony shifted. "We don't really have equivalent words in our language."

"Tell me as closely as you can," Master Diandra insisted.

While Antony used their curses and insults privately in his own anger, he didn't want to repeat such things to the group. But he was afraid that if he didn't translate them, Master Diandra would not trust him.

"Low, miserable body refuse," he whispered.

Antony introduced each of the ants and read a formal greeting from the Intercolonial Council.

Randal read greetings from the South East Roach Control Board. "It is hoped that this joint project will be the beginning of better relations and that it will promote understanding between us. Sincerely, Sir Reginald, Supreme Executor."

Sir Rex twanged his mandibles in a gesture of contempt. Antony returned it with another that meant he understood every word and could not be fooled.

Sir Rex spoke directly to Antony, using the most complex gestures and words, an obvious test. "What low-life traitor taught you our language? Answer me and don't lie, for your nervousness betrays you."

At the same time, Antony watched him give Randal a gesture that meant, "Shut up."

Antony turned to Master Diandra. "He has complemented my use of their language and would like to know where I learned so much."

"Go ahead and tell him."

Something inside Antony warned him not to say too much, while another part was tempted to boast. He decided to say it in Ant and let Randal translate. He wanted his own to trust him.

"I am Antony Dairier, son of Dorothy and David of South Dairy Colony 50. Your traders often stopped and exchanged products with us. I also had contact with one of your outcasts who scrounged out a living at the edge of our surface area."

He watched Sir Rex's reaction as Randal translated his statement, not perfectly, but good. Antony realized he knew more Roach than Randal did Ant.

"Oh, that family," was all Randal said of Sir Rex's reply. Antony heard more, but he kept it to himself. He caught a look in Sir Rex's eye that expressed an angry realization. Was this the one Old Rodger had warned him about?

Randal said, "Our archaeologists wish to locate a liquid sometimes buried in synthetic stone tanks. They want to study the liquid to see if we can gain the type of technology we need for better machinery. This may do for us what tunnel liquid did for you."

Master Gerald broke in. Antony translated. "We have found many plastic models of machines. We think the liquid was used to make larger ones of metal move. We have been working on chemical analysis."

Master Diandra turned to Master Gerald. "I would like to start in the area closest to the market complex, so Henrietta can learn basic excavation techniques. Could you look for this liquid there?"

"He says that will be fine," Antony replied. "They will go back to their camp and get their tools."

When they reached the market area, Master Roland, the senior roach archaeologist, explained that they should dig a path about one f-unit wide, perpendicular to the transport line toward the market area. They would dig other parallel paths about every five f-units. He would look for the signs that they had seen in other places where they had found tanks. He chose the most likely place to start, near the remains of a bridge over the transport lanes.

"We have found them in other places where a smaller transport lane crossed a larger one. The machines moved on the transport lines, then came off to get more liquid," he told Antony.

They found that the deposits of sediment were only half an f-unit deep and easy to excavate. The synthetic stone beneath, although crumbled, was easy to follow. By the end of the day, they had completed two parallel paths.

At supper, the ants discussed their successful first day.

"Master Diandra, may I say something?" Antony asked, his voice shaking.

"Of course."

Antony knocked over his mug of honey dew. "I'm sorry."

"It's all right."

"I don't want anyone to think I was holding out on translating everything today. There may be times when a complete, literal translation is inappropriate. Please, trust my judgment. I'm not comfortable repeating their insults. There was one other thing Sir Rex said to his group after I told him my background, 'Watch out what you say to him. He knows too much.' He resents my being here."

Master Diandra gave Antony another of her penetrating looks.

"Why don't we choose a signal for such situations?" Captain Alexander asked.

"No signal will work, Captain. Randal and Sir Rex aren't fools. They would catch on. Trust me. I'll tell you anything I overhear, like I did tonight."

"I'm sorry I offended you today," said Master Diandra. "I'll trust your discretion from now on."

*   *   *   *

Late that evening, Henrietta pondered the events of the day. Sir Rex's insults shocked her. The size of the roach warriors frightened her. Her father's words echoed in her mind: *"There are many things you don't understand."*

The next several days were spent digging more of the parallel paths. Henrietta tried to work as hard as the others. Master Diandra seemed to know when she tired and often called her away from the group for private instruction. Gradually, she ached less and worked more. She noticed that the roach warriors lounged the days away, while their own guards were always busy digging, bringing flasks of water, carrying their noon meal to them or improving the camp.

Curiosity got the best of her. "Master Diandra, why don't their warriors help out?"

Master Diandra smiled and called out, "Antony, Henrietta would like to know why the warriors don't dig."

Antony asked the nearest roach and replied, "He says, 'Why should I? I don't get paid to dig. I get credit to guard and that's what I'm doing.'"

Each evening after their meeting, Antony would look at Henrietta with longing in his eyes, and she would hurry toward the female dome before he could approach. She could ignore him when she was working, but she didn't want to be near him in the evenings.

About mid-afternoon the following firstday, when both groups began to think they would not find what they sought at this location, Master Roland uncovered a redish-brown stain on the synthetic stone.

He explained through Antony. "The Duo Pods had to have something to pump the liquid out of the storage tank. We think it was made of plastic and metal. The plastic was taken long ago by primitive scavengers. Sometimes only patches of rust like this remain. Now comes the more difficult task of breaking through as much as two f-units of synthetic stone to get into the tank."

Sir Rex asked Antony something and he turned to Master Diandra. "He says it would be much easier to get through the synthetic stone if we would get some tunnel liquid."

Master Diandra paused and tapped one back pod in thought.

Henrietta turned to her. "Master Diandra, we couldn't do that. Even if we had some in camp, no one here is trained to use it. When I spent my quarter time frame with my father, he was very strict about its use. He made me wear protective breathing gear even though I was watching from fifty f-units away."

Antony related this to Sir Rex, who looked at Henrietta strangely. Master Gerald, the roach geo-chemist, spoke to Antony, who translated. "Tunnel liquid would be a bad idea. There's no telling what might happen if it worked too quickly and somehow mixed with the liquid fuel. The synthetic stone is quite crumbled here. I don't think it'll take long to get through it."

Master Gerald was correct. When their picks broke through and they had a small hole, one of the roach workers gave the edge another strong blow. A large chunk gave way. The worker slipped and nearly fell in. The pick fell from his pod as he scrambled away. A loud splash and a noxious odor told them they had found what they sought.

Antony reached out to help the roach worker up. Sir Rex pushed him away and yelled at the worker. He hit the worker in the head with his front pod, then kicked him several times while he continued to curse over the loss of the tool.

The roach scientists turned away. Henrietta stared in disbelief, never having seen such brutal treatment.

The roach scientists lowered a bucket on a rope and drew up some of the fuel. They set it to one side so that the chemists could begin their work the next morning, since it was late in the day.

*   *   *   *

Daniel and Aaron, the ants' chemists, had their equipment in place early the following morning. They had already poured some of the foul smelling liquid into a rounded open basin when the roaches approached. Aaron was about to set the heat to it when Master Gerald shouted in badly pronounced Ant, "No! Stop! No!"

It startled Aaron and he spilled some of the liquid onto Daniel and himself. Master Gerald grabbed the heat applicator. He threw it into the dirt. "Stop! Wait. Antony tell."

Guards on both sides stood high on their pods. Antony ran toward him.

Master Gerald stooped humbly and explained in Roach. "I'm very sorry. I did not mean to frighten everyone. This liquid is so dangerous. Your chemists could have ignited themselves and perished just now. They must go and wash thoroughly. There has been enough tragedy to both of our kinds with these ancient remains. Your colony should not have perished. Our lab should not have exploded in flames last season cycle. It happened right after I left one evening. I felt so helpless. Everyone inside was killed. I do not want to see tragedy here. Please, trust me. Let me train your chemists to work with this liquid safely."

Antony told the ants what he said and everyone relaxed. Daniel and Aaron left to wash. Antony sat down with Captain Alexander to wait for them and Master Gerald to return. The archaeologists left with Randal to dig in the market complex.

Master Gerald returned with a roach worker who carried the equipment. Sir Rex was with him.

"Why did you tell him all that? Why didn't you let those two stupid ants ignite themselves and act surprised about it?" demanded Sir Rex.

Master Gerald stopped. "Because I am not you. I came on this project to cooperate and to learn. That was The Board's intent. You know only a few others on The Board took your side. You're in the wrong era, Sir Rex. You block needed progress and change with your ways of fear and control."

Sir Rex forgot how close they were to Antony and shouted, "Traitor! I could get you banished. You should watch what you say. The information you are about to give them could be considered treason, you low-life pond scum. Cooperation is foolishness. I will always be against it. You know what I can do to you." Rex shook his ornaments in anger.

"Don't threaten me, Sir Rex. You weren't there that day. Those weren't your friends. That's right. You have no friends, only loyal employees. Well, I don't work for you. I work for Sir Reginald. I don't give a fly's egg what you report to The Board. Stay out of my way and let me do my job."

Master Gerald turned away from him and approached Antony. "Not listen to him," he said in Ant, with a look that begged Antony to be silent about what he had witnessed.

*   *   *   *

"Antony, I imagine you have a good deal to share this evening?" began Captain Alexander.

"Yes, too much. Let the others make their reports first."

Master Diandra began, "Master Roland and Master Gerard are open and pleasant to work with. Randal's translations are adequate. When we first began to excavate this area last season cycle, we had high hopes of finding new things. It doesn't seem that way now. Although there are three levels in the market complex, little is left but empty passages and chambers. Whatever there might have been was scavenged long ago or they've been here digging since last season cycle. We did find a lot of well preserved writings. I'd like to train Henrietta with imaging equipment and let her work on her own there for a while. The rest of us will investigate the lower levels of the tall building. Captain Alexander, will you assign her two guards?"

"Consider it done."

"Master Roland indicated that there are more promising sights farther east. It will not be necessary to spend much more time at this location," Master Diandra concluded.

Hanna, one of the geologists, added, "Arnold and I have been studying the soil layers and the water lines on the stone pillars to establish how high the sea rose in this area, but we can study that anywhere."

Daniel began, "It's obvious that we hadn't the least idea what we were doing today. We were fortunate that Master Gerald intervened. His equipment is much better that what we brought. We need to send an order back with the carriers on firstday for completely different equipment from our main lab. It will take another quarter time frame to get it back here. Meanwhile, we'll proceed as we did today. Master Gerald plans to bring more equipment to collect the after-burn fumes. He told us they were working on toxicity studies when their lab blew up. He is anxious to use the equipment he designed and built in the safety of the open air. We will have plenty to do, if Sir Rex will just quit interfering."

"Sir Rex," said Antony, "is going to be a constant problem. Master Diandra, does the political agreement include Board supervision?"

"It doesn't say one way or the other," replied Master Diandra. "We were told a Board Member would greet us. We had no idea he would be staying."

"He's very powerful. I still haven't been able to count the number of ornaments he wears. He knows I understand everything he says and it irritates him. He was extremely angry with Master Gerald this morning. Sir Rex told Master Gerald he should have let Daniel and Aaron ignite themselves, and then act surprised about it. You don't want to know the insults. He stated he was against 'this silly cooperation' from the start. Master Gerald countered him at every turn, reminding him that he had been in the minority when The Board decided in favor of the agreement, and was standing in the way of progress. Master Gerald told Sir Rex to go back to The Board and tell them anything he wanted, but 'stay out of the way and let me do my job.'"

They all sat quietly a few minutes, thinking about the best way to handle this situation.

Captain Alexander said, "Involving ourselves in the roaches' internal arguments might be the excuse Sir Rex wants to say that cooperation won't work."

There was a long silence and then Master Diandra said, "Henrietta, you've been sitting so quietly this evening. What are you thinking about?"

Henrietta hesitated. "I know I don't understand their ways. In fact, I find Sir Rex's manners revolting. So why should we lower ourselves to his level? Why give him the satisfaction of not cooperating? If Master Gerald had the courage to tell him to leave him alone to do his job, why don't we ignore Sir Rex and do what we came here to do? He probably wouldn't listen to reason anyway. Another thing, why must we always stand back silently when he mistreats their workers? How can those miserable workers know we aren't like that? Certainly, we could say a kind word or two without it being considered interference. Maybe they would begin to realize that there's another way."

Master Diandra looked at Antony. "You're the expert in how they think. Would it work?"

"Old Rodger once told me that things between the roaches and us needed to change. It may seem simple, but Henrietta is right."

Before the meeting ended, Antony had taught them all to say, "Thank you," and, "Good job," in fairly understandable Roach.

7.

*H*enrietta spent the next few days making dozens of images of all the writings she could find in the market complex, and writing reams of notes. Her guards always held the lantern at the right angle for a good image and high enough when she was making notations. Their curious questions helped her clarify her thinking.

The most interesting things she found were several triangular stands at key points in the complex. They were too well anchored to be carted off by scavengers, even though the writings were on plastic. There were groups of square shapes with three symbols in each with matching symbols and more writing below.

Axel, one of her guards, asked, "Aren't the square shapes in the same pattern as the chambers? Could this be a location chart?"

She looked closely and scurried up and down the passageway. "Of course, like a domicile location chart for a small colony."

They scurried back and forth, matching the symbols on the stands with each other and with those on the walls above and next to some of the empty chambers. A few h-units later, Henrietta returned to the others.

She found them all grouped around the chemists. Master Gerald had set up an elaborate piece of equipment. It looked like a large lightning bug lamp, but it had a glass dome over it and several tubes attached. Its wick burned hot and the dome gathered the smoke and fumes. After letting it burn several minutes, he cut off the fuel supply, allowed it to cool and opened the dome so they could test the residue left on the inside surface. Antony was busy translating the results.

Daniel whistled. "In an enclosed space, these fumes would poison even the strongest ant in a few moments. It seems to change the atmosphere around it."

"We have found evidence that the Duo Pods had millions of transport machines," Master Roland said. "Now I'm sure this liquid made them move."

"Can you imagine what the fumes would have done to the atmosphere over time, even in the vastness of the open surface?" Daniel asked.

"Maybe their breathing organs were different," suggested Carl.

Master Gerald went on to explain other experiments they had done before their lab blew up. He told how they had found small pools of this and other similar liquids amid some of the ruins in the bog areas by the sea where nothing seemed to survive well. They thought the liquids must have been stored somehow, but the sea and the air had destroyed the containers, unlike this carefully buried tank. The roaches believed that a thick, black liquid and this yellowish fuel were related, and they wanted to find out how.

Henrietta couldn't contain herself any longer. "Master Diandra, you must come and see what I've found."

Master Diandra left the others and followed her.

"Excuse me," said Randal, running to catch up. Sir Rex was with him.

Master Diandra stopped. "What can we do for you, Randal?"

"Sir Rex would like to know why you left the others to pay attention to the young female's silly babbling."

"Henrietta's work is not silly," Master Diandra said. "She has some excellent theories about decoding the Duo Pod symbols. She seems to have found something in the market complex that the rest of us overlooked. He may come with us if he chooses."

Sir Rex laughed long and loud when this was translated, but he followed them, talking to Randal.

Master Diandra whispered, "I wish Antony were here to tell us what they're saying." Then louder, "Is there a problem, Randal?"

"No," replied Randal. "All this time, Sir Rex thought that Henrietta was only a nymph, because of her small size. I reminded him of the difference between ant and roach life cycles. Many roaches of importance train their young to follow after them. He wants to know if you have any other young besides her."

"I am Henrietta's mentor, not her mother. She is the very gifted daughter of Henry and Adeline of South Harvester Colony 45."

Randal related this to Sir Rex, who scrutinized Henrietta, smiled and said something to Randal.

Randal paused before speaking. "Sir Rex says you are very lucky to have two talented young adults like Henrietta and Antony with your group."

They reached one of the triangular stands and Henrietta explained. "Axel suggested this could be a location chart for the complex. See these little boxes with the symbols in them? They match the shape and position of the chambers and passageways. I'm sure these symbols are numerals. That would be logical for a location chart. They match those that are written here below," she said, pointing.

"Furthermore, there is a pattern to them, similar to our own numbering system. I think this represents nothing, this one, and so on. Then I began to match the written symbols on the chart with some of those that remain on the walls near the chambers. I've revised the symbol frequency chart and now feel fairly certain there are twenty-six large and twenty-six matching small symbols which represent phonemes—the actual sounds of the language. On the chart they are written with one large and the rest small, but on the walls they are often all large. So this large one must match this small one in meaning." She pointed out another example.

Then she took them a short distance down the passageway. "Last, see these curving, swirly ones? At first I was confused and thought they were completely different symbols, but now I realize they are only fancy versions of some of the others." She drew an example on parchment.

"I'm sorry, Henrietta," said Randal, "You spoke so fast I didn't comprehend much of what you said and I hated to interrupt. Would you please repeat it?"

So she went through it again, slowly this time, pausing often so Randal could translate. Sir Rex stopped smiling about half way through. He kept looking at Henrietta more and more strangely. It was no longer his size, his hateful expression, or his abuse of the workers which made her afraid of him. It was something in the way he looked at her, and she could not put it into words.

That evening in the ant camp, the meeting ran very late. They praised Henrietta's discovery, and discussed what the others had learned from the roaches. A few days of sky water followed, giving them time to write reports to send to the science facility in South Harvester 45.

A quarter time frame passed. The chemists' equipment arrived and they decided to begin work near the roach camp. During the second time frame a subtle change occurred. The ants' use of a few words of encouragement to the roach workers spread a feeling of respect through the roach camp.

They developed the ability to ignore Sir Rex and his protests. While he spent more and more time brooding alone on the side-lines, the ants and roaches built a truly cooperative spirit. The ants might even have moved their camp, except for the water well and the emergency underground shelter that the guards had completed. Though infrequent, they did have to be prepared for the possibility of severe summer storms.

*   *   *   *

One day early in the summer, Sir Rex announced that he was leaving to make his report to The Board.

"Now we are free to show you an area we think may have many things," Master Roland told Antony.

Master Roland led the group, and Master Gerald whispered to Antony. "Next time you see your parents, tell them some of us know what it is to be alone. My parents were killed in a severe summer storm when I was a nymph. My father's sister took me in and saw to it that I was well trained with the credit my parents left, but never really took an interest in me. I have no mate either." His voice grew even softer. "Things with the Control Board are not stable right now. Many want to try new ways, more like yours. But they all fear the power of Sir Rex and his lot. One never knows what may happen."

The area Master Roland took them to was another, even larger market complex. Henrietta found more of the triangular stands and went right to work on the symbols, confirming her ideas.

In the lowest level, the other archaeologists excavated two Duo Pod skeletons. Master Diandra interrupted Henrietta's symbol work so she could see what they had found.

Carl was talking to Carrie when they arrived. "See these thin pieces of metal? They must have been very sharp. Probably some sort of weapon. These Duo Pods died fighting. Look how the sharp metal goes from this one's pod into that one's vulnerable area, and that one's pods grasp this one's neck."

"Yes, I see," Carrie replied. "What are these round, shiny disks in this one's pods?"

Antony translated Master Roland's statement. "The disks are probably their form of credit. I'd say this one was stealing from that one. That fits with the other precious metals and things we found over here. The kind of clay they were buried in is typical of that left by the mud of flood waters. It seals out the air and settles hard, preserving things well. I'll bet they had this fight in the midst of a storm and the flood waters covered both of them. This lowest level would have been vulnerable to that sort of thing."

*   *   *   *

"Captain Alexander," Antony said that night on the way to their sleeping dome, "walk with me. I need to tell you something,"

"What is it?" the captain asked when they were alone.

Antony told him about his conversation with Master Gerald.

"This is very good news. I think both of us can relax. Sir Rex has left and Master Gerald is confiding in you. If they are plotting anything, I think he'll tell us. These scientists are so open. We've never gotten information from them like this before." Captain Alexander patted Antony's thorax. "Keep up the good work."

At ease with the group and his job, Antony tried to reconcile himself with Henrietta. Unfortunately, she would have nothing to do with him.

The few times he went politely to the female sleeping dome, her icy response was, "I'm busy!"

Master Diandra advised him, "Be patient. She needs time to get over it."

The following time frame, the archaeologists found an inner chamber with a very thick, metal portal, tightly sealed. With all their strength, the ants could not break it open.

"Maybe we could explode it open," Master Gerald suggested. "If the yellow liquid could blow up our lab, it could certainly break open this door."

"I thought you didn't want any more accidents," Antony said.

"I think I can do it safely. I could put some of the fuel in a clay jar with a long, thick strand of thistledown in the top like a lamp wick. All of you get way back. I'll set fire to the strand and throw it."

"Won't the fire also destroy whatever is inside?" Master Diandra asked after Antony had translated the suggestion.

"We won't get in at all if we don't try. What have we got to lose?" Master Gerald said after Antony related Master Diandra's concern.

It worked. When the flames died, they found a small chamber, filled with little box shaped cupboards. The ants were able to break them open with their pods. Inside, amidst the dust, were beautiful decorative chains of rare metals and clear crystal stones. The ants placed such things on display in the public area of the science facility. In Roacheria, such finds were owned only by those with the most power and credit.

"We should divide all these things equally between us for study," Master Diandra said.

The roach scientists nodded. But when the division was made, the roaches put the largest stones in the ants' pile.

*   *   *   *

In spite of all the progress Henrietta was making with her theories, she was far from being at peace with herself. Her unresolved anger with Antony continued to smolder. She tried to pound it off in her morning scurries up and down the arches. Time did not lessen it. The only ant she could have told was Master Diandra, who spent more and more time talking to Antony. The whole camp respected and looked up to him. She seethed inside. How could he be so content and sure of himself while she still felt so injured?

On top of this, her parents had sent word that her sister, Hilda, had emerged from pupation. They sent an image of her. Instead of the joy she should have felt, Henrietta was filled with a sad longing she had never imagined possible. She found it hard to get up and face each day. She was constantly tired. Tired of trying to avoid Antony. Tired of saying that she must not be used to the heat and humidity when asked by others if she was ill. Tired of hiding her feelings.

One evening, as they sat at the top of the arches watching the sunset, Carrie asked, "Henrietta, I don't mean to press into what may be none of my business, but what is the problem between you and Antony? Every time he approaches, you turn ashen and scurry off while he sighs and hangs his head."

"Nothing."

"If it's nothing, then why are you so upset? I know you two came from the same training facility. I'm not trying to be rude in asking. I'm worried about you. You don't seem yourself lately. Were you involved in some way that didn't work out?"

Henrietta longed to spill everything. What could she say that would address Carrie's genuine concern without breaking her agreement to keep the matter secret?

"Yes, we knew each other during training. I went to the Leisure Center with him a few times. I guess you could say, it didn't work out." She clenched her front pods for control. "I'm sorry. I know you mean well, but I really don't want to talk about it."

Carrie put a front pod on Henrietta's back. "I didn't mean to make things worse for you. You don't have to say anything, but if you ever want comfort, I'm available as your friend."

A few nights later, unable to sleep, Henrietta went for a drink of water and found herself face to face with Antony.

"Please, don't scream," he whispered. "I couldn't sleep and saw you."

"Antony, it's so late. What are you doing here?" she whispered back, starting to leave.

"Don't go. Don't run off this time," he pleaded. "I'd like to talk to you."

She stared at him, unable to move or speak, in the same frozen anguish she had felt that day in Master Alex's work chamber.

He whispered on, "Please, listen a moment. I never got a chance to explain things to you. Can't you see I'm trying to make amends?"

In the moonlight, his face reflected the anguish she felt, but she could not deal with it. She found her voice. "No, I don't want to hear it. Not now, not here like this."

"Then when and where?"

"I don't know. Leave me alone for a while. I can't handle my own feelings, let alone yours." He sighed and stood aside, antennae drooping. She returned to her dome and cried herself to sleep.

*   *   *   *

Antony kept his distance the next morning as they went to their worksite, but he saw Master Diandra talking to Henrietta as they proceeded. Concerned with private worries, he was totally unprepared to see Sir Rex firmly planted in front of the roach scientists.

"Here, you slimy maggot," Sir Rex snapped. "Read this, since you think you're so smart."

Antony took the parchment from him. It was from the S.E.R.C.B., but not signed by the Supreme Executor. It stated that the two groups should no longer work together, but pursue separate projects and share the results in reports, which Sir Rex would personally deliver.

The ants stood, stunned by the news. Antony realized the censorship that Sir Rex would exercise over the reports.

Master Diandra appealed to Sir Rex. "Why is The Board displeased with the knowledge we have shared with you? Much learning has been accomplished by both sides. We have gained so much from your greater experience with chemicals, and we have freely offered all our knowledge and new findings. Surely, you can see what we accomplished during your absence."

Sir Rex directed Randal, not Antony, to relate her concerns to him. His reply reeked of deceit. "All the more reason to make our findings more permanent in reports. More could be shared. Time is wasted while directions are explained and then translated. The Board feels this will increase efficiency and productivity. Here is some previous work." He handed Antony a stack of parchments.

All the enthusiasm both sides had shared over the last few time frames evaporated. They worked near each other in silence. The summer dragged on. The daily reports were exchanged.

Antony was not as good with parchment work, because the only writing he and Old Rodger had done was in the mud at the edge of the pond or in the dust of late summer. After spending many h-units on a report, he would find out that it was information the ants already knew. By the end of the eighth time frame, he was much better at it but thoroughly frustrated.

"This process is ridiculous and clearly designed to keep me away from the group and any good I could really accomplish. It's a total waste of my time and I hate being stuck inside this stuffy dome all day long."

Captain Alexander offered a solution. "We can be just as sly as Sir Rex. The interpreters in the colony can read these. Let's request one of them to work here in the dome on these reams of parchment. Antony, you place yourself between the groups with a portable work surface, pretending to work, but listening. We'll continue to send them accurate reports."

"Captain Alexander," said Antony with a chuckle, "you're starting to sound like them. What if it comes back on us?"

"This is a war of ideology and wits. We are not deceiving them, nor are we withholding information. We are merely giving our friends an opportunity to communicate."

Master Diandra's statement held a tone of warning. "Be sure it does not escalate beyond wits. Antony, back off with proper apologies if you sense any animosity. You've mentioned more than once how powerful Sir Rex is."

The following morning when Antony accepted the day's pile of parchment, even Master Diandra smiled at the look of consternation on Sir Rex's face as Antony set up his work surface. Sir Rex spoke with fake politeness. "Why are you doing your work here?"

"This end of the summer heat is too much. Our shelters are sweltering. I prefer the open air and the company of my group."

"Then sit with them."

"I may need to ask one of your Masters a question. Sometimes the script is difficult to make out. When I find something of vital importance, I can inform my group immediately."

Sir Rex said no more. The roach scientists raised their voices and so did the ants. The following morning, Randal set up a similar work surface a few f-units from Antony.

A few days later, as Sir Rex handed Antony the day's reports, he said, "I see what you mean about the script. I must tell Master Gerald to make his more legible. I can't make this out. Would you like it re-done?"

"I think I can manage. I'll give it back if I can't."

He labored over its contents most of the day, but never approached Master Gerald for clarification. After the first statement, he realized that, in his own way, Master Gerald had circumvented their censor. He related its contents to the group that evening:

"Most cooperative friends:

"If Sir Rex ever manages to make this out, I'll be condemned. I hope that you can. Acknowledge this by asking that my next one be re-done. I'll send more of the usual stuff and then continue, as here, the next day.

"The others wish me to share this with you. You told us your theory that extinction may have begun with a series of natural disasters. We know that this whole southern region along the sea is prone to severe storms. We believe that they were even more frequent and severe 20,000 season cycles ago. Not here, but in other ruins in our territories, we have uncovered much evidence to support this: many groups of small buildings utterly destroyed, shards of glass, corroded metal beams of collapsed buildings, sometimes many skeletons buried in the mass of rubble. The bog areas are full of these things. In one place, near the great river delta, we found remains of earthen walls, probably built to protect communities from the sea and the river. What we don't understand is why the sea was rising and why the storms were more severe."

Antony stopped. "That's as much as I've managed to make out. The rest of it is a lot of chemical analysis statements. Daniel and Aaron, I need your help with it, because I don't comprehend the words I'm translating. It seems to be more information about the liquid fuel and the pools of black stuff they keep talking about."

Master Diandra said, "This is almost too good to be true. Walls to keep out rising seas, whole areas destroyed by storms. If these things occurred around the same time that much of the western coast was destroyed."

Carl broke in. "Such multiple disasters, within a relatively short period of time, as we've noted, not only here, but planet wide, might have weakened their ability to recover and rebuild. A societal breakdown and a collapse of central authority could have occurred. Total chaos might have resulted. That would account for the evidence of battles so often found."

"I hate to break into this discussion of theory," Captain Alexander interrupted, "but there is an immediate, practical problem here. Master Gerald put himself at great risk revealing this. I wonder what our risk is, if we continue to accept it."

"I think we should," said Antony. "He told me once that many roaches are ready for change, and he said that the others wanted him to share it. Sir Rex and his group won't be around forever. I should follow his instructions exactly. If I feel that Sir Rex suspects anything, I'll simply approach Master Gerald, tear up his work in front of him, and insist that he make his script legible. He'll get the message."

A nerve-wracking game began. The military interpreter arrived to work on the routine writing. Antony worked only on Master Gerald's reports, which he realized were a clever combination of ant and roach symbols. He continued to sit between the two groups and remained alert to all conversation. Occasionally, he would send back a report to keep Sir

Rex from suspecting. Never was a single word exchanged between him and Master Gerald.

*   *   *   *

Fall equinox arrived, but the days remained stiflingly hot. The air felt particularly heavy one fifthday around noon. Ominous clouds had been building all morning. They were filled with the tingling sensation that signaled the coming of a severe summer storm, rather than an ordinary sky water shower. Henrietta had never experienced a severe storm. She panicked.

Master Diandra spoke sharply to her. "Get your things. Now! We must get back to the camp. We've only about an h-unit before it hits."

The ant guards who had remained at the camp that day had already dismantled the domes. Most of the equipment had been taken into the underground emergency shelter when the others arrived. The shelter stood like a small colony mound a little away from the camp and the water well. A waterproof portal stood on an angle in the side of the mound. Inside, a ramp of hardened earth sloped to the floor of the chamber. Sky water began to fall in torrents as expedition members grabbed the remaining supplies.

Although the underground chamber was larger than the dining dome, with all sixty of them in it and all the equipment, it was quite crowded. Lamps were turned on and the ants settled themselves. Several began joking about past experiences when the alarms had sounded, sending every ant scurrying into the nearest domicile or emergency shelter, before water poured down the colony tunnels. Someone mentioned a mated pair they knew, who had first met in an emergency chamber.

Shaking, Henrietta sat down near the wall farthest from the portal. She felt a gentle touch on her back and turned to see who it was. Antony could not have picked a worse moment to attempt to be kind. The suave tone Antony used in dealing with Sir Rex was a constant reminder of how he had deceived her. The conditions outside were nothing compared to the storm of emotions raging within her.

She turned on him. "Antony, don't you touch me!"

A surprised hush fell over the entire chamber. Master Diandra intervened. "Never mind, Antony. Henrietta has been quite overwrought lately. Find the floral herb tea and heat some water, please."

"Sure."

Master Diandra put her front pods around Henrietta. Henrietta wished she could crawl into some hole and die.

"I'm sorry," she stammered. "I didn't mean to shout."

"It's all right. Go ahead and cry," replied Master Diandra, handing her a soft square of woven thistledown. Henrietta would not allow herself to vent her feelings in front of everyone.

Antony returned with the cup of hot herb tea and stood awkwardly. Master Diandra reached for the cup. "Thank you. We'll talk later," she said and waved him off. "Henrietta, drink this. It will calm you and help you sleep."

Henrietta accepted the cup, sipped its bitter contents slowly, and stopped shaking. She was just about to nod off when Carrie approached, carrying a sleep sack. She accepted it. Feeling like a pathetic larva, she went to sleep.

*   *   *   *

Antony waited a long time before Master Diandra motioned to him that they were free to talk.

"I couldn't stand to see her so afraid," he whispered.

"I know. It isn't you. I noticed her depression some time ago, but she wouldn't talk to me about it."

"No. It *is* me. You didn't see the look in her eyes. She accepted your comfort. What am I going to do? I appreciate all you've done for me, but none of it matters if Henrietta won't forgive me. I've tried everything. I've waited. I've left her alone as she asked, and it's getting worse. I've been thinking about it a lot lately. I can't go on if she won't forgive me."

"This is a new experience for me, too. I've never been a mentor before or held a probationary contract like yours. I realize now, that I should have given the two of you the time and privacy you needed to work things out long ago, but I didn't. I misjudged the depth of her anger and hurt. The problem now is where to let her confront you. I can't let you go far from camp without guards, and you certainly don't want them around, even if they are wonderful about keeping things confidential. I suppose you could stay in here after the storm is over, but that would destroy the privacy of your contract. Right now, the others think her reaction was panic. I'd like it to stay that way. You've really changed, and I'm glad you're here."

"Will she even listen to me?"

"Your feelings for her have grown deeper, haven't they?"

"Yes. Every time she turns away from me, I hurt so much." He clutched his head and looked down.

"I can convince her to listen to you, but you had better prepare yourself. I'll have to give her back her right to extinguish you. I honestly don't think she will, but we had both better be ready for the possibility."

"What about the trail to my parent's dairy? Suppose we went with the carriers on firstday and branched off? You could say we were going to visit and check on them after the storm."

"That might work. I would still need a couple of guards somewhere for Henrietta to find, just in case. I'll have to talk to Captain Alexander."

"You can tell him anything you need to," Antony replied sadly.

She rubbed his back for a while. "Would you like some tea?"

"No, thank you. I think I'll just meditate for a while."

8.

*H*enrietta kept her eyes closed, unsure she wanted to wake up. Pretending everything was fine would no longer work. Trying to control her feelings had not worked. She might as well admit she needed help. She roused herself and looked around.

"Good morning." Master Diandra's voice was reassuring. "The storm is over. We'll be able to go out soon. You and I need to talk. Here, have a grain cake and some honey dew. Don't be so hard on yourself, Henrietta."

By the time she finished her breakfast and freshened up with a basin of water, they had opened the portal. Patches of sunshine poured through the breaking clouds. She started to pick up her sleep sac, but Master Diandra stopped her.

"The others will take care of it. Come with me."

She set her sack down again and followed her mentor up the slope to the top of the arches.

Henrietta sat down and sighed. "I'm sorry I've let you down. I really thought I could manage, but every time Antony came near me I boiled with anger. I thought it would pass in time, but now I feel worse." Her voice trailed off and she finally allowed herself to cry.

Master Diandra handed her a cloth. "Go ahead. We're alone now."

Henrietta soaked the cloth with tears.

"Why didn't you come to me sooner? I'm your mentor. Did you think I wouldn't understand?"

"I don't know. You aren't going to cancel my training contract, are you?"

"Cancel your training contract? Where in the world did you get such an idea?"

"I don't know. I thought."

"Is that why you tried to suppress your feelings? You thought I would send you home?" She rubbed Henrietta's thorax. "So much knowledge and so little wisdom. If that's what you've been afraid of, don't worry. I wouldn't dream of it, but I do want you to listen to me."

Her voice was gentle but serious.

"You and Antony need to talk. Firstday, when the carriers leave for South Harvester 45, I want you to go with them. When you reach the cross path, you and Antony head north toward his parent's dairy. Stop somewhere and work this out, one way or the other. Vent your rage! If you must, take the option you passed up in Master Alex's work chamber. Captain Alexander will instruct two guards to remain at the cross path for three h-units. If you have not returned alone by that time, they will assume you have gone on to the dairy. They will return there the following seventhday at noon, and wait to escort you both back here. Antony and I discussed this last night while the others slept."

Henrietta stared at her and began to shake. Although hurt and angry, she could not consider the option of extinguishing Antony. "I can't do that." She broke down again.

Master Diandra comforted her, and then looked into her eyes. "Of course you can't, and I'll tell you why. You care deeply about him. I could see it the day we met. The problem is, you haven't admitted it to yourself. What's more, he cares very deeply about you. Why do you think he was so anxious to take full responsibility? It was the look in both of your eyes that made me question him further that day. My mistake was not giving you the time and privacy you needed to talk things out."

Henrietta dried her face with another cloth. "How can you know me better than I know myself?"

"I've had a good many season cycles of experience in living. You can't learn to live by studying a manuscript. Life is experienced, the pain and the joy. It's our ability to feel these powerful emotions, to care, to cherish, to be compassionate, to forgive, and, yes, to be angry and hurt, that makes us unique among life forms."

Master Diandra paused and the two of them looked out at the ruins.

Then Master Diandra continued. "Did you think you could improve yourself somehow by trying to carry your burden alone? Forgive me if I gave you that impression the day we met. Our strength, to the most ancient of our antcestors, lies in helping each other. I have failed you in that. I did not make myself as open to you as I did with Antony."

Master Diandra put one pod below Henrietta's mandibles and raised her head until their eyes met. "Listen to Antony. He's changed. Give him a chance. I'm glad I did. Did you think he felt no remorse? He expressed his sorrow immediately. In fact, he vented his feelings much more easily than you did. He wants to explain and ask your forgiveness. He condemns himself each time you reject his attempts at kindness. Look beyond that front he put up when you first met. You'll find a very caring and sensitive young male who would endure anything for you. You can't go back and change things, so move on."

Henrietta lowered her head. "All right. I'll go with him. I feel so confused, but I haven't gotten anywhere trying to figure it out for myself. What about here? Aren't we needed?"

"You need the time more. It will take the roaches a few days to clean up after the storm since they don't go underground. I'm sure Sir Rex will be delighted not to see Antony around for a while. Antony also needs this time to heal, and he hasn't seen his family for two season cycles. I'll send two carriers today to let them know you'll both be there by evening on firstday."

*   *   *   *

Captain Alexander directed several guards as they set the ends of the grassfrond poles back in place for the dining dome. Antony helped bind four poles together to bend into one of the tallest arcs. He kept looking up to where he could see Master Diandra and Henrietta.

Unable to concentrate on his task, he approached Captain Alexander. "May I talk with you, please?"

Captain Alexander looked at him kindly, sensing Antony's need for a friend. "Of course," he replied. Then he said to the guard assisting him, "Axel, take charge of the dining dome. You know what to do."

"Yes, Captain."

"Antony and I are going to start on the smallest bunking domes, alone."

"Yes, Captain."

"Grab about ten of those poles, Antony, and come over here." He picked up several poles himself. "This is a little quieter. What's on your mind?"

"I didn't come on this project voluntarily. Master Diandra holds my probationary contract and right now she's up there giving Henrietta back her right to extinguish me. I'd like someone to know I really tried."

"I haven't known you all that long, but I can't imagine you doing anything seriously wrong."

"Well, I did." Antony handed the captain a pole and explained what had happened.

"Sit down and rest a minute," said Captain Alexander, putting a pod on Antony's back. "First of all, you are certainly living up to your agreement and I admire you all the more for sharing this with me. Don't think you are the only ant who has ever made a mistake. I hold contracts on three of my guards right now. In the last five season cycles, three others have completed contracts with me. Whenever trainees get into trouble, my superiors always say, 'Give 'em to Captain Alexander. If he can't straighten 'em out, no one can.' I guess they feel someone who has been through it is the best prepared to help someone else. I think you and Henrietta will work this out. She's too gentle and caring to extinguish you, or any creature for that matter. I guess everyone but the two of you can see how you feel about each other."

"What?"

"It's those we care about the most that we end up hurting. When we are hurt by someone we care about, the pain and anger are that much greater. Think about it. Master Diandra only told me you two had a personal problem when she asked me to have two guards wait at the cross path to your parent's dairy for a few h-units. She also said she planned to have the two of you spend a quarter time frame with your family. You'll work it out. In fact, I'll wager you'll come back promised to each other."

"I'm not in the mood for jokes, and I don't have anything to bet. I'll be lucky to come back at all."

"Don't be offended. If you win, I'll give you my most precious possession. If I win, I'll only reserve the right to say, 'I told you so.' That's how sure I am." He rubbed Antony's back. "Come on. Shall we get back to work on this dome?"

"Thanks for listening."

"That's what I'm here for." Captain Alexander tied a woven rush mat onto the frame they had completed.

*   *   *   *

Henrietta and Antony scurried along with the carriers in silence. The sun shone in a bright blue autumn sky, but neither of them noticed. Henrietta only heard the tapping of pods on the path and the shifting of the carrier's baskets. Their brisk pace brought them to the cross path in a little over an h-unit. They turned from the main trail. The two guards sat down and took out their water flasks.

"Have a good journey," one of them said. "See you seventhday."

Henrietta found herself dragging her pods in dread. Antony finally broke the silence. "Would you like me to carry your satchel for a while?"

"I guess so."

After they had gone about three d-units, they came to a stream, lined with stately grassfronds casting their shadows in stripes.

Antony stopped. "This is a nice spot ... pretty and shady. We might as well sit down."

Henrietta folded her appendages under her and reclined on the ground. He positioned himself at right angles to her and lowered his antennae. Neither of them knew where to begin.

"All right," said Henrietta. "I'm here. I'm listening."

"You could make it easier."

"Why should I?" she snapped. "Let's hear this great explanation of yours that's supposed to make everything fine again."

"I admit, that first day I came up to you, my main goal was to get information. I'd been really busy and hadn't done my research. I didn't know it then, but I was extremely depressed. By the third time we met, everything was different. Please, believe me. I even tried to write something different, but I hadn't read enough to do anything. So . . . I thought . . . with over two hundred reports, they probably wouldn't read them all anyway, and they'd all sound about the same. Who would know? By fifthday I had really begun to care about you."

"Care about me," she interrupted. "Taking my work is a funny way to show it."

"I was too embarrassed to ask you. What was I going to say? 'Henrietta, you did all the work, but can I put my name on it, too?'"

"Do you mean to say that you hadn't done enough assignments to realize how different my ideas were?"

He hung his head. "That's right. I didn't realize it until you asked that question at the end of Master Diandra's lecture." He told her about being caught in Master Alex's work chamber. "I was so ashamed. I couldn't even look at you."

"That's it? That's all you have to say?" She threw her head back and waved her front appendages wildly. "All this because you never got around to doing your assignments? Have you got any idea how I felt that day? All my work, h-units and h-units, and you came along, got all cozy, and I, like a fool, told you everything. I walked into that chamber feeling so great and found myself accused. I was so shocked I couldn't speak!" Her voice was louder than it had been during the storm. She picked up a small rock and flung it into the stream.

"I do know how you felt. You've made me feel that way every single day since. I thought you cared, at least a little. Now, I don't know any more . . . The day we left, when your father came up to me, so friendly and all; I realized you must not have told him. So, I thought you cared, and if I tried, we could get beyond it. Then you wouldn't even talk to me. It's been pretty hard to keep my promise to your father."

She stared at him. "What promise?"

"That I would watch out for you. Protect you from the roaches. I can't take it any longer. If you can't forgive me . . . if you really don't care, end it." Shaking, he turned his head away from her, exposing the vulnerable, narrow connection between his head and thorax.

Henrietta burst into tears. "No! I can't do that." Instead, she leaned over him as he lay on the ground, head turned away, and vented her rage by pounding the back of his thorax with both her front pods and yelling, "Why didn't you just ask me? Didn't you see? I would have said, 'Yes.'"

She pounded on, repeating, "I would have said, 'Yes,'" over and over until she was exhausted. Then she collapsed in a heap and continued to weep. She cried not only for her anger and hurt at his betrayal, but for her homesickness, her foolishness, her panic, and everything else she'd felt for half a season cycle.

Miserable, she would have accepted any comfort when she felt his first touch. His pods curled around her and she gave in and leaned against him. He stroked her antennae. She felt a touch so gentle, so caring, so different from the feeling she had when her mother or father did the same thing. Nothing before had given her such a feeling of peace. That was when she noticed his thorax was shaking; felt his tears trickling down her back. She looked up at him. "I've never cried like this before. I wasn't being intentionally cruel to you. I was so angry. I didn't hurt you when I hit you, did I?"

"No. I have a pretty strong thorax. How can I ever show you how sorry I am?" He reached into his satchel, took out a cloth, and soaked it in the stream. "Here, the coolness will feel good."

She accepted the cloth and wiped her face. "May I ask you something?"

"Anything."

"How long did you have to wait to come down to the colony for training?"

"Five season cycles. I had to wait for my brother, Drew, to emerge from pupation. He was to study the basics at home like I did, then leave when I returned. If I hadn't gotten in trouble, I'd have been home a few time frames ago, and he could have left."

"How long will your brother have to wait, since you can't go home?"

Antony drew a water flask from his satchel and held it out to her. "I don't know. Drew will have to wait almost as long as I did, I suppose. My mother wrote that my sister, Deedra, just emerged from pupation. Maybe she'll help my parents, so he can go for training. Sometimes I can't believe how many lives I ruined in one foolish moment of desperation and homesickness."

She took a long drink before saying, "I wouldn't call my life ruined. You did help me in a way. When you questioned me, it helped me prepare for my interview. You said you were depressed. Why?"

Antony explained how he had isolated himself.

"You chose to live alone in an emergency shelter? No wonder you always looked so unhappy."

"Did it show that much?"

She nodded.

"Will you forgive me?"

She looked around. "Yes. We're right near all these grassfronds. Maybe we should start all over by sharing a seed. Will you get one?"

"Come with me. We'll get it together."

He put out his front pod and helped her up. They climbed some twenty-five f-units to the top of the nearest grassfrond. Henrietta was afraid they would fall when it bent under their weight, but Antony held her firmly as she pulled off one seed. When they had climbed back down, she peeled back the husk and handed it to him to break.

He handed her a portion and they recited the seed ceremony's words: "May the All Powerful Force which makes the grassfronds grow from a large seed to great height in a single season cycle, nourish us now with this seed. May we grow with it, to care for each other more fully." Then they ate the seed.

They rose to go on, filled with the warm, autumn sunshine, the blue of the sky, and the beauty they now noticed around them. A lightness filled them and bubbled over into their conversation.

Henrietta laughed at his description of his first ride on a grasshopper.

"Shh," he said suddenly, "look. A Sun Spirit."

A radiant, yellow-orange butterfly with a nearly five f-unit wing span, alighted at the top of a nearby wood plant and began to lay her eggs on the foliage.

"Be very quiet," he explained. "Let her lay her eggs in peace. It's ironic. This most beautiful of all the butterflies has the ugliest and most destructive larvae on the face of the planet. There will not be one bit of foliage on that wood plant when her larvae finish with it."

"Then why leave her in peace?"

"Because she is needed. The wood plant's foliage will grow back next season cycle. Most of the larvae will end up being food for predators. Ugly though they are, look at the gorgeous creatures they become. Sun Spirits pollinate more blossoms than any other creatures, even bees, and they are the only ones who help the wind pollinate the grassfronds. My father lifts up a thought of thanksgiving every time he sees one."

Along the trail, he told her about the plants and creatures they saw. He even took her off the trail to see a spider's lair, reassuring her that there was no danger as long as they kept their distance.

"Where did you learn all this?" she asked.

"From my father. I hope things won't be too uncomfortable for you when we reach our dairy. My father and I did not part on good terms two season cycles ago. Although my mother has written to me often, he only wrote once. I really hurt him, too."

"Then another reason for this trip is to make things right with him?"

He nodded. "I have a sealed letter to him from Master Diandra. I'm not supposed to give it to him until we have worked things out. I don't know if he will accept me or not, but I know what I am going to say, and I'm not afraid."

"Everyone in camp looks up to you. Why would you be afraid?"

"It hasn't always been that way. I really have Master Diandra to thank for helping me. You don't know what my contract says, do you? That first four days, while you were flitting around like a new butterfly, basking in your well deserved success, I was trying to figure out how to put my life back together." He told her about his first four days with Master Diandra and the wording of his contract.

The trail crossed another stream and followed its opposite side through shaded glens. They came around a curve, where the trail left the stream and entered an open meadow. Ahead, in the shade of a single wood plant, they saw a lone male ant. He spotted them at the same moment and scurried toward them, shouting greetings.

Henrietta guessed that this must be Drew. Antony hurried forward and found himself tackled. The two of them rolled in the meadow grass, laughing and embracing, wrestling playfully with each other. As she stood by, it was clear to her that Drew had no hard feelings toward his brother. Breathless, they stood up and brushed the grass from themselves.

"I'm sorry I took off like that, Henrietta. I forgot for a moment. Drew, this is Henrietta."

"Hello," Drew said and held out his front pods in greeting. "May I carry your satchel for you?"

"Yes, thank you."

"What took you so long?" asked Drew. "I've been waiting since noon."

"We had a lot to talk about and we stopped a lot."

They started on their way again. Antony said, "Drew, I'm sorry I'm not back to stay. I've ruined things for your training for a while."

"Don't worry about it. I don't want to go any more than you did. You saved me all the arguments you had with Dad."

Antony stopped and looked straight into his brother's eyes. "Don't think that way, Drew. It's only postponed. Don't make the same mistakes I did."

An awkward silence followed. Drew shifted his pods and began to walk. "All right. I know. Let's forget it."

Antony changed the subject. "How is everybody? How bad was the storm here?"

"I was terrified, but Dad said it wasn't as bad as some he's been through. We had an awful lot of sky water. The stream flooded some. We had a few downed wood plants, but nothing serious. Deedra is great. Wait until you see her. Mom is all excited. She can't wait to see both of you, and has she got a surprise for you. Allen has gotten really big. He won't stay in a larva coop any more. Mom says he is almost as big as Arlene was when she pupated, but he's way too young for that."

"And Dad?"

Drew hesitated. "He never says anything about you. He harvested a huge area of grassfronds alone yesterday after the carriers brought the message."

They proceeded up a small, gradual slope. When they reached the top, they could see the dairy. Henrietta looked down and saw the smallest mound imaginable, shaded by grassfronds and wood plants, and surrounded by inward curving fences. Antony took her front pod in his and said, "This is my home."

"You said it was beautiful, but I didn't really know what you meant."

Drew scurried down ahead of them shouting that they had arrived. They reached the yard, and Antony's mother came out, threw her front pods around him and said, "It is so good to see you, even if it's only for a short time."

He returned her affection. "It's good to be here. You have no idea how much I've missed all of you. Mother, this is Henrietta. Henrietta, my mother, Dorothy."

Henrietta found herself warmly embraced. "I'm so glad to meet you. Come in and rest. Supper is almost ready. Antony, your father will be here in a minute. Drew went on after him."

A shy face appeared in the portal and Deedra came out to greet a brother she had never met. Antony stepped forward and embraced her tenderly. "Drew was right." He turned back to his mother. "What's this surprise Drew says you have?"

She laughed. "Come in and see."

They entered the mound's main chamber, which served as parlor and kitchen. Antony's eyes fixed on a worn incubator near the opposite wall. In it, nestled in thistledown, lay an egg.

"Mother, you didn't. Another one? Aren't you too... I mean..."

"Too old?" she laughed again, finishing his statement. "Not yet, obviously. Maybe I'll set a record."

Drew entered with Antony's father. Henrietta felt a sudden chill in the mood.

Antony shifted. "Hello, Dad. This is Henrietta."

"Welcome to our domicile, Henrietta. I wish the circumstances could have been more joyful." He glared at Antony and gave Henrietta a formal embrace.

"Please, don't start in on me, Dad. I didn't come to spend six days arguing."

"That's a switch."

"I'm not proud of what happened. I know I've been a great disappointment to you. I can't change that now. I can only ask that you try to understand why it happened."

"I've read all your explanations. I won't hear more excuses. It amazes me that Henrietta didn't exercise her rights. You got off too easily with a two year contract."

Antony took a deep breath. "There was one thing you never even considered. You and Mother couldn't stay away from this place, and you had each other to comfort and lean on. I had no one I really knew. I didn't know how to cope with loneliness."

"Loneliness?" David shook his head. "You spent most of your life here off by yourself."

Antony took another deep breath. "Being alone in the meadows with the herds, and being lonely in a colony aren't the same. And I was usually with Old Rodger. In hindsight, it's a good thing. If I hadn't learned so much from him, Master Diandra would have had no use for me, and I don't care to think about where I would be right now. I'm doing good work, Dad. A lot of ants are counting on me. I have a talent I can be proud of, even teach others. I'll be free in one and a half more season cycles. I can't go back and change what happened, but I'm trying to make it better."

David's expression softened. "I don't think I'm talking to the same brash young male who stormed out of here two season cycles ago not even waiting to travel with the carriers."

"No. You're not. I'd like to stand beside you, cared about and forgiven; proud of who I am, and from where I came, instead of hiding from it. Will you forgive me?"

David looked back and forth from Antony to Henrietta, with the same searching expression Master Diandra had given him in the beginning. Antony met his gaze with a steady, pleading look. Could his father see how much he cared and that he was hurting too?

Allen wailed in hunger. Deedra's antennae twitched. Drew shifted his middle pods.

David broke his rigid stance and embraced his son.

Dinner relaxed everyone. Recent events were pleasantly related. Antony's mother brought out a honey cake for dessert.

"I knew we would celebrate tonight," Dorothy said.

Antony reached into his satchel, which he had forgotten to take off is back, and handed his father Master Diandra's letter.

David unsealed and read the parchment.

"My Dear David and Dorothy,

"I want to thank you for your son, Antony. As I look back, I think it was a fortunate accident that we met. This project could not have enjoyed such success without his talents as an interpreter and his willingness to be of real service to all of us. Yet, I know that his work here prevents you from sending your other young adults for formal training. I have taken the liberty of contacting the Colony Council to see if they can find two young adults who would be willing to work with you as their mentor, enabling Drew and Deedra to leave as originally scheduled. Please accept this small token of help. You two have accomplished so much against such overwhelming odds.

"With warmest regards,

"Diandra"

David laid the letter on the table. He looked at Antony, started to peak, stopped, and lowered his eyes. Finally he said, "Well, the aphids an't stay up in the wood plants all night. Come on, Drew and Antony, et's go get them down."

*   *   *   *

In the morning, Antony left early to help his father and brother arvest the grassfronds. It felt good to be in the fields again. Many of the tems were bent or broken from the storm, but the seed was still good. At oon, when David asked Drew to return to the mound to get their lunch, Antony took the opportunity to speak to his father alone.

le picked up a seed from the nearest basket. "For all the times before I eft, and everything I should have been and wasn't, I would like to share a eed with you. There are so many things I would like to forget."

David put his front pod on Antony's back. "Before we do, I have omething to say. Until last night, I never realized how many times you tried to tell me about your problems. Even your letter last winter was a cry for help, but I wasn't listening. For that, I'm sorry. Put all this behind you, but don't forget it. Someday, you may have a son or a daughter who cries silently for help. Perhaps with the wisdom of your experiences, you'll listen better than I did."

He took the seed, broke it in two, and handed half to Antony Together, they recited the same words that Antony had spoken with Henrietta the day before, and ate the seed.

"Do you really like this interpreting work?"

"If I had my choice, I would rather be here with you, but yes, I do like it. Sometimes it worries me, though. It's so much responsibility.' Antony told his father about the conflicts with Sir Rex.

"You're asking the wrong creature for advice on that one," David said. "In many ways, I was glad when the roaches moved their trade route farther north and stopped coming here." He looked off into the distance and said, "Forgive my getting personal, but you really care about Henrietta, don't you?"

"I can't even begin to explain what I feel."

"The word you're looking for is 'cherish.' Twenty-nine season cycles ago, I was about to stop seeing your mother. She said to me, 'We're as different as night and day. You like the surface and I like my underground lab, but I'll never feel for anyone else what I feel for you. If you cherish me as well, make a promise with me, and somehow, we'll make our lives work together.' So we did, and two time frames later, we had our ceremony, and two time frames after that, along came Arthur. I hasn't always been easy, but our life has been good. If you feel that much for Henrietta, don't keep it to yourself. Tell her. Don't make a second mistake."

Antony wanted to ask how, but Drew returned with fungus muffins and honey dew. When they had eaten and had drunk their fill, David told Antony to take the honey jugs and check the bee hives.

"Be sure you show Henrietta how to keep from being stung," David said as Antony left.

Thirdday David sent Antony and Henrietta off by themselves "Take your time. Be back by sundown."

Antony checked on the grasshopper herd out of habit.

"Ride one of the hoppers with me," he suggested.

"I've always been afraid, even of the partly tamed ones in the hopper ride at the Leisure Center."

"I'll hold you. You won't fall."

Off they bounded in a wild ride across the meadow.

"You were right," Henrietta laughed. "It *is* fun."

Later, they relaxed by the stream. Antony had never seen Henrietta quite so happy. They talked about everything: her work, dairying, the beauty of the surface...

*   *   *   *

Fourthday at supper Antony said, "Dad, remember my first autumn as an adult, and the game I made of scattering grassfrond seeds for you?"

"Yes, I remember."

"Well," he glanced at Henrietta and they broke out laughing. "You won't have to plant any seed next spring."

"You didn't."

"We're sorry," Henrietta apologized. "I guess we got carried away."

David smiled and put his front pod on his head.

Later that evening, Antony watched Henrietta play with Allen as he tried to help Drew with some problem solving. His father and Captain Alexander were right. He did cherish her, and he did want to ask her to make a mating promise with him. Long after Drew fell asleep on the thistledown mattress they shared, he lay awake thinking about it.

*   *   *   *

Sixthday evening arrived too soon. Supper was quiet. Antony asked Henrietta to go out to enjoy the evening air.

"Keep alert," said his father. "I know there is a mantis about somewhere. I haven't seen Old Rodger for about a time frame, and he didn't look well. I've been too busy with the harvest to find him."

"We'll be careful. Don't worry, we're only going to the top of the slope," he replied and then explained to Henrietta. "Old Rodger always kept the mantises away from our dairy. We'll leave extra early tomorrow, visit the memorial and then I'll take you to meet him. I know where to find him."

They sat at the top of the rise and looked down at the dairy and up at the autumn moon.

"This has been the best quarter time frame of my life," Henrietta said. "I really understand why this place and your family mean so much to you. Part of me wishes that we didn't have to go back tomorrow."

"That's good to know."

He pointed out several constellations to her and named them. They flopped onto their backs for a better view. Suddenly, Antony bolted upright, tense and alert.

"What is it?" whispered Henrietta.

A giant cricket leaped up only ten f-units away and then bounded off into the dark meadow. It was still again, but Henrietta's heart continued to pound.

"It's all right," said Antony, putting his front pods around her. She leaned against him. Contentment flowed through her.

Antony fumbled for words. "When we left the camp, I only wanted to get your friendship back. Now ... I feel so much more. I keep looking at my mom's new egg ... and watching you with Allen, and I wish it were our egg, our larva, our domicile. Then ... I remember that we have to go back. We both have obligations, and we would have to wait a very long time. Yet, I don't want to lose this moment. Would you come back here with me when my contract is finished? Would you make a mating promise with me?"

"I've come to care about you very deeply the last few days, Antony. There is nothing I'd like more than to let this lovely dream go on forever. Are you sure about this, knowing what my obligations are? My training contract is for three season cycles. I might have to be gone for long periods of time, even study in the northern ruins during the warm seasons. I've chosen a career that may not mix very well with being mated."

"I know, and I don't want to take that from you. You're too good at what you do. Look at Carl and Daniel. They both have mates and families, and they manage. Maybe you could spend half your time there and half here. It's not so far to travel. A lot of your manuscript work you could do better here, with a proper work chamber and a good place to store things."

"What about the young we would have? What if I laid an egg in the middle of some archaeological dig?"

"Males raise young all the time. There would be other families here by then. When we get a couple of workers out here from the colony, they'll want to stay. Eggs get laid in all kinds of places. Other ants always help. You could send me an emergency message, and like our ancient antcestors, your faithful worker would come to his queen and carry that egg carefully to our domicile to nurture it."

He stopped and looked at her intently. "I can wait for your contract to end. I can wait if you are called away. In the colder seasons, when things are dormant here, I can go wherever you are. Waiting isn't so difficult when you know what you are waiting for. We can overcome anything together."

She looked into his eyes and saw the sincerity there. Master Diandra was right. Why had it taken her so long to realize it? "I will make a mating promise with you. You don't have to ask Master Diandra first, do you?"

"I don't think so, after her letter, but she should probably be the first ant we tell."

The position for a mating promise demonstrated the interdependence between two ants from that time on, for no ant could stand alone on only two appendages. They rose, uncertain of their future, stood on their back appendages, joined their middle pods for balance, and lifted their front pods above their heads. Antony glanced down toward the dairy for a moment, and then turned his eyes to hers. Together, they spoke the words of a mating promise.

9.

*D*avid handed Henrietta a plate of grain cakes smothered in honey. "You'll need a good breakfast before your journey back."

"Thank you."

Dorothy packed fresh wild fruit, bread, and two flasks of honey dew into Antony's satchel. "Are you sure this will be enough for lunch?"

"It'll be plenty. The sun won't rise for another h-unit."

"Are you sure you won't come back this way and take the trail?" David asked.

"It will be shorter to cut across the meadows after we talk to Old Rodger."

"Be careful. I have an uneasy feeling. I don't know why. Will you take these with you?"

Antony took the letters his father held out. "The carriers can take this one to the council tomorrow. I'll give the other one to Master Diandra myself."

They finished eating and rose to leave. Drew and Deedra stumbled sleepily out of their chambers to say good-bye. When David embraced Henrietta, the stiff formality of their first meeting was replaced with a warmth that reminded her of her father.

David held Antony close and whispered, "Should I start digging another domicile?"

"Not now. We'll have a long wait."

David handed Antony a lantern. "It's still dark. You'll need this. Keep it."

They left the mound, crossed the stream and headed off across the meadow. Half way there, Henrietta could see the old mound against the rose-colored dawn sky. After reading the inscription on the main entrance, Antony led Henrietta to the top, where they sat in silence and meditated as the first rays of sun poured over them.

Antony pointed back in the direction of the dairy. They could see the tops of the wood plants in the glen and the slope on the western side where they had stood the evening before and spoken their promise.

"This has always been good surface area for dairying," Antony said. "That slope will be the entrance of a new mound. That's where our domicile will be. Long after our time, it will rise like this one, and we will have been its beginning."

"The surface is so beautiful here. The meadows seem to go on forever."

They meditated in silence and then headed east toward the grove of wood plants where Old Rodger lived. A swarm of flies buzzed around it.

"What are they doing?" asked Henrietta.

"Laying their eggs on something ... Oh, no ... Please, not ... Wait here." He set down his satchel and ran toward the wood plants. A few moments later he returned and slumped to the ground.

"Old Rodger is dead. By the look of him, it was several days ago."

Henrietta put her front appendages around him. "I'm sorry. Maybe we should go and cover him."

They walked to the glen together. Antony waved his front appendages and shouted. The flies took off with a loud buzz. Together, they dug a hollow. Antony dragged the remains of his first friend into it and pushed dirt over him.

He raised his pods in meditation. "Old friend, I'm sorry I wasn't here. I wish you hadn't been alone. There was so much I wanted to tell you and ask you. Perhaps if I meditate on the things you taught me, I'll find the answers to my questions. I'm trying to do what you asked, so send me a little of your wisdom when I need it. I'm sorry I was angry with you when I left. You were a true mentor and I did not appreciate you. One day I'll be back with a proper marker."

He wrote the words, "My Mentor," on a piece of parchment Henrietta had in her satchel and left it under a stone.

Antony led Henrietta in the general direction of the cross path where they were to meet the escort guards. He couldn't say why, but he felt drawn by some unseen force. Henrietta took his front pod in hers.

"I can't imagine what you're feeling, but I'm here."

"There was so much I wanted to tell him. Now I can't."

They came to a stream and Antony stopped, as if he didn't know where they were. It shook him back to reality from the empty, dream-like state of the last h-unit.

"This is the same stream that runs by the dairy. Further on, it flows into the stream that sets the border with Roacheria. It must have flooded worse here during the storm. The banks are usually gentle, but they're sharply eroded. Look how the mud is caked on the grass."

"What's that? It looks like a corner of synthetic stone."

"There are some ruins around here but nothing important."

"Could we look anyway?"

"I guess so. Be careful," he said, helping her pick her way down the slippery bank.

She began pulling more soil away from the synthetic stone with her front pods. It fell away easily, already loosened by the water.

"What is it?" asked Antony.

"I don't know. Have we got time to find out?"

"Plenty. It's not even mid-morning yet."

They worked their way along the edge of the wall facing the stream. The synthetic stone ended and gave way to metal. They dug around it and found an area of metal about seven f-units high and four wide, with the stone all around it. There was a round dial on the lower right side, with symbols in a circular pattern. Henrietta recognized them as numerical from her work on the location charts in the market complex.

"This portal looks like the one that we found in the building near the roach camp, but that one didn't have this dial and the numerals."

She slid her front pod gently over the surface. "I can feel a direction pointer. It's pointing at the dial. There are more symbols at the end of it. I can't see them very well, but I can feel where they're etched into the metal. Hand me some parchment from my satchel."

She laid the parchment over the symbols and rubbed the side of her pod over it, making a clear print. "Can you turn that dial?"

He worked at it a minute. "Yes, but not easily."

She felt around its edge. "Here's another direction pointer. I think we need to move this dial back and forth to each of the numerals in order."

She pointed to the numerals one at a time. He turned the dial back and forth.

"That's all," she said after she had finished the sequence.

They heard a click and then a hissing sound.

Antony felt around the dial. "It's sucking in air."

"Can you pull it open?"

He tried, but even with all his strength, he couldn't budge it. The hissing sound continued for several minutes. It stopped. Another click.

Antony gripped it securely again, pulled as hard as he could. They heard a sucking sound, then a pop. A crack appeared at the edge. They both grasped the edge and pulled harder. Slowly, the thick metal portal swung open. They faced the darkness within.

"The lantern." Antony reached for his satchel and untied the lantern they had used earlier. Both of them gasped at what they saw before them.

The chamber was fourteen f-units deep, twenty wide, and eight high. Each of its walls was a full image, depicting a different scene of plants and life forms as they had been over twenty thousand season cycles before: tropical forest, grassy plains, and arid desert. The ceiling was covered with a night sky. All along the base of each wall were shelves, covered with objects. In the very center stood a sculpture of a female Duo Pod, seated on a wide, tall chair. It was so life-like that Henrietta caught her breath.

Pod in pod, they stepped in, eyes wide, mandibles open.

Henrietta whispered, "It's like moving back in time. Look, we've been fairly correct in what we thought their world looked like."

"Why are you whispering?"

"I don't know."

Antony turned around to see that the wall around the portal was also a painted image, a northern forest and its life forms. Henrietta moved toward the sculpture. The form and details were exquisite. The eyes seemed to be gazing right at her. Henrietta gasped when she saw what lay in the sculpture's opened, upper pods.

"Parchment! Master Diandra said they must have had it, but it would not have survived the eons. But here, sealed in this place. This must have been planned to preserve these artifacts. There isn't even any dust.

The air must have been removed. That's why we heard that hissing sound as we broke the seal. The numerical sequence was not only to open the portal, but to allow the air to enter slowly, so the things would not be destroyed. It's a gift from the past. See how she is holding the parchment, as if reaching out to us."

Gently, she lifted the single parchment. Under it were three bound manuscripts. She picked up the first and turned its pages carefully. Like the single parchment, it seemed to be covered with a thin film that felt like raw plastic.

"What is it?"

"We've stumbled into the most important artifacts ever found. From my first research, I knew something like this must exist, but I thought it would be in some large edifice dedicated to science. These are the keys I need, the keys to decode their symbols. Here are all the symbols and images to clue their meanings. It appears to be a basic guide for training, but look at the images. They must have trained their young."

Antony stared at it and then at the shelves.

"Look! There are more over here."

On one shelf, lay dozens and dozens of books. They looked at them briefly and then moved on to the other shelves, wanting to touch everything, yet afraid of spoiling something. Henrietta had no idea what some objects were.

"This looks like a small video wall," she said looking at a strange machine. "It has the written symbols on it." Nothing happened when she touched the tabs.

"It must require some kind of energy. I wonder if lightning bug power will make it work. There is another one of those manuscripts right next to it. When you figure out how to decode the symbols, maybe this will tell you how it works."

Henrietta moved on. "At least I know that these are dishes. Isn't it wonderful to find some that we don't have to piece back together? Aren't they beautiful?"

On the next shelf were several curious objects, some wood and some metal. One of the wooden ones had long fibers stretched across its surface. Antony picked at it and a pleasant sound filled the chamber. Fascinated, he picked up another, a long, thin metal tube with holes and gadgets all over it. He blew into several.

"What are you doing?"

"Didn't you ever blow on a hollow reed? I used to think of all kinds of things to do to amuse myself when I was alone with the grasshoppers."

He blew into it over and over, then finally found the right angle. A soft whistling sound emerged. They both smiled with delight. These music makers were very different from theirs.

Antony's mood changed abruptly. "We need to carry these things back to camp right away. Would you consider the manuscripts the most important?"

"Yes, but there's more here than we can possibly carry by ourselves. We should go back to camp and get some help."

"Then we'll just take the manuscripts. We can't wait. This place is only a few d-units from the roach border. The only reason they never bothered my family, or tried to claim this part of the surface, was that they didn't think there was anything valuable here. The moment they know this place exists, they will claim it and tear up the surface looking for more."

He roamed about the chamber, looking for some sort of container or basket to carry the manuscripts. Then he began to examine the sculpture. He beat on the back of the chair with his pod. A hollow, clanking sound filled the chamber. He lifted one edge of the statue.

"Antony, be careful."

"It's hollow." He tipped it until it lay on its side. "We could turn it upside down, put all the manuscripts in it and carry the whole thing on our backs."

"Let me make images of everything first, just the way it is."

He returned the sculpture to its upright position and held the lantern as she directed him. She made images until she had used all of the materials she had. She wished she hadn't taken quite so many of Antony's family and the dairy.

When she had finished, they loaded all the manuscripts into the upturned sculpture, including the one next to the machine with the symbols. They considered loading the machine, but Henrietta was afraid it might be damaged without some thistledown to cushion it. They put in a few of the sturdier looking artifacts and placed their satchels on the top.

Antony lifted one side and Henrietta crawled under it, holding it briefly while Antony joined her. It was heavier than Henrietta expected and she groaned and shifted herself into a more comfortable position. Once outside the chamber, they set it down again and pushed the portal almost shut. They could not manage to get the sculpture up the steep slope, so they headed down the stream. Henrietta was panting before long.

"Are you all right?"

"I think so."

"It will be easier once we get away from the stream."

The stream bed widened about a d-unit later and they made their way up a more gentle slope. The meadow wasn't much easier. Henrietta stopped trying to talk and concentrated on the task. They went along at an average pace for about an h-unit and then Henrietta stumbled.

"My thorax hurts a little. I'm not used to this. How much farther is it?"

"It's only two or three more d-units. We'll rest a while and eat."

After a brief rest he said, "Let's push on. Place yourself a little closer to me. Then I'll take on more of the weight."

"What's wrong? You seem so nervous."

"I don't know. I have a strange feeling. I'm afraid we'll come across some wandering roach. I'll be glad when we're back at the camp."

Henrietta tried to go a little faster. She kept her breathing steady, in spite of the growing pain and stiffness in her thorax, abdomen and front pods, which she had never used against the ground. Finally, Antony stopped at the top of a gentle slope and they set their burden down. They could see the cross path and the two guards, sitting in the shade of a small wood plant.

"They won't be looking for us in this direction. Wait here and drink the last of the honey dew."

She watched him scurry down the slope, whistling to attract the guards' attention. One of them looked up and pointed. In a few moments, they were all back with her. The guards insisted on carrying the sculpture. Antony helped Henrietta up and they began the final portion of the journey.

*   *   *   *

"Master Diandra, you'll never believe what we found," Henrietta burst out as they entered the dining dome. "Manuscripts! Dozens of them. And so much more that we couldn't carry."

Antony gulped the mug of honey dew someone handed him. "Get me a location chart. Captain Alexander, you've got to go now and get the rest of the things. If wandering roaches find them first . . ."

"Slow down. What in the planet's name?"

They explained briefly between gulps of honey dew.

Antony pointed to the stream on the chart the captain handed him. "Here, right in this curve of the brook, a few d-units from where it joins the border stream."

Henrietta bubbled. "The things are perfectly preserved. The artifacts will easily fill four large baskets. Take a lot of thistledown. Some items are very fragile."

"Master Carl, take Carrie, ten guards and four large baskets. Leave now," Master Diandra instructed.

"Captain Alexander, after you have everything, go on to my parents' mound for the night. Could some of the guards stay there? If the roaches find out about this before we're ready to tell them, my family may need protection."

"I'll leave five guards and have more sent as soon as possible."

The excitement gradually died down. Master Diandra gave Antony and Henrietta a knowing smile. "You two have had quite a journey."

In the late afternoon quiet, they related the events of the last quarter time frame, including their promise.

"You finally realized what you felt for each other all along. If you thought you needed my permission, Antony, you didn't. But I do hope you're prepared to wait a while. I wish the quarter time frame had gone so well around here."

"What do you mean?" Antony asked.

"Master Gerald is gone."

"Where?"

"Randal said he had a family emergency."

"That's a lie. Master Gerald doesn't have any family. Sir Rex must have found out what he was doing."

Master Diandra continued. "They haven't worked since the storm and they told us to stay in this area. I've requested a formal meeting so we can air our concerns. We're to meet the day after tomorrow. Should we tell them what you found?"

"Have the guards noticed them watching our camp? Do they know Henrietta and I left?"

"We told them you were away. I said you needed to check on your family. I don't think they have been watching. Why?"

"I don't trust Sir Rex. I think he may be the one Old Rodger warned me about. The carriers should take the sculpture and the manuscripts back to the colony in the morning. Henrietta should go with them. We could process the images she made here. If the meeting with the roaches goes well, we can show them the images and tell them we'll share the results in reports. The guards should be ready for anything."

10.

*H*enrietta cringed with pain as she rose to get the imaging materials from her satchel. Master Diandra caught the look in her eye. "You strained yourself carrying that sculpture didn't you?"

"It's not so bad. It feels about like my appendages did that first morning here."

"Let me see. There is a big difference between swelled muscles in your appendages and those in your thorax and abdomen." She examined Henrietta carefully. "When appendage muscles are strained, they only put pressure on your exoskeleton, causing pain. Your other muscles swell inward, pressing on your internal organs. Severe strain can be fatal. Breathe deeply."

Henrietta took a deep breath and winced.

"You're going to have to be very careful. Antony, see if the guards can find some container large enough to hold her, and have them heat plenty of water. I'll get some pain potion. If we don't treat this as best we can now, the carriers will have to put her in a basket along with everything else. Henrietta, don't even pick up your satchel tomorrow. When you get back to the colony, go straight to the medical facility for a complete examination."

"Why didn't you tell me you were hurting?" Antony asked. "I would have stopped if I'd known."

"I guess I was too excited. I thought it was because I wasn't used to it. I've never had much strength, but nobody ever told me it was dangerous."

Before long, Henrietta sat soaking in a large vat. Master Diandra gave her a mixture of herbs and honey to ease the pain and swelling. They reheated the water after dinner.

*   *   *   *

"Master Diandra," Antony said as they entered the darkness of the emergency shelter, "I wouldn't have let her carry it, if I'd known."

"Don't blame yourself. Here, hold this pan while I pour the chemicals into it. Let's process these images. I'm dying to see what else you found."

An h-unit and a half later, Master Diandra stared at the first few images. "No wonder she didn't want to stop! I've been studying the ancient past for twenty some season cycles and nothing this well preserved has ever been uncovered. Do you realize what this could mean for us?"

Long after everyone else had retired, they sat, discussing the images and taking preliminary stock of the manuscripts. Antony was relieved that Henrietta felt better. He listened in wonder to Master Diandra's explanation of some of the items they had found.

"It makes sense that they would have trained their young. With no pupate stage of life, they simply grew into adulthood gradually, like nymphs, but without molting. Learning things must have been a slow and gradual process like their growth."

Antony groaned. "I can't imagine spending so many season cycles in training."

A clamor of voices outside the dome ended their discussion. Captain Alexander burst into the dome with the guards and carriers. They lifted Master Carl and Carrie out of empty baskets. Both looked sick. Captain Alexander slumped onto a stool, shaking.

Master Diandra rushed over to the captain. "Captain Alexander, what happened? What is wrong with Master Carl and Carrie? Antony, get them something to drink right away."

The captain took several gulps of water from the mug Antony handed him. "Everything is wrong. Rouse the whole camp. I want all the guards on the perimeter, except those who were with us. They need to rest. Carl and Carrie need some herb tea, and I could use some too."

Within minutes, the whole group gathered in the dining dome. Carl had calmed down some, but Carrie was still shaking as she sipped her tea. Henrietta sat next to Antony. He braced himself for what could only be bad news. Captain Alexander took a few sips of his tea, then placed the rest in front of Antony.

"We found the chamber easily, Antony. Your notes on the location chart were perfect. We even had a good h-unit of daylight left when we got there. The chamber was empty when we entered it. There were roach tracks everywhere in the mud. They had trampled a path both ways from the stream. There must have been many of them. We left immediately, following their tracks toward the dairy. We were probably a d-unit away when we saw the smoke."

He stopped a moment and placed his front pods on Antony's back. "They were renegades. They attacked your family. I'm sorry. All of them are dead."

Antony began to shake. Henrietta put her appendages around him.

Captain Alexander continued. "When we entered the glen, it looked like a battle zone. All of your fall harvest had been set on fire. Your father and brother had defended themselves as best they could. They took down three. I've seen plenty over the season cycles, but nothing like this, not to the innocent and unprotected. Carl and Carrie were both ill. I thought I would take them into the mound to rest, but when I entered the mound to check the situation out, I found the rest of your family. I was sick myself."

Antony turned and looked up at him. "It's all my fault. If I hadn't"

"No, it's not your fault. If you hadn't gone up there, we wouldn't have that," the captain said, pointing to the sculpture and the manuscripts. He handed Antony the mug of tea. "I had the guards dig one large hollow and we placed your family together and covered them. I'm sorry I couldn't take more time to do a better job, but I knew we must get back here immediately."

Antony gave up trying to control himself, threw the mug of tea across the dome, and yelled, "**No!**" Then he collapsed in shock and grief.

Caring appendages surrounded him—Henrietta's. Without a word, she embraced him, stroking his entire body with her middle appendages and softly stroking his antennae with her front pods. He pressed his head against her thorax and wept, accepting her comfort and emotional strength.

After a while, she said, "Nothing I say will help right now, but you know I'll always be with you. Please, try to drink a little tea."

He took another mug and sipped slowly, while she continued to hold and stroke him.

"I wish we had gone ahead and told your parents we made our promise."

Antony sighed and shook his head. "My father knew. He was watching us. As we rose last night, I happened to look down and saw him standing in the yard, looking up at us. This morning he asked me if he should start digging another domicile."

"Then I'm glad he was watching."

Antony forced his mind to concentrate on their predicament. The whole camp was in danger. If any of them were to get back to the colony safely, they needed his knowledge more than ever. Silently, he lifted his thoughts. "How do I beat Sir Rex, Old Rodger? How can I save us? Where in all you taught me, lies the answer?"

They returned to the group, and each member expressed his or her sorrow and support, embracing Antony. Although only Henrietta grasped the full meaning of Master Diandra's comment, it meant the most. "I'll provide you with another chamber for your grief and stay with you. This time I'll repair it. Are you strong enough to help us decide our next step?"

He nodded. "I had a bad feeling, even though I saw no signs of wandering roaches today. Maybe Sir Rex sent renegades for me. I know he hates me for my knowledge of the language."

"Let's not worry about why right now. Would they expect us to travel at night?"

"No, they know it's not our usual pattern. However, they might be out there."

"We think that you and Henrietta should leave immediately, with the sculpture and the manuscripts and twenty guards. You could be back in the colony by dawn. You could have them send two more brigades to help us. We can pack up everything here and be back at the colony by tomorrow night. Would that be best?"

"I wouldn't say 'best'. It isn't good for us to be split up, but the sooner someone gets back to the colony for more help, the better all our chances will be. They know we'll act only in defense. It's time to make the first move."

*   *   *   *

Henrietta realized that the others would be putting themselves at risk for her sake and wondered if she would have the courage to do the same. They decided that it would be easiest to keep the manuscripts in the sculpture. Four carriers volunteered to take it, saying that they could travel faster if they shared the burden. Those leaving ate a quick meal of fungus muffins while Master Diandra and Captain Alexander gathered Antony's and Henrietta's personal things and loaded them in with the manuscripts. By rearranging the Duo Pod books, Master Diandra managed to fit in all Henrietta's other notes and materials.

It was two h-units after midnight when they headed out of the camp. Antony whispered to Henrietta, "If you get tired, tap me and I'll carry you."

They slipped along the grass at the edge of the trail, not a sound coming from their pods. The pace was so brisk that Henrietta ran to keep up. The moon, still nearly full, shed its silvery light on the path. Rigid with anxiety, Henrietta glanced around. Looming grassfronds. Groves of wood plants. Open meadows. Hurry.

They stopped briefly at the cross path leading north to the dairy to drink from their flasks. A few of the guards fanned out, looking for signs of roaches. Nothing.

They had gone one third of the distance. Henrietta forced herself to go on. She would make it. A short while later, she found it difficult to keep up. The potion was beginning to wear off. Her thorax and abdomen throbbed with pain. She reached forward and tapped Antony. Without a sound, he scooped her up. A cloud covered the moon.

Antony moved even faster. His antennae twitched. He tapped one of the guards. The tap spread. Antony had Henrietta climb onto his back. He stroked her in reassurance. The guards formed a tight circle around them. She strained her eyes looking across the dark meadow. Nothing except a long, low ridge. A single wood plant stood where the trail turned and ran along the ridge. Henrietta remembered the place from last spring. Not much farther to the main trail. Two thirds of the way home.

They reached the wood plant. Screeching sounds echoed in the night. A horde of renegade roach warriors poured over the top of the ridge.

"Both of you, climb up into this wood plant," the closest guard said.

Antony pushed Henrietta up ahead of him. They reached a safe height as the roaches fell upon the guards. Henrietta looked down on the confusion. It was difficult to tell who was winning. The roaches were much larger, but not as strong. A fire ant could kill a roach with one sting, but there were so many more roaches. Two or three would set upon one guard, taking care to avoid both mandibles and stinger. They'd pin him down and crush him, or tear him apart with their strong mandibles.

Henrietta leaned against Antony and closed her eyes to the horror, but she could not shut out the terrifying sounds of battle. The cracking noise of splintering exoskeletons and the guard's screams of pain rang through her. Roaches wailed as deadly poison burned through them. It seemed like an eternity, but the whole battle was over in a quarter h-unit. It was quiet again. She opened her eyes and looked down. Bodies lay everywhere. Nothing moved.

"Wait here," said Antony.

He looked around and eased himself down the thick center of the wood plant. As he reached the ground, Henrietta saw a large roach warrior raise himself from the ground on the other side of the wood plant behind Antony.

"Antony! Look out!"

He whirled. The roach lunged at him. He braced himself too late. The roach caught Antony's mid-right appendage in his mandibles. There was a loud crack. Antony cried out in anguish and fell backward. The roach pounced.

Henrietta watched Antony struggle. He held the roach as far off as possible with his front pods. The roach's mandibles snapped at him. Antony had no poison, only his mandibles, and his were not nearly as large as the roach's. He had to penetrate some vulnerable area of his opponent. They were directly below her.

Without thinking, Henrietta jumped out of the wood plant, landing on the roach's broad back. The warrior turned his head. Antony seized the opportunity and sunk his mandibles into the exposed crack between the roach's head and thorax. The roach collapsed.

Henrietta slid off the roach's back. With strength born of desperation, she heaved the dead roach off of Antony. She knelt down and listened for his breathing. Life juice poured from his mangled leg.
"Don't move. I've got to bind this."

She scurried over to the closest dead guard, knowing there would be emergency supplies in his satchel. Fighting off a wave of nausea, she grabbed the satchel, closed her eyes and pulled, falling backward as the bag freed itself. She hurried back to Antony and dumped out the contents.

During her emergency medical training, she had fainted at the sight of life juice. She willed it not to happen now. She wound binding material around his nearly severed appendage. His life juice stopped flowing out.

She looked closely at the angle of the crushed joint, climbed back up the wood plant, and scurried about its twisted branches. She found one with the right angle, broke it off, climbed down, and splinted his leg. She dumped two packets of pain potion into a flask of water and held his head so he could drink it. Then she held him close and rested.

The potion took affect and Antony pulled himself up a little. "Are you hurt?"

"No. What are we going to do?"

"One thing is certain. We can't stay here."

"But you're injured. How can we leave?"

"I think I can manage on five legs if you support me on that side. Can you get some more binding material and tie my leg up against my thorax so it won't drag?"

"Why not wait for help to come?"

"We're too far from the main trail to be found. Nobody in the colony knows what's happened. They won't expect the carriers to arrive until this evening. By then the camp could look like this." He swept his front pod toward the destruction around them. "While we were up in the wood plant, I saw two of them slip away when they began to lose. It's only a matter of time before they come back with more. If we can get to the main trail, we'll be all right. It will be dawn soon and the earliest carriers will be out. How does your thorax feel? Do you think you could help me carry the sculpture again? We can't leave it here."

Henrietta weighed her options. Since the trauma of the battle and the exertion of lifting the roach from Antony, breathing had become very painful. But her choice involved more than herself. Twenty guards and four carriers scattered around her had sacrificed themselves to get her this far. The rest of the group was counting on them to send more help. She could not even begin to calculate the possible impact on millions of lives from the information in the manuscripts. With her notes, others could decode them.

"You're right. We can't stay here. We have to try."

She moved uncertainly toward another dead guard. Once again, she closed her eyes to the horror of his crushed body and pulled his satchel free. Antony turned onto his side and she carefully looped bindings around his thorax, under his injured appendage, and tied it up. She turned her back to him for a moment, so he wouldn't see her dump two packets of pain potion into a water flask and drink it. Antony rolled onto five pods.

They moved toward where the sculpture sat in the midst of several mangled bodies. "Can you lift one side enough for me to crawl under?"

"I'll try."

"Once I'm under, place yourself very close beside me and support my right side. Let me take on all of the weight."

Concentrating, she lifted the side of the sculpture. Antony rolled under and into position. She joined him and they rose slowly. Henrietta lifted up a silent thought, pleading for strength. The sculpture seemed much heavier now, and it had been twenty-four h-units since she had slept.

With agonizing slowness, they moved along the trail. Henrietta kept her breathing quick and shallow. She concentrated on each step, keeping in rhythm with Antony. She didn't want to jar his leg. He would probably lose it anyway, but she didn't want to give him any extra pain. She felt numb from the pain potion, but her breathing was labored and she felt dizzy.

"Do you want to stop and rest?" Antony said.

"No," she replied. She knew if she stopped, she would not be able to get up again.

The sky began to lighten as they struggled on. The longest two d-units of her life passed. Antony slowed down and began to let out long whistling sounds of distress when they reached the main trail. They heard an answering whistle. Henrietta's world went black.

*   *   *   *

When Henrietta stumbled and fell, Antony realized she had been holding up much more than he thought. The entire weight came down on him. His back-right leg cracked. He fell, groaning. Beneath the crushing weight, he continued to try to press upward with his four remaining legs, hoping that his slightly greater size would protect Henrietta. A stabbing pain shot through his thorax. Another through his abdomen.

"What is it?" he heard.

"There's someone under here!"

The weight was lifted. There stood Denton, whom he hadn't seen in at least a season cycle. "Antony! What's happened? Adell, emergency supplies. Quickly."

Antony gasped, "Renegade roaches attacked ... twenty guards with us ... all dead, two d-units back ... send more guards ... the expedition ... communication ... my satchel."

"We'll find it. Lie still now. Thanks, Adell," Denton said, taking the materials and starting to bind Antony's thorax while another carrier splinted his back appendage. "Can you find his satchel in that thing?"

"Here it is," shouted Adell. "I'll leave with it now."

"Break your own record. Tell them to be ready at the medical facility. Antony has several critical fractures and this young female is swelled like a fungus muffin, severe carrier strain syndrome. She's already lost consciousness. This thing must be terribly important."

Adell scurried off with Antony's satchel. They pried the lids off two crates and bound them together. Antony was carefully moved onto it and secured with bands of woven thistledown.

Antony grabbed Denton's pod. "Please, don't let Henrietta die. They murdered my whole family. I've no one. We're promised to each other. Save her."

"Be still now. You'll only hurt yourself more. We're doing all we can."

They placed Henrietta in a basket. Denton climbed in with her to monitor her respiration. Three times they stopped so he could restore her breathing. Antony became more hysterical each time.

About five d-units from the colony, they met the brigades of fire ants headed out. Whistles cleared the path ahead of them straight to the fire ant facility and medical center.

Medical assistants surrounded Antony, all shouting. Fluids! Hurry! Binding material! Now!

Antony's only concern was Henrietta. He kept yelling that they were promised to each other, and to leave him alone and save her. Strong pods restrained him, insisted that he calm down. Someone held his head and looked into his eyes while injecting something into his neck.

"You're going to be asleep soon, Antony. If you wish to live to fulfill your promise, lie still. This young female is Henrietta Harvester, correct?"

"Yes."

"Master Henry, our chief tunnel engineer, is her father?"

"Yes."

The face turned away for a moment. "Amy, have some one notify her family immediately." The eyes focused on him again. "Antony, we're doing all we can. They have a breathing mask on Henrietta now. Did she take any pain potion?"

"Yes, no, I don't know. Maybe." Antony told what they had done the evening before. "I don't know if she took anything after the attack. I passed out for a while." The chamber swirled around him.

"I'm going to tell them to assume that she did and wait the proper time before giving her anything else. A double dose with her small stature could be worse..." Antony heard no more.

11.

*P*ain throbbed in every part of Henrietta's body. A mask over her face forced air into her, causing a sharp, stabbing pain with each breath. She opened her eyes and saw an ant guard looking intently at her.

"Doctor, she's awake."

In a moment another face looked into hers. "Don't be afraid, Henrietta. Don't try to speak. You're safe now. You're in the military medical facility. You've been unconscious for several h-units. Antony will live. Our best surgeon is attending him now, trying to save his appendage. You did a very good binding job, by the way. The brigades of fire ants sent to help the rest of the expedition have not returned yet. I'm going to inject a very strong potion into your neck. One part of it will put you into a deep sleep, while another part works to reduce the swelling throughout your body."

The pain from her swelled muscles was so great that she did not even feel the injection. The blackness swept over her again.

      *   *   *   *

Antony awoke to a dull aching throughout his body and the touch of gentle pods on his head and antennae. He moaned and opened his eyes. The male ant before him looked fuzzy. He shook his head, trying to clear the confusion.

"Guard, tell the surgeon he's awake," he heard. The face looked into his. "Antony, it's I, Henry. Do you remember?"

Events came back in a rush: Henrietta's father, the battle, the crushing weight, her collapse... He tried to nod.

"Be still now. It's all right. Hearing of your promise surprised me, since Henrietta hasn't mentioned you in her letters, but that's like her. She never told us about her mentorship either, until she was sure she had it. But we're family now. Adeline and I are truly pleased."

Antony sighed. "Is Henrietta going to be all right?"

"Thanks to you, she's still alive. She regained consciousness briefly a couple of h-units ago. Each moment brings more hope for the next. Adeline is with her. I didn't mean for you to end up like this when I asked you to watch out for her."

The surgeon entered, carrying a mug with a sipping tube, which he held out to Antony. "Drink this. It's warm honey dew with liquid nourishment and more powdered herbs for the pain. You're one very lucky ant. It took me seven h-units to put you back together. You've got five major and over twenty minor fractures, but you still have all your body parts. Don't even try to move. All of your thorax and most of your abdomen, and two appendages are covered with plaster. That roach just about destroyed your main support joint. Your other legs are swelled from the strain of carrying that thing. You'll be in this body cast for two or three time frames and can look forward to about nine time frames of therapy after that. But you should be able to lead a fairly normal life."

"What about Henrietta?"

"If she makes it through the night, I'd say her chances are good. I'll be honest with you. Most carriers with strain that severe die within a few h-units."

He checked Antony's respiration. "Commander Ferdinand wants to talk to you."

"Should I leave?" asked Henry.

"No, stay with me," Antony pleaded.

Antony spent an h-unit of going over the events since they had left his parents' dairy on seventhday morning, explaining his relationship with Old Rodger, the reports from Master Gerald, and the problems with Sir Rex. "Commander, I think the roaches will try to justify the attack on my family by saying we helped a banished one. Don't let them. Their laws concerning banishment don't include murder. I'll be glad to help communicate with them. What did you do with the sculpture and the manuscripts?" Antony's front pods shook. He fought for control.

Commander Ferdinand held Antony's pods. "I had the them placed in the chamber with Henrietta. I'd better let you rest now."

Emotions churning, Antony turned to Henry. "This is all my fault."

Henry held his head and stroked him. "Don't blame yourself. From what you said, you prevented things from being worse. You did what you had to do. You knew it then and your intellect knows it now. Release your grief. I'm here for you."

Antony hurt too much to move and couldn't anyway. He let his tears flow.

Henry stroked his antennae. "While you were still in surgery and Adeline and I were sitting with Henrietta, I took a brief look at those manuscripts. Henrietta would never have left them behind. I know my daughter. She would do anything to prove her theories. I will grieve greatly if I lose her, but I would grieve even more if she hadn't tried."

Adeline entered. "Henry, I must go home for a while. I don't think anyone notified Hilda at the training center, and Andrew was upset when I left the nursery without him. There's nothing I can do here..."

Henry held his mate close. "Don't go alone. I need to stay with Antony for a while longer."

Adeline looked at Antony and burst into tears. "Antony, I'm so sorry about what's happened."

Henry called to the guard at the portal. "Send for some tea and find someone to escort Adeline home."

An attendant arrived with the tea. "I'll take Adeline. My duties for the day have ended. Your domicile is on my way home."

Henry returned his attention to Antony. "Tell me about your family. Memories can be healing."

Antony remembered how much better he had felt after talking to Master Diandra in the beginning, and the sense of relief he experienced after he confided in Captain Alexander. He decided he didn't want anything hidden between himself and Henry and told him about his contract and why they had gone to the dairy in the first place.

"I never meant to hurt Henrietta," he said when he finished his story. "I really do cherish her. Don't think ill of me for it. I was so lonely and desperate. I thought I had everything made right again, but now it's worse than ever."

"It certainly explains a lot of things that didn't make sense before, but it doesn't change what I think of you. You had the strength to tell me, now let go of it. Leave the guilt behind and move on with your life. You and Henrietta need one another now more than ever. Things will be right again in new ways. Don't give in to despair."

A female medical attendant entered. "Please, excuse the interruption. I'm Amy and your surgeon is my mentor, Antony. You'll be seeing a lot of me. I have more liquid nourishment for you and some herbs to help you sleep."

Henry rose to leave. "I'll see you tomorrow."

Antony gave himself up to Amy's care.

*   *   *   *

When Antony awoke, Amy was still there. "Good morning," she said. "Time for more liquids. Try holding the mug yourself this time." She propped his head up with a cushion and handed him the mug. He took it awkwardly.

"What day is it?"

"Secondday. How are you feeling?"

"I ache everywhere but it's not as bad as last night. How is Henrietta?"

"She made it through the night," Amy answered as she lay warm packs over his four unbroken, but strained legs. "In fact, her doctor removed the breathing mask a little while ago."

Amy massaged one appendage and then another, replacing the warm packs every few minutes.

"Were you here all night?"

Amy nodded. "I slept on that pallet over there after reviewing this procedure. You'll be my final therapy exam for the next season cycle. Master Surgeon Clint says I'll know everything about joint and muscle repair by the time I'm through with you. The rest of the expedition got back safely about two h-units before midnight. Master Diandra came in to reassure herself that you were alive. She told me to tell you not to worry." Amy continued to work some of the stiffness out of Antony's appendages, and told him a little about herself. "I've completed three season cycles of my mentorship and have two to go. I want to remain here as a physician and surgeon when I finish. Master Clint had me watch every minute of your surgery. He quizzed me as he went along."

Antony could move each of the strained appendages one fourth of their normal range when she finished. Amy carefully changed the woven coverlet under him, and washed all of him that wasn't in plaster.

"This is embarrassing," said Antony. "No wonder larvae whine."

She laughed. "You might as well get used to it. You'll be cared for like a larva for the next three time frames and you can't crawl out of this coop."

"I'm hungry. Can I have some real food? This liquid stuff takes care of the pain, but it isn't very satisfying."

"Sorry, not until this evening. But I'm glad you feel well enough to complain."

"Good morning," Master Clint said as he entered. He checked Antony over carefully. "Amy, good work on the strain relief therapy. Antony, Master Diandra is here. Are you ready for company?"

Antony nodded.

"I'll send her in. Amy, let's go. We have others to attend."

Master Diandra greeted him with affection. "I've been so worried about you. We spent the rest of the night packing. In all my season cycles of digging, I've never felt our lives were in any real danger. It was difficult to remain calm."

Master Diandra paused and reset the cushion under Antony's head. "When the three units of guards arrived, they couldn't tell us whether you were alive or not. Over one hundred roach warriors approached us, but scurried away when they saw our reinforcements. We did not bother to pursue them. We spent quite a bit of time at the scene of the attack, covering the bodies and making a complete list so families could be notified. It was awful. I don't know how you..."

She stopped and turned away for a moment, and took a few sips from her mug before she continued. "I had hoped to say this under happier circumstances, but I want you to consider your contract completed. I knew I would never need it after the first time frame. I was only waiting for you to make your own peace. I hold no further claim on you, but I hope you will choose to continue to work with us. You are a master interpreter, and I intend to refer to you as Master Antony when I release information to the colonies today. As soon as possible, I'll have the director of your former training facility join us here to consume that parchment. If I had ever mated and had a son, I wish he could have been like you."

Antony savored the moment. "Why don't you go back to sleep for a while. You look like you could use it."

The hint of a smile crept over her face. "I don't suppose it would do to go on Intercolonial Video Wall looking like this. Captain Alexander will be in to see you as soon as he finishes his meeting with Commander Ferdinand."

She went to the portal and returned with a crate. "I brought you something. When you feel the need, throw a few of these at the wall."

The crate was filled with mugs like the one he'd thrown across the dining dome. She placed the crate so he could reach it with his front pods, stroked him once more and left.

About half an h-unit later, Captain Alexander arrived. He walked around Antony. "What's this? They missed a spot. There's no plaster right here."

Antony laughed, even though it hurt to do so.

"Humor is a necessary ingredient in my life, Antony. It keeps me sane. I feel so responsible for what's happened. I should have been more on top of the situation. Many I cared about are tragically gone and you're lying here glued together with plaster. Can you ever forgive me?"

"It's not your fault. I missed a few cues, too."

"I didn't want to bring you more work until you felt better, but we need your help. Right before we left, Axel and another guard found Master Gerald's body about a d-unit from camp. Axel spotted this behind his right mandible."

He handed Antony a bit of parchment. "Our best writing interpreter spent most of the night trying to read it. He even looked at some of Master Gerald's reports and your translations of them, trying to get a clue to his script. How did you make it out?"

"He mixed ant and roach symbols. I got used to it after a while," Antony replied as he studied it. The ink was smeared, the parchment creased and torn, making it even more difficult to decipher. Commander Ferdinand came in, but said nothing.

An h-unit later, Antony lay his head back on his cushion and sighed.

"What is it?" asked Captain Alexander.

"It's the proof we need. It's dated last fourthday. 'My friend, Captain Alexander, you must heed this warning. Sir Rex plots against Antony and your young female trainee, Henrietta. He rejoices to know they are alone at South Dairy 50. I overheard him tell two of our warriors who owe him loyalty to take twenty of his renegades and wait, hidden on the trail, to ambush them as they return on seventhday. You must send many of your guards to bring them back before then. He despises Antony's abilities and wants him dead. He desires Henrietta's knowledge and theories. He would abduct her and force her to work for him. Guard them well. Don't let this happen. Your friend, Master Gerald.' Captain Alexander, if I hadn't decided to go and look for Old Rodger, if we'd been on the trail instead..."

Antony's voice faltered but he continued. "They probably got impatient waiting on the trail... Tried to force my father to tell them which way we went... Were the pieces of my family big, or little?"

Captain Alexander hung his head. "Big."

"Was it Allen, Arlene, and my mother's egg that made you ill?"

Captain Alexander nodded.

"They would have held my father till last... He was the only one who could speak to them... and he speaks very little Roach..." Antony reached down and picked up a mug. He wailed in agony. One by one, he threw the mugs at the wall.

*   *   *   *

A flurry of communications kept Antony's mind off of his grief for the next few days. His doctor said that moving him risked further injury, so Commander Ferdinand had communications equipment and a video wall installed in his chamber.

The Intercolonial Council sent a strongly worded message to the South East Roach Control Board. They condemned the attacks on Antony's family and the group returning to the colony as acts of war and demanded the offending roaches be delivered to them for justice. The reply came not from The Board, but from Sir Rex. As Antony predicted, his family was accused of aiding the banished. Antony and Henrietta were also accused of stealing artifacts from Roacherian territory. Sir Rex went so far as to demand that Antony and Henrietta be sent to Roacheria for a Formal Inquiry, or more attacks would follow. When an image of Master Gerald's letter was sent via video wall, it was discredited as a forgery. Master Gerald's murder was referred to as justice for treason.

The colonies prepared to defend South Harvester 45. All the dairies connected to its main tunnel system brought as much of the harvest and herds underground as possible. Bands of roving renegades set fire to fields of grassfronds, slaughtered and scattered remaining herds of aphids and grasshoppers. Legion upon legion of fire ants arrived through the intercolonial tunnel system, bringing supplies from other colonies with them.

*   *   *   *

Fifthday, a strategy meeting took place in Antony's chamber. Captain Alexander, Master Diandra, Commander Ferdinand, Helen— South Harvester 45's Council Chief—and the plastic and commodities supply administrator for South Harvester 45 sat around Antony.

Master Alexandra, the Intercolonial Council Chief, had contact with them via video wall. "We're concerned about plastic supplies in the southern region. We must have Roacherian plastic and they know it."

Antony lifted his head from his cushion. "I've been thinking about that and everything I learned from Old Rodger. Several times, my family misjudged our plastic consumption and ran low before the carriers arrived with more. My father always quit eating it and said to give his to Arlene and later Allen, because he didn't need it as an adult. My mother and I would do the same. Maybe we don't really need Roacheria's plastic. Suppose all adults in the southern region gave it up until this is settled. Would our mines supply enough if it's only given to larvae and pupas?"

Everyone looked toward the commodities administrator. She thought for a moment and then replied, "Yes, we'd have enough plastic, but our other food products are in short supply as a result of these raids."

"We can live on fungus for a while. It's nourishing enough," said Antony. "You're all forgetting how much food Roacheria gets from us. They'll be short too, and they won't be getting any credit from us for their plastic. If we can manage, why not let them worry for a change? They'll worry plenty when we continue to demand justice and say we don't need their plastic. We could let them think we have found the secret to producing it. They don't know what we found in the chamber."

Master Alexandra signaled another comment over video wall. "There's no need to sink to their level with untruths."

"I'm not implying that we be dishonest, only that we let them wonder. Besides, maybe the secret is in those manuscripts. A season cycle from now, Henrietta may have it for all of us. Isn't a season cycle of sacrifice worth the possibility of beating Roacheria?"

The commodities administrator spoke up again. "But what if Henrietta doesn't recover?"

Antony had been denying that possibility for five days. He continued to live on hope. She was still alive, but the first potion was only supposed to have kept her asleep for a day. She had overreacted and been in a coma for three days. She had been able to speak when she awakened, but could not move at all. Her doctor tried a second, weaker potion. It had been two more days. Instead of waking up, she alternated between what her doctor thought were trauma induced dreams, and a coma-like state.

Master Diandra answered the question. "If that happens, we assemble the best scientists in all the colonies, take her notes and get to work on it."

Antony struggled to maintain emotional control. Master Diandra caught the anguish in his eyes. She looked at him with steady reassurance and then continued. "We think that one whole manuscript is nothing but location charts. We could get our best geologists to compare them to present-day surface graphics. There's a lot of uninhabited surface area on this land mass. There may be Duo Pod ruins and plastic deposits no ant or roach has dreamed of. The areas that were covered by the sea have changed some, and we know that the western coast is drastically altered, but other than that, 20,000 season cycles is a tiny dot in geologic time. We could find new supplies away from roach control."

Captain Alexander supported Antony as well. "I agree. A temporary sacrifice is worth it. Sir Rex thinks he has us isolated. Roacheria doesn't know about our intercolonial tunnel system. We are united and we know from Master Gerald that they aren't."

The others agreed to the logic of their arguments. The Intercolonial Council would seek input immediately from all the Colonial Councils. Support came quickly and was overwhelming. They would band together and stand against Roacheria's greed.

                    *   *   *   *

Roacheria stopped the attacks and ceased all communications. Antony tired of staring at the plain earthen walls of his medical center chamber, rereading supportive messages that arrived from all over the colonies, and watching video wall. Although Henry came every day and reassured him, his anxiety over Henrietta increased. Her condition remained unchanged. Although her muscles were no longer swelled, she did not awaken. Early seventhday, after Henry talked to her unconscious form for an h-unit, she had moved one front pod slightly.

Antony was sure she would respond to him and begged to be moved into her chamber. His doctor did not want to risk moving him. Firstday morning, when Amy came in to wash him and change the bed clothes, he tried again.

"I'm almost immobile. You have to move me every day when you do this and it hasn't hurt anything. You could slide me onto a portable couch. I'm going to go insane if I have to look at these same walls one more day. She needs me, and if she never comes out of it, I at least ought to be able to be with her once more."

Amy convinced her mentor to move Antony. That afternoon they arrived with a portable couch and two other medical assistants. They slid him off of his clinic bed and onto the couch, and took him into Henrietta's chamber.

Henry and Adeline had gone home. Except for two guards at the portal, he was alone with her. Her stillness frightened him. Was she real? His couch touched her bed. He reached out, stroked her antennae and spoke softly.

"Henrietta, it's Antony. I know you can hear me. Please, wake up. I need you so much. My life has no meaning without you."

Her doctor entered to check on her. "I wish I knew of something more I could do. Every so often she cringes and cries out as if in terror. Then she thrashes about before sinking back into this vegetative state. Do you need anything before I leave?"

"No, thank you."

"If anything changes, call to the guards. They'll have a medical attendant here in moments."

Antony continued to talk to her about anything and everything for the next two h-units. She flinched and cried out. He held her as closely as he could.

"You're safe. I'm here. Don't think about the attack any more. Think about good things. Remember riding the grasshopper and jumping from the grassfronds. Dream about us."

He took her front pods in his and held them. "I promise myself to you as your mate, to cherish and support, no matter what joys or sorrows may occur. I will nurture with joy all new life that may come from our union. I promise this freely for as long as we both live in this world."

Over and over he spoke their promise. "We are each other's now. Remember when I said that we could overcome anything together? I'm with you."

On and on he spoke and stroked her. She lay still, but seemed more relaxed. His voice grew tired. He stopped talking but continued to stroke her antennae. The h-units dragged on. He longed to sleep, but would not end his vigil.

About two h-units after midnight, Henrietta stirred and opened her eyes. After all his plans, he only said, "Are you really awake this time? You aren't going to pass out again and leave me all alone, are you?"

She reached out to stroke him and they both cried.

12.

*T*he bliss of being with Henrietta lasted only half a day. Captain Alexander entered with a red desert ant. "Henrietta, it's wonderful to see you awake. Antony, this is General Arnold. He arrived this morning from West Desert Colony 15 with several hundred of his guards and supplies from the western colonies. They captured two roach warriors not far from the main entrance. Would you help interrogate them? Your surgeon says since they moved you safely once, it's all right to carry you in the portable couch."

"I'll be glad to. General Arnold, excuse my surprised look when you entered. I've never met an ant as large as you."

"Don't worry, you aren't the first. We may be twice a fire ant's size, but we've only half the venom."

Several more cushions were placed around Antony. They carried him carefully to the confinement chambers in the center of the military complex. The two roaches were tightly bound when Antony, the general and Captain Alexander arrived.

"I remember these two," Antony said as they set down his couch. "They were with the roach scientists from the start."

"You're right," Captain Alexander agreed. "I didn't have time to look at them carefully before. That fits with Master Gerald's letter about Sir Rex sending two who were loyal to him."

"Turn them around a moment," Antony said. "I think they're the same two I watched slip away from the attack on us. Both of them winced at the sound of my voice, even though I know they don't understand what we say. I'm probably the last ant they expected to see again in this world."

Antony heard the larger of the two whisper to the other, "Shut up. You'll live longer."

Antony addressed them in Roach. "What makes you think we're about to kill you? What are your names? We need to inform the S.E.R.C.B. that we have you. Maybe Sir Rex will bargain for your release."

The smaller one flinched.

The larger roach said, "I'm Gerry and he's Renae'. We won't tell you anything."

Antony related his response to the general.

"I have an idea," General Arnold said, "Place them unbound in the same confinement chamber. Maybe they'll talk to each other if they think they're alone. Antony could listen closely. We could use a voice imager too."

The general waited while the two prisoners were removed, then said, "If you get tired, Antony, we'll separate them until tomorrow and try again. Guards, keep alert. If they start to fight each other, separate them immediately. I don't want them killing each other. The roaches will say we extinguished them without due process—as if they don't. The time will come for that, but by our laws, even if they don't deserve it."

He showed Antony several pod signals. "Be very quiet. If they know you're listening, they might not talk freely."

In perfect silence, they placed Antony's portable couch close to the chamber where the two roaches were confined. He listened for two h-units, but the only thing he heard was Gerry angrily telling Renae' to shut up. He signaled his desire to stop.

"How did it go?" Captain Alexander asked when they had carried Antony to the guards dining area where he and General Arnold were waiting. The general handed Antony a mug of tea.

"Gerry intimidates Renae'. I think Renae' will eventually talk. There was something about the look in his eyes before we left them together, as if he wanted to tell me something. I'm not sure why, but I'll believe him when he does."

"Instead of going back to the medical facility, would you like to stay with me in my living quarters?" Captain Alexander asked. "It's close to here and to the confinement chambers. We wouldn't have to move you as far every day. Amy will come early every morning. She'll also teach me how to care for you."

"I'd like that, but what about Henrietta? How will I get to see her?"

"Don't worry. I'll make sure somebody brings her down here as often as possible. Commander Ferdinand would like to know if you would be a mentor to the interpreter who was with us in the ruins and two others. They will come to my quarters four h-units a day. All of them are pretty good at it on parchment, but we need more who can speak Roach like you can."

"Sure. I can't stand lying around all day with nothing to do."

"I had a feeling you'd say that."

When they finished eating, Captain Alexander and Axel carried Antony to the captain's quarters. The curving earthen walls of the cozy parlor were covered with images of the southern conifer forests near Captain Alexander's home colony and members of his family. Axel rearranged the floor cushions so Antony's couch faced the images and the video wall. He placed a small work surface with parchment and ink where Antony could reach them.

*   *   *   *

The ants continued their practice of questioning the two roaches formally each day, allowing them to be together while Antony listened, then separating them again.

Antony spent the afternoons with his three trainees, Fred, Carter, and Cathy. He knew Fred from the ruins project. Carter and Cathy were a mated pair. Carter had attempted to translate Master Gerald's letter. All three were eager to learn. Sometimes, they sat silently with Antony as he listened to the two prisoners.

For a few days, the roaches continued their silence. Then they began to speak about their lives. Although it did not help the ants establish guilt or innocence, Antony gained important background information.

Antony knew from Old Rodger that Roacherian society was sharply divided. There were the privileged ones who had more credit than any creature could possibly need or use and all of the political power; those who did most of the work; and finally there were large numbers with absolutely nothing, who scrounged and starved, their young often suffering from plastic deprivation.

Old Rodger had rarely spoken about himself, but Antony knew he must have been one of the privileged. The master scientists who worked in the ruins, though they were not among those with the most credit, were definitely well off. The two warriors ranked at the bottom. It was difficult for Antony to explain this system to his trainees.

"Look at it this way. During job exploration, did you like and find yourself well suited for every job you tried?"

The three laughed.

"Because you tried many things and failed at some, you came to appreciate the work of others. The roaches do not train that way. The Board Member's servant has no idea about the pressures a Board Member faces when making difficult decisions. Likewise, the Board Member has no appreciation for the one who serves him. Neither sees that both are important to the whole. The Board Member looks down on the servant and the servant envies the one who looks down on him. Board Members do not serve each other as we do. Often, their decisions benefit only themselves. So the servant is even more resentful. They don't give out credit according to need. The servant gets next to nothing, while those in so called 'important' jobs, are given more than needed. Their system runs on greed and selfishness."

Antony listened as the two roaches talked about the desperation that pushed them into becoming renegades. Neither Gerry nor Renae' had any formal training or any hope of getting any. They counted themselves lucky that they had gotten enough plastic in their nymphood to be intelligent.

Renae' had seen only two season cycles since his final molt into adulthood. He became a warrior because he had the size and strength required, and had been promised training. But he was only trained to kill. His dream had been to better himself and he felt deceived and angry.

Gerry's mother had booted him out half a time frame after his final molt, saying she had too many nymphs to support, and told him it was time he fended for himself. He had lived by stealing for five season cycles before becoming a warrior. He had no illusions. He was cold and cynical, often laughing at Renae's naiveté.

*   *   *   *

Twice during the next time frame, roach forces assaulted South Harvester 45. The first time, ant scouts spotted them coming a long way off. Everyone was directed to stay in domiciles or emergency shelters. The ants allowed the invaders to proceed down the main tunnel. Then hundreds of fire ants poured out of side tunnels and chambers, cut off the roaches' escape and killed them all.

Antony's message to Sir Rex was brief. "Those who come to retrieve the bodies from the meadow east of the main entrance will not be bothered, as long as they come no closer."

The second time, fire ant guards and desert fighters poured out of all colony entrances, ringing the entire mound several times. The roach warriors turned and fled. The ants grew confident that this time they would prevail against Roacheria.

                    *   *   *   *

Although busy, Antony still grieved. Only Henrietta's presence, his growing bond with her family, and Captain Alexander's constant care kept him going.

Master Diandra often came by in the evening when Henrietta was too tired. It would be a long time before Henrietta regained what little physical strength she'd had. One evening, Master Diandra brought him another gift, a thick, oval shaped slab of wood about five f-units wide and three high.

"Grief has its phases. First, I gave you the mugs to release your anger. This is to help you remember with fondness and renew yourself. Picture it in your mind, or sketch it until you are out of your body cast and able to work on it. This will be the memorial marker for your family."

She handed him a carving tool. "I know what it is to lose someone. A time frame before the date of our ceremony, I lost my Promised One in a tragic accident. He saved me, but I panicked and lost him. I withdrew in guilt and grief for many time frames. It wasn't until his parents asked me to make his marker that I found the strength to live again without him."

"How long does it take?" he asked, recalling his mother's occasional bouts with sadness his first year of adulthood.

"Everyone is different, but in time, the aching goes away. There will always be an emptiness, but peace will come."

He looked at the tool, fashioned in the shape of a carpenter ant's mandible, the natural tool of those who knew wood best. "Thank you. When Henrietta and I have our ceremony, will you take my mother's place?"

"I'd be honored."

                    *   *   *   *

The day to remove Antony's body cast arrived. It had been difficult for him to accept helplessness. Now, he thought he would have himself back. Amy lowered him into a tank of warm, swirling water to loosen the plaster. She was in the tank beside him pulling away chunks of plaster and dropping them outside the tank when Master Surgeon Clint arrived.

"This phase of your recovery is over, Antony. I hope you weren't planning to scurry out of here this evening. You'll be very weak. Even your uninjured legs will lack the strength to support your body, since you haven't been able to use them. You'll remain in the portable couch for quite some time, but I promise it'll get better."

"Master Clint," said Amy as she removed the last of the plaster from his thorax. "Some of the plaster is sticking in the scar lines. What should I do?"

"Leave it for now. You could re-open the fracture if you scrub too much. It will loosen on its own over the next several days, since you will begin each therapy session in the tank. Wait a moment. I'll guide you," he replied, climbing in with her.

Antony sighed with relief as they finished releasing him from his plaster prison. Master Clint had Amy watch as he worked carefully on Antony's midright appendage. His expression grew more serious.

"What's the matter?" asked Antony.

"It hasn't healed as well as I had hoped. I'm afraid you're going to have a lot of pain in this joint. We'll have to adjust the plan I made for your therapy. I know you value your independence, but you'll have to accept the fact that you will always need help. All the scar tissue is very delicate. If you try to do too much and strain yourself, you could split the scars open. If that happens, you could find yourself in a portable couch permanently."

They lifted Antony from the tank. He twisted and turned, looking at himself. Each scar showed up plainly with the bits of remaining plaster, two long stripes down the back of his thorax and one down the front. There were two more scars down his abdomen and scores of smaller ones crossing them.

His voice shook with disappointment. "I look like a turtle."

"Believe me, the scars won't show up so much later. Take things slowly," Master Clint said as he helped Antony turn himself over on the couch. That was all he accomplished that night.

A long, painful process began. Henrietta came every evening. She arrived as Antony finished soaking and held his front pods while Amy worked the muscles in his legs. Strength came quickly to the uninjured appendages. He made steady progress with the healed back leg, but his midright appendage continued to be a problem. The joint ached constantly, often aggravated by the cold, damp, winter weather.

"You can do it, my cherished one," Henrietta said whenever he wanted to give up. "Remember, we can overcome anything together."

In early spring, he finally abandoned the portable couch. He walked on five legs with his thorax and head lowered. The useless midright leg dragged.

*   *   *   *

The persistent knocking awakened Henrietta. She was alone. Master Diandra must have fallen asleep in the research center again. She crawled from her sleep cushion and went to the portal.

"Henrietta, I'm sorry to wake you," Axel said. "Captain Alexander sent me to fetch you. Neither of us can manage to comfort Antony. Climb on my back. It'll be faster."

Henrietta clambered aboard. "I was afraid this might happen. He's been so discouraged with his therapy."

Captain Alexander held open the portal. Henrietta crossed the familiar parlor and entered Antony's sleep chamber. He lay on his cushion moaning that he wished he were dead. Henrietta reclined beside him and wrapped her legs around him. Behind her, she heard the portal shut. Captain Alexander usually left it open.

"Don't talk this way, Antony. Remember what you said. We can overcome anything. You must keep believing that."

Antony turned toward her, huddling like a larva. "Why? I've no family. Look at this body... covered with scars. I'll never be able to walk normally again..."

"Because I cherish you so much." Henrietta stroked his thorax and abdomen, then his antennae. "You will get better."

He relaxed and wrapped his front pods around her. His eyes pleaded. "Then let me give myself to you now. Let there be some shred of joy in my life."

She pushed herself away slightly and shook her head. "No. Giving yourself to me now will not change anything. It won't take away your grief. Nor will it give you any more strength. It will only rob us of the joy we should have when the time is right. I will stay with you and comfort you until you sleep, but we will not join, even though Captain Alexander has left us alone. You mean more to me than that."

He shook as she continued to stroke him. "I'm sorry," he said. "I shouldn't have..."

"Never mind."

It wasn't the only night she spent with him.

*   *   *   *

Henrietta made rapid progress decoding the Duo Pod manuscripts. She brought one with her each evening and told Antony the simple stories. He laughed at some of the more fanciful ones, in spite of his pain. Amy listened, too, often asking Henrietta questions.

One evening at the beginning of the fourth time frame, Master Clint arrived with a wrapped parcel. Amy said, "Henrietta, do you remember that story you read a time frame ago about the injured Duo Pod nymph? I couldn't get the image out of my mind, and it gave me an idea. Master Clint helped me invent something we think will help Antony."

Antony removed the wrapping and saw a shell of his appendage, made from metal with short strips of pliable plastic in place of the joint. The inner sides were lined with thistledown. Softly twisted hemp laces tied the opening from top to bottom.

Master Clint explained. "I measured your appendage some time ago for a different purpose and hope this fits properly. I have friends who work in the plastic mine. They watched for pieces that would bend just right when I explained what I needed. The thistledown should prevent any abrasive action to your exoskeleton. Hopefully, this brace will give your joint the strength you need. Put your pod in. Let's try it."

Antony placed his mid-right appendage in the brace. Master Clint helped him up. He raised his head and thorax, lifted his front pods and stood uncertainly on four pods for the first time in over half a season cycle. Henrietta took his front pods in hers.

"It works. I can walk like a regular ant again." He dropped Henrietta's pods and tried going faster, but tripped and fell.

"Slow down," Master Clint said as he helped Antony up and checked him over. "Don't try too much too soon. This is completely experimental. Let's start by wearing it two h-units a day and increase the time gradually."

*   *   *   *

The silent stand-off with Roacheria continued. Under heavy guard, the dairies planted the grassfronds and tended their herds. Food became more plentiful and all the colonies grew more hopeful. That fall's harvest was abundant and none of it went to Roacheria.

A season cycle from the date of the attacks, Antony and Henrietta sat together in a conference with their doctors.

"How is the brace working out, Antony?"

"I can't go very fast, but it's much better than before."

"And the aching?"

"When the weather is good, I don't need any pain herbs at all, but I can always tell when there is going to be sky water."

Master Clint laughed. "We'll give you another job as chief weather announcer. You'll always be given all the pain herbs you need. Henrietta, has Amy shown you how to massage occasional stiffness out of his joint?"

"Yes, she has."

"Good. You need to know how to take care of him. I no longer have any medical objections to your formal mating, but I have some restrictions. Antony, your exoskeleton will always be weak. You are like one of Henrietta's repaired artifacts, one slip and it shatters. Any injury will be serious. I don't want you taking chances. No climbing wood plants or riding grasshoppers. You can walk by yourself in level tunnels, but I want someone to carry you up or down any slopes. Henrietta, if he complains, you put your pod down and stop him, if you want him to be around to a ripe old age. When can I look forward to an invitation to your ceremony?"

"It depends on my manuscript work for the next few time frames," said Henrietta.

"Now it's my turn," began Henrietta's doctor. "I'm afraid I don't have good news. Your strength tests last quarter time frame weren't encouraging. Half your own weight is all you'll ever carry safely. Antony, you know she pushes herself too hard. You must protect her from herself. Henrietta, you will not survive another bout with strain. Keep your head in your manuscripts and let others do the digging. Like Antony, you should be carried through sloping tunnels."

He looked down before continuing. "There is one other thing you must both know and consider before mating. The female reproductive organs are particularly vulnerable to damage when abdominal muscles swell with strain. I'm sorry to say that records throughout all the colonies regarding female carriers who suffer even mild carrier strain syndrome, show that eighty percent are infertile. Your chances of laying an egg with life are not very good. If you do have larvae, Henrietta may not carry them beyond the second season cycle, or whatever point they reach half her weight."

Antony took Henrietta's front pod in his and looked at both doctors. "We will do as you say. Thank you for everything you've done for us."

They left and ambled down the passageways that led to Captain Alexander's quarters. Antony was glad he wasn't home. They reclined on the floor cushions, holding each other.

"I'm not the same ant with whom you made a promise," Antony said. "I'll understand if you want to call it off."

She reached up to stroke his antennae. "I didn't make a promise with you because of your strength or good looks. I made our promise because I could see that you cherished me enough to share me with a commitment I had already made to my training. I made that promise no matter what joys or sorrows, and I intend to keep it. Do you still want me, knowing we may never have any young?"

"What would I have if I didn't have you?"

They sat in silence, clutching each other, struggling inwardly to accept their limitations.

"Be patient a while," Henrietta said at last. "I may be very busy and unable to spend as much time with you. I think I'm on the verge of finding out why the Duo Pods died out. Daniel and Aaron will join us again, and a geologist from South Dairy 40. They'll help Master Diandra and me study some of the scientific writings. Remember the first parchment I found? I decoded it yesterday and its message was most disturbing."

13.

*T*he strategy of letting the two captive roaches be together each day so they would talk about the attack had not worked. Commander Ferdinand had decided to leave them isolated. Now, Antony suggested they try again.

"Gerry," said Renae', when the two roaches were reunited, "I'm really glad to see you. I was afraid you were dead."

"I wish I was," Gerry replied. "Now we start this stupid game again. I hate this. I hate it underground. I wish they'd extinguish us and get it over with! We were both dead from the start anyway."

"What are you talking about?"

"In all this time, you haven't figured it out? You really are stupid. I don't think we were sent here to count how many fire ants entered."

"What do you mean?"

Antony and the others listened intently, the three writing away. Antony started the voice imager.

"I don't care any more," Gerry said. "I think we were supposed to get caught. I think we were the justice offering. Sir Rex probably figured the ants would extinguish us and be satisfied and everything would get back to normal. I realized a long time ago Antony's been out there listening every time we've been together."

"Then stop. I don't want to die. It's not so bad here. I've even gotten to like that fungus stuff. It's better than starving or facing him again."

"Not for me! Antony, I know you're out there. Here's what you've been waiting for. We were there, both of us. Want to know who killed your family? We did. The whole lot of us. Sir Rex always hated you and so do I, you pond scum. I don't care any more. I was one of the ones holding your father, that stupid, stubborn piece of body waste. All he had to do was say which way you went. It's his fault they all got killed. He hated you for it, too. He died cursing you, screaming your name. Your father was angry. 'Liferme, Antony, liferme!' he screamed. Now you know. Send one of those guards in to finish me off."

Renae' shouted, "No! No! Listen to me! Let me explain. I didn't kill anybody. I tried to stop them. Please, believe me. I don't want to die."

Antony said, "Separate them. Get Renae' some tea. Calm him down so I can talk to him."

The guards moved quickly. They dragged Gerry back to his own confinement chamber where he ranted and raved, begging for death. Two others held the hysterical Renae'. When the tea arrived, Antony took a sip of it himself, and then held it out to Renae'.

"It's not poison. It will calm you down so you can tell me the truth."

The guards let go of Renae's front pods. He took the mug and drank. "Please, don't kill me. I'll tell you the truth."

Antony turned to the others. "Carter, put another pack in the voice imager and all of you write down everything. I'm fine. For the first time, I really am all right."

They only stared at him.

"Didn't you hear the last thing Gerry said. My father's words were in Ant. He was saying 'Live for me, Antony, live for me.'"

"Let's start at the beginning, Renae'," he said in Roach. "You're a regular warrior. Why were you working for Sir Rex?"

"I wasn't at first. When I got assigned to the ruins project with Gerry, he asked me if I could use more credit. He said all I had to do was swear loyalty to Sir Rex and maybe work a little extra once in a while."

"Tell me about it."

"At first it was easy and I had more credit to send home. I even saved some. You probably won't believe me, but it was for my younger brother to get training." His eyes pleaded.

"I believe you. What did Sir Rex tell you to do?"

"We spied on your camp. We spent lots of nights in that one tall ruined building. We counted how many fire ants every day, things like that. He... He always hated you and said things about you that I didn't understand."

"Who said what things?"

"Sir Rex. Things like, 'That old one haunts me through him.' Sir Rex always told us that if we ever saw you leave camp alone, to kill you right away and dump you in a spider's lair we knew about. He started talking about Henrietta after that day he went in the market complex with her and Master Diandra and Randal. That night he yelled at Master Roland and Master Gerard. He said they had all that time and why hadn't they figured out the numbering system or something. I didn't understand. He called them idiots for letting a silly female trainee outdo them. He told us if she ever left camp alone, grab her, but don't hurt her, and bring her to him. Only neither of you ever left camp, so he got angry and went back to Roacheria for a while."

Antony told the guards they could relax their grip on Renae'. Then he asked, "Did he have you do anything else?"

"No, that was all until after the storm when he found out that the two of you had gone to South Dairy 50. He laughed and said that now was his chance. He told us to go to where his personal warriors were camped."

"The renegades?"

"Yes, we were to get twenty and wait for you on seventhday, kill you and take her. I told Gerry it wasn't right. He kicked me and said I had to. I already got the extra credit and now I had to earn it. Sir Rex had told us to erase our tracks afterwards and use mantis pods and leave a few pieces of you. He wanted it to look like a mantis so nobody would go looking for her. He said we better not even bend one of Henrietta's antennae or we're dead. He said nobody better see us, especially not your family. But Raul, the renegade commander, got tired of waiting and said he had his own plan."

Antony's antennae drooped. He had been right in his first guess. He requested some tea for himself and then nodded for Renae' to continue.

"I told Raul we shouldn't, that we were supposed to wait. He kicked me hard, right here," Renae' said, pointing to the vulnerable area where his back leg joined his body. "And we went on to where your family lived. Raul told your father we were supposed to escort you back to camp because we were all working together. Your father said he didn't believe that and you were gone anyway. Raul asked which way and he said he didn't know, that you made your own trails. He told us to leave. He kept talking to the other young male in Ant. I backed off. I wanted to run."

Renae' glanced at all the guards around him, twitching. "I swear, Master Antony, I didn't do anything. I told Raul we should go and he told me to shut up. Then it all happened. Your father and the other one sprang on two warriors and they dropped. Your father jumped a second and then all the others grabbed him. There was a lot of yelling. It was awful..."

The mug fell from Renae's shaking pods.

Antony requested more tea and waited while Renae' drank it and calmed down. "Cooperating will help you live, Renae'."

"Raul killed the young male first. Then someone broke down the portal of the mound. They dragged your father inside. I stayed away. There was a lot of screaming. I don't know what all happened in there, because I didn't go in. Raul and Gerry dragged your father back out and asked him one more time where you were. That was when he started yelling what Gerry said, and Raul killed him."

Antony took several deep breaths. "What happened then?"

"Raul told the others to set everything on fire and we left."

"What about the chamber and the artifacts?"

"We found that place on the way back to the renegade camp. Raul was happy when we saw all that stuff and said it was almost as good, so we took it. On the way back to camp, Raul said for us not to say anything and let him talk to Sir Rex."

"What did Sir Rex say?"

"He wanted to know where we got those things and why we didn't have Henrietta. Raul made up a pretty crazy story and kept looking at me to be quiet. Sir Rex caught it. Three of Sir Rex's other guards grabbed Raul and two grabbed me and held me down. Sir Rex put his back pods behind my head and said tell him or die, so I told him. He was furious and started hitting Raul, saying he should have let it go. There would have been another chance the next time you went home. Sir Rex said it would probably turn into a war and he would have to figure out some way to make it your fault. He said Raul would know the pain of all of them. He killed Raul slowly."

Old Rodger had told Antony about such torture. The corpse ended up in tiny pieces. Knowing that Captain Alexander had told him that he had covered "big" pieces of Antony's family was a small comfort.

Renae' continued. "After that, he stepped on me again and wanted to know exactly where we found the stuff. I was afraid he would do to me what he did to Raul. When I said it was by a stream, he got interested and asked me to describe it. I said it had steep banks. He asked which side of the stream. I said toward us. He started laughing that it was ours anyway. He let me up and said now he had his reason. I didn't understand, but I was glad he let me up. The dent behind my head really hurt."

"Wait a minute," Antony said. "Did you cross another stream within a few d-units, also with steep banks?"

"Yes."

"Did you tell Sir Rex about it?"

"No, he never asked. I still don't understand why it mattered anyway."

Antony stopped and addressed the others. "No wonder Sir Rex accused us. He actually believed the chamber was on the Roacherian side of the border stream."

He turned back to Renae'. "Tell me about the attack on us."

"It was almost evening then, and Sir Rex sent three to spy on your camp. They watched the others come back late at night. When they saw you and Henrietta getting ready to leave, they scurried back to us. Sir Rex was angry that you found out so soon and cursed you again, but he was glad that the group was split up. He told us to take fifty and kill everybody, but don't hurt Henrietta. We waited behind the ridge. That's about all. When he sent Gerry and me here, he said we were supposed to count any fire ants who entered from other colonies, because he was planning a big attack. That's the truth, I swear it. I didn't kill anybody. I was there, but I didn't do anything."

"One more question. Who killed Master Gerald?"

"Master Gerald is dead?"

"Yes."

"I don't know, honestly. He was alive when we left the ruins."

"Thank you, Renae'. You're going back to your confinement chamber now. Your cooperation will be taken into account when all of this is settled."

Antony turned to the others. "Fred, Cathy and Carter, get all this written up. Use the voice image and get it exactly as they said it. I'll check it for accuracy before we make copies. Then Gerry and Renae' will put their marks on it. Guards, keep them separated. Let Gerry have his anger. I'm going to the nearest meditation chamber and the only ants I want to see are Henrietta, Captain Alexander, or Master Diandra."

*   *   *   *

For three days, while they waited for the other scientists to arrive, Henrietta and Master Diandra looked through the scientific writings, picking out things that had environmental images or key title words relating to the use of fuels. Henrietta found several likely ones and started to work on them while Master Diandra gathered some of the other reports.

Master Diandra, Master Dawn—a geologist from South Dairy 40-- Daniel, and Aaron, listened as Henrietta read the quote and poem she had found lying on top of the books in the pods of the statue when she and Antony first entered the buried chamber that fatal day:

"Lift up your eyes to the heavens.
Look down at the earth.
The heavens will vanish like smoke,
The earth will wear out like a garment,
And its inhabitants die like vermin." Is. 51:6 NJB

Demise
Our mechanical locusts descended on the fields
And sucked the juices of the earth
To fuel all our desires.
When poisons fill the water and air,
And forests lie in ashes and sawdust;
A ravaged planet will take its revenge DKOF

They discussed everything that Henrietta had translated. She stayed up late every night, translating more for the next day's discussion. They talked about every theory and still came back to the same idea: a long string of natural disasters and their consequences. Disasters usually disrupted safe supplies of food and water. Too many disasters too close together would result in economic collapse and the inability to rebuild. Central authority would no longer be able to function. Anarchy would result. Henrietta wasn't satisfied.

"Look, Henrietta," said Daniel. "I'm not trying to be critical, but living beings can't cause a natural disaster. You can't say, 'I think I'll make a summer storm next quarter time frame.'"

"Then why was this particular parchment in such a prominent position? Why go to all the trouble to construct that chamber and seal out the air? Why coat parchment with plastic for the sole purpose of preserving it, if it weren't significant? That portal was designed so intelligent creatures could figure out how to open it. That parchment was placed so it would be noticed immediately. There has to be something we're all missing in these references to the planet. Daniel, remember the experiments with burning the fuel in that dome thing? Remember how you said it seemed to change the atmosphere? Could that change set off some of the disasters?"

"Henrietta," asked Master Dawn, "if this one was on top, what was under it?"

"The first three training manuals."

"Of course!" broke in Master Diandra. "To teach us to read it. Where were the other manuscripts?"

"They were arranged on one of the shelves."

"Which ones were first on the shelf?" said Master Dawn.

"I think it was the rest of the training manuals and the literature."

"What then?"

Henrietta sighed. "I don't remember. We loaded them so quickly I didn't look. They shifted as we carried it. They've been rearranged so many times since, there's no telling."

"When did you make the images, before, or after you moved the manuscripts?" Master Diandra asked.

"Before!" Henrietta left the work surface and quickly found the image of that section of the shelves. Using an enlarging glass, she looked at the order of the manuscripts on the shelf. "It's a small one with a yellow edge."

Master Dawn went over to the piles of scientific manuscripts and looked for one like it. The others began to look, too. Master Dawn held up one with a yellow cover Henrietta had missed and began to look through it.

"If position is important, then this is what we should be studying. The images are full of graphs and location charts like some of the others you translated. Here's an image of a burning forest. Some of the passages seem to be marked." She handed it to Henrietta.

The group put in many h-units over the next several days. Again, Henrietta stayed up late every night. When she had completed decoding he article, and they had the answer they sought, they sat in silence, wishing it had come out differently.

Master Diandra put one pod on Henrietta's thorax. "How much ime will you need to prepare your report for publication and a formal announcement to all the colonies?"

"My report? My announcement? I don't think it's my place as a rainee..."

"Of course it's your place," Master Diandra insisted. "It was your heory to study the writings. You figured out the numerical sequence in he market area of the ruins, and that's what got you into that chamber. You were willing to give up your life to get these manuscripts back to the colony. It was your persistence the last few time frames that kept us all searching. Don't be so reluctant to take pride in your accomplishments. You deserve the honor and I will be pleased to stand behind you."

"But I didn't do it alone."

"Of course not, but the rest of us would never have reached this point without you."

*   *   *   *

Copies of the renegades' confessions had been sent to Roacheria via video wall with a demand that Sir Rex and any other of his renegades still living be turned over to The Colonies for justice. Antony kept himself busy with his trainees. He wished Henrietta weren't so busy, but he knew he importance of her work. She'd sent him a brief message each day, but he worried about how hard she was working.

Knowing his father's last words had helped Antony decide what he wanted to write on his family's marker. He had carefully inscribed their names and dates of hatching. Curving upward at each side, he carved grassfronds.

One evening in the middle of the thirteenth time frame, as he finished the last of the words: "Your courage and your dream are still alive," Henrietta arrived unexpectedly.

Her antennae drooped, but she smiled and embraced him. "It's beautiful," she said, looking at the marker.

"So are you."

"I'm sorry I've been gone so much, but now we'll be together more. Remember the poem I translated? It was correct. I've got one time frame to prepare a report for publication, and make a speech in the council chambers, but Master Diandra said we can set the date for our ceremony now." She embraced him in a way she never had before. "Captain Alexander isn't here, is he? Let's skip the ceremony. Give yourself to me right now."

Antony backed off from her embrace, in spite of his own longing. "Don't tempt me. This isn't like you. What's wrong?"

Henrietta slumped to the floor and wept. "I'm sorry. I'm really tired. I'm afraid to make the speech and I'm disappointed at what we found out about how the Duo Pods became extinct. I can not comprehend why such intelligent, inventive, creative creatures would do that to themselves. All the pieces we've had... the natural disasters, the battles, the evidence of mass disease, deformities in skeletal structure among the young; all of it was tied to their destruction of the environment and their greed over the fuels. How could they poison the very air and water they needed to survive, and destroy huge areas of vegetation vital to the interdependent chain of life? Where did they think they were going to get more? Such short sighted greed!"

Antony wrapped his appendages around her and stroked her.

"I think I can see how. I don't know as much as you do, but to me they seem to have a lot in common with the roaches. Not all the roaches are selfish and greedy. A lot of them are pretty much like us. But it only takes a few to ruin things. Probably not all the Duo Pods were selfish and short-sighted either. Maybe in the beginning they didn't realize what they were doing, and once they knew, it was too late."

She sat up and looked at him. He continued. "Remember that little story you read me the first time you brought a manuscript to my therapy sessions? It had hilarious images and was about a little creature who sneezed. One thing led to another until everything was out of control. Maybe it was like that, like ripples that spread out when you toss a stone into a still pond, and they couldn't stop what they had started."

"You mean the funny story could be a metaphor of what happened?" The idea settled. She stood straight up. "Oh, Creative Spirit... The roaches and we could do the same thing if we aren't careful about how we work with what they left behind. We've already made some tragic mistakes. If we continue to develop our own technology without regard to our environment, we could destroy ourselves too! Some of their toxic waste probably began our evolution. I've got to go back and tell Master Diandra." She began pacing. "It won't be difficult to demonstrate that to the Combined Colonies, but how will we ever convince the roaches?"

She started toward the portal. Antony reached out and pulled her back to him. "Slow down. I don't know how we will convince Roacheria, but it can wait a few days. You're pushing yourself again. You came in here depressed and ready to skip our ceremony. Now you want to run off. The last time you got worked up like this you got yourself sick. I'm going to make you some tea and supper. Then I'll have Axel take you home."

*   *   *   *

In half a time frame, winter solstice would end the season cycle. Henrietta scheduled her speech for the fifteenth day of the first time frame. She and Antony set the date of their mating ceremony a time frame later. Henrietta worked on her report and speech every morning and spent each afternoon with Antony.

Roacheria would not answer any communications, despite Antony's efforts.

Seven days before Henrietta's speech, Antony had an idea. "Suppose you made images of all the manuscripts you've done so far, bound the images, sent the whole thing to Roacheria. Let them come to their own conclusions. Remember some of the things Master Gerald told us? They were on the same path."

"What if they don't catch on to the decoding system as quickly as I did?"

"We offer to train them ourselves."

"After all that has happened, what ant is going to take it to them?"

"Not an ant, Renae'."

"What?"

"He's desperate enough to live that I think he would. When you make your speech, our images can be sent side by side over open video wall, with you speaking in Ant and me in Roach. All of Roacheria will hear it, not just The Board."

*   *   *   *

At the end of a day-long conference with South Harvester 45's Council, and communication with the Intercolonial Council, they agreed to try Antony's idea.

Antony went to the confinement chambers.

"Renae', do you want to live badly enough to risk your life for both our kinds?"

"What do you mean?"

"Henrietta has learned something of vital importance to the future of ants and roaches. We need someone to take this information to

Roacheria, but I cannot guarantee what might happen to you there. The only thing I can say is that if my request for you to be returned to us for justice is granted, I will not ask for you to be extinguished for your guilt when our justice council meets."

Renae' didn't hesitate. "I will do this thing you ask."

"Do you know where Sir Reginald, the Supreme Executor of The Board, resides within the city of Roacheria, as well as the surrounding area?"

"Yes."

"Good, because it's directly to him that you are to go. Take a route that will keep you well away from any of Sir Rex's renegades or any others who might recognize you. Can you do that?"

"I think so."

Antony gave Renae' his own time piece and taught him to use it. He instructed Renae' to arrive at Sir Reginald's residence five to ten minutes after the scheduled end of Henrietta's speech. "My request that you be returned to South Harvester 45 for justice will be on the top."

*   *   *   *

Twenty minutes after Henrietta's antstoric speech, a message came into South Harvester 45's communications chamber in the military complex:

"The courier has arrived and will be kept alive for now. The parchments will require many time frames of study. Our decision about them will be sent to you later. Sir Reginald."

It was the first communication that had come from someone other than Sir Rex.

14.

Captain Alexander tapped on the portal of Antony's chamber. "Are you awake?"

"Yes."

"I'm leaving to go to the science facility to get the blossoms you wanted. Will you be ready for the oil when I get back?"

"Yes, thank you."

Antony returned his attention to the image of his family, one that Henrietta had taken during their visit, and continued to meditate. "I wish things had been different, but I know I will feel you with me today. Soon, I will not belong to myself and it feels good." He continued to meditate, feeling a mixture of contentment, excitement, and nervousness.

He ate the graincakes Alexander had left for his breakfast and thought about the last time frame of planning. He would have preferred a small, private ceremony. But that became impossible after Henrietta's speech. They had to arrange for the colony's largest meditation chamber and celebration area. Henrietta reminded him that everyone would bring food to share. She said her family would make an enormous honey cake. Antony and Captain Alexander had prepared batch after batch of grassfrond seed ale.

When Antony said he thought it was too much, Alexander quipped, "There's never too much ale at a mating celebration."

Finding a domicile had been another problem. With all the extra fire ants and red desert ants, there were no vacant domiciles in the main part of the colony. Although there was still one guest domicile in the science facility, Henrietta knew it might be needed if any more specialists were called in to work with her. New domiciles in the lowest section of the colony were available, but they were too far from both of their work sites. Finally, Antony recalled how spacious the emergency chambers were. The Colony Council granted permission for one to be re-excavated to meet their needs. Henrietta and Antony chose one half way between the science facility and the military complex, so neither of them would have to be carried to their jobs.

Breakfast finished, Antony immersed himself in a tub of warm water to relieve the pain and stiffness in his mid-right appendage. Several dreary days of sky water left it aching almost as much as it had the previous winter when he first got out of his body cast. He massaged it and tried to relax in the warmth. He heard Captain Alexander return.

"I put the blossoms on the dining surface. The botanist on duty said to consider them a gift in thanks for all your work."

"Give me a few minutes to lace up my brace and I'll be ready for the oil."

"I'll fix your pain herbs, too."

"No."

"You can't hide it from me. It's been hurting all winter. I can tell by the way you move."

Antony sighed. "If I have pain herbs, I can't drink ale. I would rather share a mug of ale with Henrietta, so no pain herbs." He looked at the blossoms with surprise. "These are summer blossoms. How did they have them now, even in the lab? They're perfect."

"They've been experimenting with varying the light to simulate summer conditions."

Antony sat down on a stool and began to weave the stems together to form a circlet. Alexander rubbed Antony's head, thorax and abdomen with grassfrond seed oil until his exoskeleton glistened, and his scars barely showed.

Alexander looked at the circlet of blossoms. "It's beautiful."

"When I was in therapy, Henrietta often brought one of the Duo Pod manuscripts. She would read me the fanciful stories. Some of them were about male and female Duo Pods called kings and queens, who ruled others. They wore circlets of shiny metal and crystal stones which they called crowns. Some of the stories were about having great courage to overcome tremendous difficulties before finding true joy. Henrietta is my true joy and she has helped me through a lot, so this is a crown for my queen."

"A fitting symbolic gift. It's been good sharing my quarters with you. I haven't been a very good chaperone though."

Antony smiled as he remembered all the times Alexander had brought Henrietta to him, even in the middle of the night, and left them alone. "You are a good friend and that's more important. I wouldn't have made it without her."

Master Diandra arrived a little later as he put the last of his belongings in his satchel. All of his other possessions had been taken to their new domicile the day before.

"It's nearly midday. Is our drone ready? Your basket awaits."

Before climbing in, Antony put his front appendages around Master Diandra. "Thank you for everything you have done for me. Don't ever stop being a part of my life."

She returned his embrace. "No one gets rid of me easily. I'm proud of you, Antony. Thank you for honoring me today."

The families of a male and female about to be mated carried them from opposite directions in separate baskets to the portal of the meditation chamber for their ceremony. Master Diandra and Captain Alexander picked up Antony's basket and started down the tunnel. Others joined the procession as it passed.

Henrietta's family reached the final tunnel curve a little ahead of Antony and stopped, so that the two processions could merge. Antony and Henrietta stepped out of their baskets when they reached the meditation chamber. They joined pods as Captain Alexander and Henrietta's sister, Hilda, held the portals open. Pod in pod, they proceeded to the front of the chamber and stood beside a long narrow surface, piled high with grassfrond seeds. Family, friends, and other colony members filled the large chamber until it overflowed. Hilda and Alexander left others holding the portals and took their places beside Antony and Henrietta. When it grew quiet, Alexander handed Antony the circlet of blossoms and Antony spoke.

"You trusted me and I betrayed you. You forgave me. I tried to protect you and you saved my life instead. You comforted my grief and made me feel whole. I come to you now to give you myself and begin to fulfill our promise, because you will always be my queen." He placed the blossoms carefully over her antennae and around her head.

She smiled at him and held out her gift. "The Sun Spirit's larva spends its time consuming foliage without thought for any other creature. Then it enters a chrysalis and changes, allowing its inner beauty to emerge, a glorious winged creature, giving joy and inspiration to all. I come to you now to give you myself and begin to fulfill our promise because you changed yourself for me." She placed the curved side of a Sun Spirit's cocoon, which she had cut and shaped to fit him, over the back of his thorax.

They rose onto their back pods for their promise. Henrietta placed her mid-left pod gently under Antony's brace, supporting it, as they rose higher and lifted their front pods above their heads. Together, they recited the words they had first spoken to each other over a season cycle before.

"I promise myself to you as your mate, to cherish and support, no matter what joys or sorrows may occur. I will nurture with joy all new life that may come from our union. I promise this freely as long as we both live in this world."

The seed ceremony took quite a while, since the chamber was so crowded. Everyone waited patiently as Antony and Henrietta, helped by Alexander and Hilda, passed the seeds around. The entire community recited the seed ceremony's words together, reaffirming the dedication of all ants to each other.

Antony and Henrietta spoke together again. "To each other we have given ourselves. To you we give our talents and our work. Confirm our gifts and pledge to us your help in anything we cannot do for ourselves."

All those gathered responded. "We accept your gifts and pledge our support to both of you."

The colony's *Record of the Mated* lay in its place at the side of the chamber. Antony and Henrietta went to it and made their inscription: "Antony, son of Dorothy and David, of South Dairy Colony 50, to Henrietta, daughter of Adeline and Henry, of South Harvester Colony 45, this thirteenth day of the second time frame, 188th season cycle of the Combined Colonies of Insectia."

The pair faced their family and friends and sang a mating song:

cycle of water and life

essence of ardor
water of two
gathered and rose
swirled into the sky
flowed one to the other
condensed and grew
creating new life
cherished essence
locked in solids
released in the end
to gather again
essence of ardor

Ceremony completed, Hilda and Alexander opened the side portals which led into the adjoining celebration area, and made sure all was in order. Antony and Henrietta stood and welcomed those who had come to share their joy. The chamber filled with happy conversation. Food overflowed the surfaces. Several guests helped take more surfaces from their storage compartments. The banquet began.

When no one could eat another bite, Captain Alexander raised his mug of ale and signaled for quiet. "As Antony's 'first friend' and stand-in family, it falls to me to say a few words. I'll keep it short." He spoke slowly and distinctly. "Antony, I told you so."

An awkward silence followed. Antony broke into gales of laughter, rose and explained. "Captain Alexander can really pick his moments. At a certain point, Henrietta and I had a personal problem. Captain Alexander listened to me, and said he was so sure that we would work it out, that he bet we would end up promised to each other. Obviously, he won the wager, and his prize was to say, 'I told you so.'"

The two of them continued laughing and soon it echoed through the chamber. Mugs of ale were refilled as others rose to speak. The oval mating cake looked like an enormous honey comb, because Henrietta and her family had stuck so many smaller ones together, but there was more than enough.

Henrietta's parents cleared the center of the floor for Antony and Henrietta to perform their mating dance. The ancients had swarmed into the air, but since ants had lost their wings in the evolutionary process, the dance was played out on the ground. The distinctive music of pea pod shakers, cricket violas, and bee's wing hummers began softly and slowly. As the pitch and the tempo increased, Henrietta and Antony spiraled inward from opposite directions. The closer they came, the higher and faster the music, until they swirled together at the center and stood nearly upright, twisting and breathless. Henrietta caught and supported Antony before anyone saw him trip in his brace. The cheers were long and loud.

The music slowed and the two of them swayed gently back and forth, then released their hold of each other. Henrietta drew her father into the dance while Antony took Master Diandra. Then Henrietta pulled in Captain Alexander as Antony led her mother onto the floor. The dance spread until everyone, even larvae in the pods of their parents, swayed back and forth.

"Henrietta, you look tired. Let's rest and enjoy watching the others," Antony said, only because his leg ached so badly he thought he might faint.

"Yes. You look like you should rest too."

The celebration continued into the early evening when some of the larvae began to whine with exhaustion. Hilda and Captain Alexander put left over food into containers for the newly mated pair. Amid more cheers, the two climbed into a down-lined basket. Whistles and light-hearted joking echoed down the tunnels as the procession made its way to Antony's and Henrietta's new domicile. Their families carried them in and left them alone.

Captain Alexander closed the portal behind him with a final, "I told you so."

Henrietta embraced her mate, but accidentally leaned on his aching joint. He groaned.

She pulled away. "I'm sorry. I noticed it was bothering you before, but I forgot. Didn't you take any of your pain herbs today?"

He lay back in the basket and shook his head. "I wanted to be able to drink ale with you. It's all right."

"No, it isn't. We have one time in our lives to give and receive the gift of life. I would not let it be in your grief, and you wouldn't allow it in my frustration. It shouldn't be in your pain now. Another few minutes won't matter. Where are the herbs and do you want one or two packets?"

"In my satchel and I need three."

She helped him from the basket and into their sleep chamber. While he unlaced and removed his brace, she mixed the herbs in a mug of warm honeydew. He sipped it as she massaged his joint.

"Is that better?" she asked when she completed the movement sequence Amy had taught her.

"Much better, thank you."

She took the empty mug and set it on the floor. "Come, my drone. Your queen is more than ready."

15.

*A*ntony was happier than he had ever been in his life. The music of the mating dance echoed through his head each day as he loped along the tunnels to the central communications office in the military complex. He worked with Fred, Carter, and Cathy, expanding their Roach vocabulary and developing training materials for others.

Henrietta continued to study the Duo Pod manuscripts. A team of geologists worked with her on the ancient location charts. Plastic deposits were always associated with Duo Pod ruins. By early spring, a group of surface explorers left North Carpenter Colony 15 for one prospective tract.

Antony and Henrietta began to make plans for their eventual return to South Dairy 50. The days lengthened and grew warm. Antony thought about it more and more. He wondered how much longer their problem with Roacheria would prevent another attempt to rebuild the colony.

"Master Antony, incoming message," Fred called out.

Words in Roach flashed across the video wall. "Prepare for transmission from Sir Reginald, Supreme Executor of the South East Roach Control Board."

Carter and Cathy reached for clean parchment and more ink. Fred put a packet in the voice imager.

"Watch and listen," Antony instructed. "We can go over it later."

The video wall blinked twice and the image of a large, light brown, middle-aged roach appeared. His steadfast gaze told Antony he could trust this one.

"I am Sir Reginald. I speak to you personally, Master Antony, for I know that it is through you that all the colonies will understand my message. You and Master Henrietta extended yourselves as a gift of trust and sent materials so that we might see your words were true. There is but one who could have taught you our language so well, the former Sir Rodger. In my youth, he was my mentor. As he must have told you, the charges against him were false. I knew who was behind it, but I could not prove it. If I had spoken out during his inquiry, I would have found myself in his place within a quarter time frame. With his eyes he told me to be silent and wait for a better time. That time is now. As you trusted him, trust me.

"A Formal Inquiry has found Sir Rex guilty of conspiracy, murder, and provoking hostile conflict. Many of those loyal to him have been condemned and received their punishment. The one you want will be returned to you and you may keep the other. However, we must insist that one of our surgeons come and administer necessary justice for acts of violence. Sir Rex will be delivered to you as well.

"The South East Roach Control Board wishes to pursue a fair settlement with the Combined Colonies of Insectia. We ask that you receive myself and two other Board Members, Sir Ralph and Sir Raymond, to negotiate an end to the hostilities between us. Calculate all your losses. They will be paid in full. Choose the place to meet that makes you feel safe.

"Master Roland and Master Gerard report that they will be able to decode the Duo Pod symbols, but that it will take many more time frames. The say they can see by the images that Master Henrietta's conclusions are correct. They would like to accept your offer of training. Randal will accompany them to assist with translations if you will allow it. Please, acknowledge receiving this transmission."

Fred, Carter, and Cathy sat still, mandibles gaping. Antony reached forward to the control panel, switched it to "send" and entered the words, "Message received. Basic premise accepted. Details of arrangements will follow."

By evening, Master Alexandra had sent Antony word that she and three other Intercolonial Council Members would leave their headquarters in Central Harvester 12 the following morning and arrive in a quarter time frame. Master Alexandra also instructed Antony to draft a preliminary agreement for discussion and seek help from Commander Ferdinand in determining a meeting location.

Allowing for a day of rest for the Intercolonial Council Members after their arrival, and time for their own meeting and preparations, Antony sent further instructions to Roacheria:

"On the twenty-fifth day of the fourth time frame, three h-units past noon, your group should be in the middle of the meadow one d-unit east of the main entrance of South Harvester Colony 45. There, in the midst of our protecting guards, we will meet and escort you into our colony. We will provide for your needs as our guests and begin our discussions the following morning in the comfort of our council chambers."

*   *   *   *

Antony looked at the calendar again before leaving the communications chamber. It had been more than sixty days since he and Henrietta had mated. The first egg came to most pairs between days fifty-four and sixty. Henrietta's doctor had told them that if she laid no egg by day seventy, she probably never would. Henrietta and Antony did not talk about it, but Antony had convinced himself that they would overcome the odds. After all, she had lived when no one thought she would, and he had recovered better than expected. Roacheria had agreed to his instructions. Things were going his way. He said a cheerful goodnight to his trainees and headed home.

He opened the portal and saw Master Diandra pacing about their parlor. He heard Henrietta moaning. He dropped his satchel and rushed toward the closed portal of their sleep chamber.

Master Diandra stopped him. "Wait, Antony. Sit down. Let me explain." She took his front pods in hers and led him to a cushion.

"What's..."

"I hardly know where to start. I should have sent for you, but Henrietta wanted to wait. She kept talking about how surprised you had been when you went to visit your parents and your mother had laid that last egg."

Antony nodded at the pleasant memory. He had been so happy for his parents, because the egg had life, in spite of his mother's age. He had wished so much that the egg had been his and Henrietta's. It had made him realize how much he cherished Henrietta and that he wanted to be her mate.

"Well," said Master Diandra, "the feeling came over Henrietta this morning. I said I would send for you, but she asked me not to. She wanted to see your face when you came home and saw it. Then the pain began and we knew something was wrong."

Antony bolted for the portal. "I'm going to get her doctor!" In his haste, his brace snagged on the edge of the cushion, and he tripped.

"He's already here," Master Diandra said, helping Antony up.

At that moment, the doctor opened the portal. "You've explained?" he asked.

Master Diandra nodded.

The doctor gestured for Antony to enter. "She needs you. There is nothing we can do but wait. The pain is due to internal organ damage. I've given her some herbs to relieve the discomfort. I've never had, or heard of, a case like hers."

Antony limped over to the sleep cushion and wrapped his front pods around his mate. Henrietta turned and looked up at him. She spoke through clenched mandibles. "You know, it's ironic. The Duo Pod females gave birth in pain. If it was like this for them, I can't help but think it was another factor in their extinction. We're a lucky species... except for me."

Antony tried to be encouraging. "But the joy will be worth it."

An h-unit later, the egg came. All of them could only stare. It did not look like a first egg from someone young and recently mated, firm and oval, quivering with life. It was flattened and wrinkled—the type that told female ants past mid-age that the fertile stage of life had ended. Henrietta would never have to endure the pain again. There would be no more eggs.

Antony and Henrietta wrapped their pods around each other and wept.

*   *   *   *

Master Alexandra held out her front pods to Antony. "We finally meet in person."

Antony smiled as they sat down to consider his proposal. There were five key points in the document he wanted to place before Sir Reginald.

The artifacts taken from the chamber by the renegade roaches would be returned to South Harvester 45 for study. Then the archaeologists from both sides would decide on their fair division and permanent location. The needs of Master Roland, Master Gerard, and Randal would be provided by the colony during their training with Master Henrietta.

The total value of all crops and herds destroyed in the renegade raids would be delivered in plastic.

The value of lives lost would be paid in Roacherian credit.

There would be an additional charge of 25% for the insult to The Colonies. All credit and plastic would be delivered to the Intercolonial Council.

To safe-guard against future treachery by other renegades, any roach wishing to enter ant surface area would apply to the nearest colony for an ant guard escort. Any roach found on ant surface without such an escort would be considered hostile.

"I have only one concern, Master Antony," said Master Alexandra. "How can one possibly calculate the value of a life? This total is exorbitant."

"For us, such a figure isn't necessary," Antony explained. "But in Roacheria, if someone is killed, those at fault are bound to pay an assessment of credit to the surviving family members. I estimated the amount of credit used by an adult ant in one season cycle, multiplied it by the average number of working season cycles in a life time and multiplied that by the total number of lives lost. They will expect this of us. If we don't include it, they will take it as an admission of our guilt. Think of it as a return for the sacrifice of every member of every colony in giving up plastic for the last season cycle and a half, or as restitution for all past cheating. We must negotiate from an assertive position."

After much discussion, further explanation, and slight modifications in wording, Master Alexandra said, "I don't suppose I will ever understand, let alone agree with their ways, but I trust you, Master Antony. If you think this will bring peace and change, then I will stand behind it."

The others nodded.

*   *   *   *

Standing on the surface for the first time since the attack, Antony sighed. The sight of the tall conifer he'd climbed so often brought back a flood of memories.

Captain Alexander whispered, "I'll carry you, Antony."

Antony shook his head. "It's level here, and only a short distance."

"I don't think I'll be able to remember all the gestures you explained," Master Alexandra said as they drew closer.

"Relax and let me lead. Do whatever I do. I'm sure they're as nervous as we are. Let's hope that storm to the north holds off until we're back underground."

Antony surveyed the group of roaches and the empty meadow around them. True to their word, no large group of warriors accompanied them, but Antony was glad that five brigades of fire ants stood thirty f-units behind him. Sir Reginald stood in the center, wearing several polished metal ornaments. The two beside him were also adorned with symbols of their rank. Behind the Board Members, stood Master Roland, Master Gerard, and Randal, wearing only broad smiles, and a fourth roach that Antony guessed must be the surgeon.

Four warriors stood guard over Sir Rex and Renae', their pods in restraints, both without their mandibles and branded as banished. The once haughty and arrogant Sir Rex stood in disgrace. Renae' looked pathetic; his face was badly infected. With respect to Roacherian customs concerning the banished, Antony did not acknowledge their presence.

Sir Reginald and the two others stooped low, sweeping their front pods out to the sides in the customary submissive gesture of greeting. Antony accepted the gesture with a nod.

"I'm pleased to introduce Master Alexandra, our Intercolonial Council Chief; Helen, South Harvester Colony 45's Council Chief; Captain Alexander and Commander Ferdinand."

Randal introduced the roach party.

Sir Reginald nodded to those guarding the prisoners. At the same time, Captain Alexander signaled the fire ants, four of whom came forward and led the prisoners away.

Sir Reginald said, "We are honored to be treated as your guests. Accept our humility."

"It is accepted," said Antony. He pointed to the fast approaching storm clouds. "But we had better set aside formalities and take cover."

Everyone ran toward the main entrance of South Harvester 45. Antony let go of his pride and climbed onto Captain Alexander's back. The last two brigades of fire ants were drenched.

Fred, Carter, and Cathy led the roaches to their quarters. Antony took the roach surgeon to the medical facility in the military complex. He dreaded what he knew he must witness. He was pleased to find Amy on duty and told her what he needed for the surgeon. He also whispered to her that Renae' needed medical attention.

When they reached the confinement chambers, he stopped near the one he knew had been reserved for Renae' and whispered in Roach, "A physician will be here shortly to treat that infection and give you something for the pain. Trust her. I cannot come to talk to you for several days, but another will."

He heard a soft moan in reply.

The guards opened the portal to Gerry's cubicle. The warrior took one look at Antony and the roach with him and began cursing.

"Bind him securely," Antony said. He had no affection for Gerry, but he pitied him at that moment.

"You aren't in Roacheria now," Antony said to the surgeon. "No one will know. Our surgeons will provide an injection of sleep inducing herbs."

"I know you consider our practice of mandible removal cruel," the surgeon said. "But you are too merciful. I don't like what I must do, but this duty comes to every Roacherian surgeon in turn. I'm not the cold torturer you might think. This miserable creature knew exactly what he was doing, and he knew the consequences. I have no sympathy for him. My sympathy is for you. Did he offer your family an injection? What must be, must be."

Only Antony remained in the surgical area with the doctor after Gerry was placed on its flat surface, unable to speak or move. Antony looked away from the terror in the warrior's eyes. A wave of nausea swept over him. The moments dragged by.

"I'm finished," the surgeon said. "What you do for him now is up to you. I'm sorry about what I said. I didn't intend to offend you. If it makes you feel better, I did not revive him when he lost consciousness. By the way, I didn't do that butchering job on the other one. That was the work of a trainee. He'll die of that infection before you have your day of justice if it's not treated."

"I already took care of it."

The guards returned to remove Gerry.

"Keep him in the infirmary until it's healed, but keep him bound," Antony told them.

"Pardon my forwardness, but I am very curious about the device on your mid-right appendage," the surgeon said as he cleaned up after himself. "I know of one who could benefit from something like that. Would you mind letting me see how it's constructed?"

Antony looked directly into the surgeon's eyes as he thought about it. "Perhaps you would like to discuss it with those who made it for me."

"I would be honored."

"I'll set it up and arrange for Carl to translate."

*   *   *   *

At the beginning of dinner, everyone felt awkward. The ants worried that their simple life style, the way they served each other, and the foods prepared would offend the Roach Board Members, who were accustomed to being treated as more important than others. The roaches were concerned that the next day's negotiations would not be successful if they complained about anything. They were desperate for normal trade in food products and plastic. Antony and his trainees kept busy translating overly polite conversation.

Helping himself to more roasted grasshopper, Sir Ralph attempted to lighten things. "Do you know how long it has been since I've tasted grasshopper quite this tender?" he asked Antony.

Antony grinned and allowed a hint of sarcasm as he replied, "Probably about as long as it's been since I had shredded plastic salad."

Unlike their leaders, the scientists didn't concern themselves with politics and were already discussing theories through Randal.

Sir Reginald lowered his antennae and whispered to Antony. "We both know I should not ask, but I must know. Does Sir Rodger still live? He was more than my mentor. His youngest daughter is my legal mate."

"No, I'm sorry," Antony replied. "I covered him the same day Henrietta and I found the chamber of artifacts. He probably died half a time frame before that. One day I will put a proper marker there."

"Thank you. I'm glad he found you. You are a truly remarkable creature, and Master Henrietta as well."

"Yes, she is, and I'm proud to be her mate."

A wide smile came to Sir Reginald's face. "Indeed! Congratulations. We'd better watch out. The planet will soon be crawling with little Antonies."

Antony accepted the well-intentioned compliment with a smile, in spite of the hurt it caused. He glanced at his trainees. They were busy with other conversations. For once, Antony was glad that the few creatures in the chamber who knew of his and Henrietta's loss did not understand Roach. Henrietta had been right when she insisted the day after it happened that they keep their grief private because of the importance of the arrival of the roaches and the training she would be giving.

By the time Antony served the honey cake, the conversation had turned to curious, but respectful questions about ant customs. The roaches listened with open minds. When they said good night, Antony felt that change in the way roaches and ants regarded each other was not only possible, but beginning to happen.

In spite of the successful evening, he was glad to reach the privacy of his own home. Henrietta did not ask why. She had a way of sensing when he needed comfort. She fixed him some tea and stroked his antennae until he slept.

*   *   *   *

The strain of formality was back in the morning. Antony looked toward the ants at one end of the oval surface, toward the roaches at the other end, and across at Randal. He handed copies of the proposed agreement to all, giving Randal two copies, one in each language.

"You may check that they are the same."

Everyone read the document carefully and waited while Randal read both. Antony watched the facial expressions of the roaches.

Randal spoke to his leaders. "The documents are the same. Nothing is hidden."

Sir Reginald conversed with his colleagues. Antony pretended not to listen. He noticed that Fred and Cathy were attentive as he had instructed. He would quiz them later. This was their final test.

"What was the amount confiscated from Rex?" whispered Sir Reginald to Sir Ralph.

"A good deal more than this total. This is less than I expected, a very fair offer."

"What about the artifacts?"

"That could be a problem. Master Gerald said a lot was damaged. I don't even know what there was to start with."

"Even the mantis compound is too good for him. I hope they let him rot for all the trouble and needless suffering he's caused."

Sir Reginald addressed the group. "We agree to the damage assessment. It is a most fair proposal. You are wise to protect your surface area. We have captured and dealt with all those we think were loyal to him, but we cannot be sure. You will be notified if we hear of any others. Our trusted warriors will try to apprehend any without travel parchments before they enter your surface. You have many reasons not to trust us. We must work diligently to regain your trust. I would add these provisions. We should provide compensation for our scientists staying here for training. Also, I cannot guarantee that all of the artifacts can be returned. Have you a list?"

"We have images," replied Antony. "We understand if some have been lost. Compensation for training is not necessary. It is in the interests of a better understanding between us and perhaps our very survival on this planet. Such learning has no price, only benefits for all."

Fred and Cathy related their comments to the ants. Perfectly, Antony noted.

Sir Reginald dipped the tip of his front pod in the ink pot. "Then there is peace between us." He signed the document and passed it to the others.

Antony savored the moment as the copies were passed, each participant signing all the copies.

He lifted up a silent thought. "Old Rodger, it is a new beginning, thanks to you."

16.

"*H*enrietta, Axel is here. Please, come with me. I promise I won't climb it myself." Antony stroked her gently. In an h-unit, seventhday would dawn. In three more days, the Justice Council would meet to hear his request concerning the punishment of Rex, Gerry, and Renae'. He had to go to the top of the conifer. They had argued for two days since the Roaches had left. Suggesting that Axel carry him was a compromise.

Henrietta turned away from him, crying. "I still don't understand. We can meditate anywhere. Why there?"

"Please," he begged again. "I need you and I need the view, the peace, and the strength I've always felt there."

Reluctantly, she rose and went with him. When they reached the stately wood plant, Antony sighed. He wanted to climb it himself.

"Master Antony," Axel said, "do I whine because I can't speak Roach? Do I try to do your job when I can't?"

"What?"

"I don't mean to insult you, because I really admire you, but I wish you would quit complaining and let me carry you. Let me do what I am able to do, as I let you do what you do best."

Henrietta gave Axel a look of gratitude. Antony climbed onto Axel's back and held on. When they reached the top, they settled themselves on a sturdy branch, facing east. It promised to be a beautiful day with enough clouds to create a gorgeous sunrise. Antony drank it in and began to meditate.

He lost himself in the stillness around him and in memories of his first season cycle of adulthood. Searching for an answer, he recalled all the things his father had taught him. He remembered what Gerry and Renae' had said while he listened. He thought about what Axel had just said. Henrietta joined her pod to his.

It was nearly mid-morning when he lowered his pods, turned, and looked at her.

She returned his gaze. "I'm sorry. You were right. It **is** inspiring here."

"I'm sorry I worried you. I'm glad you insisted that I be carried."

"Master Antony, next time you decide to come here, will you request me again?" Axel asked.

"You can count on it."

"May I ask you something else?"

"Of course."

"Do you still hope to go back there, to South Dairy 50?"

"More than ever," Antony replied. "Master Alexandra took our proposal with her when she left yesterday."

"When will you go?"

"Next spring—if it's approved."

"Will you ... ask Captain Alexander if ... I might go with you?"

"Why not ask him yourself?"

Axel shifted in discomfort and looked away. "I'm not my own right now."

"Oh, I understand. I'll be glad to ask him for you."

      *   *   *   *

Henrietta tapped on Captain Alexander's portal.

"Antony. Henrietta. What brings you here?" Alexander asked. "Come in. Would you like some honey dew?"

"Yes, thank you. I need the wise advice of a good friend," Antony said as he stepped into the familiar parlor and sat down on a floor cushion. Henrietta curled up next to him, leaving the other floor cushion for their host.

Alexander handed them each a mug of honey dew. "What great wisdom can I offer you?"

"First, will you assign Axel to New South Dairy 50 if it's approved? He asked me to ask you."

"Really? I don't suppose he said anything else."

"Not specifically, but I'll be open if he wants to."

Alexander said, "I've already asked Commander Ferdinand to send my whole unit with you. That didn't take any wisdom. What else is on your mind?"

Antony stroked Henrietta as she leaned against him. "Hypothetically, how does one design an effective contract?"

Alexander stared at the two of them. "Are you thinking what I think you're thinking?"

"Maybe. Anyway, we need to consider all the options. I promised Renae' his life when he took the documents to Roacheria. One thing I do know, I can't extinguish any of them."

"You don't have to do it yourself."

"I can't watch either. You weren't in that chamber with the surgeon. In spite of everything, it's not an option any more."

"Then this isn't hypothetical at all." Captain Alexander took Antony's front pods in his. "Consider your own experience first, but you were easy. Master Diandra had the battle won before she started, because you were already filled with remorse. You wanted to die didn't you?"

"Yes."

"What made you want to change?"

"Fear of the alternative."

"Right. That is how it always is. Death is a coward's way out. It's living with yourself and changing that are so difficult. There are two keys to a successful contract. First, the alternative must be a fate worse than death for that particular individual. In the beginning, that's the only incentive. Be careful that they have no opportunity to end their own lives. Second, the time of the contract must be longer than you actually think it will take to accomplish change."

Antony thought of his first four days with Master Diandra and wondered who had given her the same advice. "You know the law better than I do. Would I have to specify the length of time?"

"No. Some contracts, like Axel's, are open ended. Have you considered how the other families who plan to go to South Dairy 50 with you might feel about this? What about the families of the carriers who died?"

"I'll talk to them."

"Renae' might cooperate. But what about Rex and Gerry? Always remember, if a contract fails and you enforce the alternative, it's not your fault, but their choice."

Antony set down the empty mug and rose. He and Henrietta embraced their friend. "Thank you. I knew I could count on you."

*   *   *   *

The six members of the Justice Council sat behind a counter, each holding copies of all the documents regarding the three roach prisoners. Antony and Henrietta sat to their right with the families of the slain carriers behind them. To the Council's left, stood Rex, Gerry, and Renae', with a counselor who had tried her best to work with them.

Antony was glad to see that Renae's face had healed, although it was horribly scarred. Fred stood with them to translate. The rest of the large chamber was filled to capacity with colony members representing every work area. Those from the Colonial Bulletin and the Intercolonial Information Network carried imaging equipment.

Antony whispered to Henrietta, "I wasn't this nervous the day you made your speech, or even during the negotiations."

"You'll be all right, my cherished one, because you believe in our decision, and the others are here supporting us."

Two guards entered with the Intercolonial Banner and all rose to reaffirm their loyalty. The assembly sat in silence.

The senior justice rose and said, "Rex, Renae', and Gerry, this council recognizes your guilt in the acts of war and murder on and after the fifth day of the eleventh time frame, 186th season cycle of the Combined Colonies of Insectia. Have you anything to say before Master Antony makes his request for your punishment?"

The ant counselor said, "In spite of all my advice, only Renae' wishes to speak. The other two say they are prepared to be extinguished."

Renae's voice faltered several times. Fred translated. "I was there during both ... attacks and beg for mercy ... because I killed no one. I am barely ... sixteen season cycles old, and did not understand what I was getting myself into. Please ... believe that I tried to stop it, and remember what was promised when I carried the parchments ... to Sir Reginald. I don't think I deserve to die." He looked toward Antony, his eyes filled with sorrow and fear. The other two looked at the floor.

Antony faced the Council. "Wise members of this Justice Council, I know you and most of those gathered here expect me to follow customs and call for these three to be extinguished. Those who know me better, know that the only traditional part of my life was our mating ceremony. One hundred and eighty-eight season cycles ago, other ants of courage and foresight broke with their traditions and began the Combined Colonies, uniting us all in a better life. We stand at the beginning of a new era as well.

"My father had a dream that South Dairy 50 should live again through me and my brothers and sisters. I want to take his dream a step further and establish New South Dairy Colony 50 as a place where ants and roaches will live and work together in a new understanding of care and concern for all. I refuse to ask for the deaths of Rex, Renae', and Gerry. The reason is simple. Will ending their miserable lives bring back my family? Will it give the others back their cherished ones? Will killing them give Henrietta strength, or undo the damage that prevents our having young, or give me wholeness of my body?

"No. Nothing can bring back what was lost. A friend of mine told me recently that dying is easy. It is living with the consequences of our actions that is often difficult. I have made some foolish and some good choices in my life and learned to move on. What I request is the authority to draw up a contract with each of them, designed so they will learn to appreciate what they destroyed. Perhaps they will choose to change and rebuild their lives. They are harmless now, but will wear restraints and work within the military complex, well guarded. When our proposal for New South Dairy Colony 50 is approved, they will go there with me and perform the work that I long to do and can no longer do for myself. In that way they will make restitution, at least symbolically.

"This contract is to last as long as it takes for them to show remorse and truly change, be that a few season cycles, or well into the next century. If they do not cooperate, or if they violate their contracts, then I request that they be permanently confined underground, alone and in darkness, to contemplate the misery they have caused until nature takes their lives."

Silence hung in the air, thick like fog, when Fred spoke the last of Antony's words in Roach. Renae's eyes lit up in relief. Gerry's face showed no emotion. Rex's expressed a combination of shock and outrage.

The Justice Council sat, stunned by Antony's words. The senior justice turned to Henrietta. "Are you one with your mate in this request?"

She took his front pod in hers. "Yes, I am."

"And you others?"

"We agree," responded those seated with Antony and Henrietta.

"Then I don't see how this council can object to your request, unusual though it is. Rex, Renae', and Gerry, you will be returned to confinement until Master Antony presents you with your contracts and suitable work is found for you within the military complex. This council has spoken. Let justice be done."

*   *   *   *

Renae' smiled and stooped low in greeting when Antony entered his confinement chamber. "Master Antony, thank you. I will do whatever you say."

"Sit down, Renae'. Did Cathy explain why I couldn't come until now?"

"Yes, and the female doctor, she was so kind. The way she touched me, I've never felt so good, so... I don't know how to say it."

"We always stroke each other's antennae when comfort is needed. I'm sorry about your face. You didn't deserve that."

Renae' looked down. "It could have been worse. Several times I hid from Sir Rex's warriors. Once, they saw me and I barely outran them. I didn't think I would get to Sir Reginald's at all. Those guarding his domicile wouldn't let me in. I started screaming. Sir Reginald came to see what all the noise was. I lay on the ground and cried out, 'Mercy! I am the one sent to you. Here,' and threw the satchel.

"Sir Reginald pulled me in roughly, slammed the portal and ordered more warriors to surround his home. He said, 'Get this detestable renegade out of my sight. Lock him up below until I sort out this mess,' and walked off with the satchel."

Antony sat in silence and let Renae' continue.

"They threw me in a damp chamber, gave me bad water and poor food every two or three days. I found some fungus growing in one corner and remembered eating it here. I ate some and left half for another day. It grew back. I always left some. That's why I didn't starve.

"I lost track of the days. Then they dragged me to the Inquiry. They read the paper of my own words and condemned me. I never even got to speak." He began to shake.

Antony, moved with pity, found himself able to comfort the penitent roach. Once he was calm, Antony read Renae' his contract and explained it.

"I could really be free one day?"

"Yes, it's possible."

"Where is the ink? Where do I put my mark?" Renae' scrawled a crooked line and Antony put the document in his satchel.

"I brought you something." Antony took out a slate and soft-rock marker and wrote Renae's name on it. "Practice with this. The next time you need to put your name on something, you can do it properly. You'll work in the food preparation area. The guard in charge will show you what to do. I'll be down every other evening to talk to you."

*   *   *   *

Gerry was sullen. "Now what?"

"This is your contract with me," Antony said, and read it to him. Then he said, "You have been confined here one and a half season cycles. Sometimes you have been alone and sometimes you have been allowed companionship. Now you have a choice to make. If you put your mark on this and cooperate with me in your punishment, you will have companionship, do work which contributes to the colony, be able to see the surface again one day, and perhaps more. It all depends on you. If you don't, you'll spend the rest of your life alone in the dark."

Gerry grunted. "That's not much of a choice."

"Whatever you think, but it's what you've got."

"I don't know how to sign my name."

"You could learn if you wanted to, but the mark you used before will do."

"All right," Gerry sputtered in disgust. "I'll sign it."

"You'll start work in the morning in the guards' food preparation area. They'll show you what to do. I'll stop by every few evenings, and we'll talk if you want to. Try pounding and throwing this. Perhaps you can find a better way to get rid of your anger." He handed Gerry a lump of clay.

*   *   *   *

Rex turned away when Antony entered. "Leave me alone."

"Be careful, Rex, you may get what you want and live to regret it. I suggest you examine this carefully and think about the options that remain open to you."

Rex glanced over his contract. "If you expect me to live like an ant, you're out of your mind, Antony."

"It's Master Antony."

Rex glared at him. Antony let it pass. He knew that Rex wanted to arouse his anger in the hope that Antony would extinguish him. The roach had come from a time of owning more than the value of South Harvester 45 and controlling the lives of thousands, to absolutely nothing. Antony would not have believed him if he had acted penitent.

"You can't make me be something I not only don't want, but despise. You'll wish you'd killed me. I won't sign this, now or ever!"

"I know you don't understand our ways. I will make you a generous offer. I will enforce the terms of this contract for one time frame. You will be left alone in total darkness. You may rant and rave and show all the anger and disgust you like, but you will also taste the rest of your life. You're not that old, Rex. You'll have many season cycles of your own misery to keep you company. I will return in a time frame and ask you once more if you would like to sign this."

He picked up the lightning bug lamp and left, instructing the guards to use the small opening at the side of the portal when giving Rex his daily portion of fresh food and water.

17.

*M*aster Roland expressed his feelings of gratitude the first day of training with Henrietta in the Science Research Center. "You can't imagine how wonderful it is to be able to speak freely. From the day it happened until we left, I lived in constant fear that my family or myself would share Master Gerald's fate. Many prominent citizens disappeared. We finally took refuge with Sir Reginald, since we knew he owed no loyalty to *him*."

They never mentioned Sir Rex by name and Henrietta was careful about it herself. Antony had told her that once banished, an individual's name should not be spoken again. She felt strange teaching others when she still had so much to learn herself. Master Diandra had left the colony. Henrietta missed her mentor and longed for Master Diandra's lecture tour to end.

"We'll spend each morning working on the symbols. You'll start with the easy literature, as I did. In the afternoons, you'll work by yourselves while I translate other manuscripts and plan the next day's session."

The three archaeologists kept both Antony and Randal busy interpreting. Before long, they were trying to say things in each other's languages. Antony helped Henrietta in her work as he did in her life.

"Go and rest for a while," he often said. "Don't tire yourself."

She knew he disliked all the parchment work and gave him a calendar to count off the days until they would depart for New South Dairy 50. The Intercolonial Council had approved their proposal immediately, designating most of the credit from Roacheria for the project. Her father had agreed to engineer the tunnel that would connect New South Dairy 50 to South Harvester 45.

*   *   *   *

Antony went to the military complex to check on his charges every few days. Gerry did what he was told, no more, no less. Antony noticed little marks on the chamber walls where the ball of clay had hit. Later he noticed that the clay had been molded into one shape and then another.

Renae' bubbled with enthusiasm. "Look, Master Antony," he said at the end of the first quarter time frame, displaying his slate where he read, "Grassfrond seed," as well as his name in poorly pronounced but understandable Ant. "Grind seed and foof, powder settle, so guards," he gestured, "put word." He gave up and spoke in Roach. "I will do better in time. I promise."

Antony looked at him with an amused fondness. "It looks as though you need a new soft-writing piece. I'll have one sent to you tomorrow." He taught Renae' to say a few more words in Ant.

Captain Alexander caught him as he was leaving that night. "Rex has finally stopped ranting and raving, but he hasn't touched his food or water in two days. It would be a miserable way to go, but he may be trying to starve himself to death."

"What should I do? I told him he would have no contact for a full time frame."

"You can let it go. It's his choice, not your fault. Or, you can interfere and force feed him."

Antony tapped his back pod in thought. If Rex thought he could get off that easily, he didn't know much about ants. He walked to the portal of Rex's confinement chamber and spoke calmly and clearly in Roach. "Rex, you have no right to shorten your natural life. You will be fed daily."

He turned to Captain Alexander. "Once each day, have the guards enter in silence, bind him, insert a feeding tube and give him liquid nourishment. Keep me posted."

Captain Alexander nodded.

*   *   *   *

Many days passed. One afternoon as Antony sat with Henrietta going over the next day's session, he felt a light tap on the back of his thorax. In a somber tone, Captain Alexander said, "A certain individual, whose name may not be mentioned in polite company, is yelling for you and saying, 'parchment,' in Ant."

"You'd better go," said Henrietta. "I'll have supper and some tea waiting for you."

Antony did not trust Rex. He stood and listened as Rex called out, "Master Antony, the parchment," over and over, his voice revealing desperation, rather than anger or deceit.

Antony opened the portal and entered the pitch dark cubicle. "I'm here, Rex. What do you want?"

"You deserted me. You didn't come back. I'll sign your cursed contract. Please, release me from this living death."

"What do you mean? I deserted you."

"You said you would come back in a time frame and ask me if I wanted to sign it. The time was gone long ago and you did not come."

"What day do you think this is?"

"I don't know. I can't mark it in this endless darkness. I'm losing my mind."

"So now you are ready to work, speak politely to those who control your life, and make an effort to understand our ways?"

"I'll work. I'll keep my curses private. I won't pretend to like it and I won't change what I am, but I'll do what is required if it gets me a lamp and someone to talk to."

"I appreciate the honesty of that, but let me be very clear, now that you know you don't want to be alone. If you violate this contract in any way, I won't hesitate to enforce this again, and there will be no reprieve. Do you understand?"

"Yes."

Antony called for a lamp and handed Rex his contract. "By the way, I didn't desert you. The time frame wasn't up. You had another four days. You'll be closely watched, so don't think about trying to kill yourself."

Rex groaned and signed his contract.

      *   *   *   *

"It's hard to believe nearly a season cycle has gone by," said Master Roland as he packed the last of the parchments in a basket for their trip back to Roacheria in the morning. "I'll miss both of you. I have learned much more than how to decode the symbols."

His pronunciation was still rough, but Henrietta could understand. She spoke slowly so he could as well. "We'll be able to share information easily. I'll have all new equipment at New South Dairy 50. I can help if you find something you can't decode. We can send sealed, private communications to the border exchange box, and you can come back and visit any time."

"I know, but it won't be the same. Will you be leaving soon with Master Antony?"

"No," she said with a sigh. "I'll work here for a few time frames. Antony wants me to wait until everything is completed before we move the manuscripts."

"A good decision, even though I know it's hard to be apart. I'm anxious to get home to my mate, and see this new nymph she surprised me with. You are everything to Master Antony. We all take care of precious things."

Henrietta knew he was right, but deep down she was miserable because she wanted to go. She was peeved with herself for feeling that way after all her talk about how Antony should be prepared to be away from her. She had never thought about how she might feel. Knowing that her sister, Hilda, would be with her didn't help much.

*   *   *   *

Riding on Captain Alexander's back, Antony led the way for the entire group. The trail had all but disappeared after two and a half season cycles, but Antony still knew every wood plant and bush. It was an unusually warm day for the middle of the fourth time frame.

Besides the fifty guards in Captain Alexander's unit, there were three other mated pairs who would begin the new coly. Donald and Cassie, who had been with Antony's parents the day South Dairy 50 died, were the only other survivors returning. Friends in South Dairy 40 would watch their pupating young until they emerged, and they had one larva about to enter pupation.

The second pair, Allie and Art, were newly mated. Allie had just finished her mentorship as a physician's assistant, and would provide their basic medical needs. She was not a full physician, but could consult with any of South Harvester 45's doctors via video wall. Art was a dedicated dairier. His father, Cort, had instilled in him the desire to return, although he was too ill to return. Cort and Alexa, the other survivor, had suffered permanent damage to their breathing organs and had never enjoyed good health.

Alexa's daughter, Denise, and her mate, Herbert, were an important part of the group. Herbert carried a large basket over the surface trail, but Denise was underground helping Henry complete the last several d-units of the tunnel. Herbert's specialty was domicile excavation.

Antony looked at Captain Alexander. "The meadow on the north side of the slope would be a good place for our temporary camp. Would you ask the others to set it up and would you stay with me? There are two things I want to do without the others, but not alone."

"You know you can count on me."

Antony sat at the top of the slope, looking down at his home. The wood plants looked the same, but the meadow grass had grown tall everywhere and vines covered the aphid fences.

"The last time I sat here was the night Henrietta and I made our promise. In a few days, as this becomes the new mound, this place will no longer exist. What will I find when I enter my home?"

"Dust, fungus growing in the damp corners, wild creatures who will have moved in, stains on the reed mats. Why not seal it and hold your memories?"

"My mother kept a journal. Last night in a dream she showed me where to find it, and there are some images I want. When I have those things, I will seal it. Rex, Renae', and Gerry will clean up the yard and mend the fences. The aphids always liked those wood plants and there's no reason not to use them again. Will you bring the marker and show me where you covered them?"

Alexander nodded. Antony ambled down into the yard, pushed open the portal and stepped in. At the sound, two little furry creatures scurried away. Memories flooded Antony's mind, but he felt at peace. He crossed the chamber to the work surface his mother had used and opened its storage compartment. Beneath a layer of dust and several manuscripts, lay the images and the journal. He picked them up, walked out, and closed the portal behind him. Captain Alexander arrived with the marker.

The captain went to the base of the largest wood plant, took ten steps toward the mound and said, "This is the place." They set up the marker.

Antony ran his front pods over it, caressing the symbols of each name, and then took Alexander's front pod in his. "I'm back with others and more will come next season cycle. Live in me now, as I live for you."

*   *   *   *

It took Rex, Renae', and Gerry three evenings after their regular work day to finish restoring the yard and fences. Rex and Gerry did so with their usual do-it-because-they-had-to attitude, but Antony heard Gerry say more than once that he liked being back on the surface. Rex tried not to show it, but he was glad of Gerry's company. Renae' avoided both of them.

It was dark when they finished the third night. Renae' lingered after Antony had dismissed them. Antony turned to him. "Is there something you want to talk about, Renae'?"

"Yes, but I think it's personal."

"It's all right. I know you're trying to learn."

"You seem happier now, and I wonder what it is you do there when you raise your front pods in silence."

Their conversations always began in Ant, with Renae' stumbling over his words, and ended in Roach. Over time, the amount in Ant had increased.

Antony paused. "I was meditating. When we die, our bodies go back to feed the earth, which in turn feeds new plants and creatures in a never-ending cycle, but our essence goes on. When I meditate, I speak in my mind, or recall some memory of my family. Although I can no longer see, hear, or touch them, I can feel their presence in meditation, or in my dreams, and that takes away the sadness."

"Can I learn to do that? I miss my family, too, and I can never see them again, either."

"Yes, but not tonight. I'm very tired."

*   *   *   *

The work and exhaustion seemed endless for everyone. Although some grassfronds had sprung up voluntarily, more needed to be planted, if the fledgling colony wanted to be self-sufficient. Starter herds of aphids and grasshoppers had been provided by the dairies around South Harvester 45. Hatching nymphs had to be protected from predators. Some fire ant guards found themselves learning to be dairiers, while others helped excavate domiciles in the new mound under Herbert's careful guidance. Antony found the old bee hives were undisturbed, and set out more, since some would soon swarm and form new hives.

By summer solstice they took down their temporary shelters and moved underground. Antony returned to South Harvester 45 for Henrietta.

Even though the tunnel was complete, they took the surface trail. Their joy was as great as it had been on their mating day.

*   *   *   *

On their second seventhday together, Henrietta and Antony packed a picnic and headed eastward toward the glen where Old Rodger had lived and died. Axel carried the marker Antony had finished. The words, "Sir Rodger, My Mentor," were framed with elongated open spirals. At the bottom was a carefully carved image of an ant and a roach, seated together in the meadow grass.

"Do you want me to stay with you?" asked Axel when they reached the grove of wood plants.

"No, thank you," replied Henrietta. "We'll be fine. We can get back on our own."

After placing the marker, they ate lunch. Antony told Henrietta how he had first encountered Old Rodger, some of the many times they had shared, and about their last day together. "How different things might have been if he had only lived a little longer," Antony concluded.

"Or if he had never come here at all. I often wonder if there are times when things are simply meant to be a certain way."

"I think it's more like standing where two tunnels branch and deciding which one to take. Our lives are formed by the choices we make and what we do with the circumstances placed before us by others. The problem is that we can never see what's at the end of any tunnel, and we can never go back and take the other one."

They lay down in the grass and stroked each other. A soft breeze swayed the foliage overhead. Sunlight and shadows danced around them.

Antony turned and raised his head. "Did you hear that?"

"What?"

"I'm not sure, something like a soft moan. There it is again."

"You're imagining things."

Antony sat up, straining in the stillness. "No," he whispered. "Listen. There's something by the pond."

Then she heard it. Antony gestured toward the tallest wood plant and Henrietta scampered up. When she reached a height where she could see the pond she called down to him. "It's a roach, and it's injured."

Antony scurried to the pond as fast as he could. The young, light brown female was of the large variety with an exceptionally dark brown band down her back. She had her mandibles and was not branded as banished. She reached for water with one front pod, while holding a dingy bundle of woven thistledown in the other. Half of a severed middle leg dangled. The plate behind her head had a large fracture.

She screamed when she saw him, but was too weak to move.

He spoke in Roach. "Don't be afraid. I won't hurt you."

She flinched and cried out. "Mercy! Mercy!"

"Let me help. Who are you? What happened to you?" He turned toward the wood plants. "Henrietta, bring several large, flat leaves and some long grass stems."

The roach looked at him with a mixture of fear and relief. "Are you... the one they call Master Antony? Have I reached New South Dairy 50?"

"Yes, now lie still. No more harm will come to you." He could see there was no hope for her. Anything he did would only be a final comfort. He tried to take the bundle from her.

"No," she cried, clutching it to her. "I beg you, let this egg live."

Henrietta handed him the flat leaves, which he wrapped around her mangled leg and tied with the grass stems. "Bring a little water," he said to Henrietta.

"Of course your egg will live," he reassured the dying female. "Let me finish binding this. Tell me your name, and what happened to you."

Henrietta looked at her mate intently as she handed him the water. Antony held the cup so she could sip. Henrietta stroked her.

"I am Geree'. My mate, George, was one of your enemies. Forgive them and me now. Ask Renae'... he knows. I had another nymph once, but it ate something wrong and died. No safety cage." Her breaths were short and labored. "Just as well, no credit for plastic anyway. Please, give this one a chance."

"Is that why you came here?"

"But the border warriors ... I could not outrun them ..."

She didn't need to finish. Roach warriors, in their eagerness to keep the peace, had killed many roaches who tried to enter ant surface area. Although some might have been renegades, others were probably innocent. The warriors didn't ask questions beyond demanding to see their permission parchments. Ant guards at least investigated stray roaches after capturing them.

Antony let her sip more water. "They left me for dead. I crawled on, hoping."

"Do you have any family?"

"I no longer exist to them ... because I mated George."

Henrietta understood Roach better than she spoke it. Her words came slowly. "Don't worry, Geree'. Be at peace. Antony and I will hatch your egg as our own."

Geree' allowed Henrietta to take the ragged bundle. About an f-unit long, slightly larger than an ant egg, its smooth, tough outer covering quivered with the life inside it. Henrietta recalled the wrinkled, lifeless mass she had laid, and stroked it in awe. "When will it hatch?" she asked.

Geree's pod dropped. "Half a time..."

18.

*A*stonished colony members congratulated the new parents. Antony sent for Renae'.

"Relax, Renae', you don't need to be afraid to come into our home. I need your help." He told Renae' about the egg. "What can you tell me about Geree', or her mate, George?"

"Geree'..." Renae' searched his mind. "I remember. I only saw her twice. I wasn't with the rest of them much. When Gerry and I first got to the camp, I remember Geree' running up to George, saying that she couldn't go home any more. He said something about proving to her father that he could be a good mate. I think she was from some rich family. George was a huge warrior, biggest I ever saw. He was with us when we came here. Like me, he stayed back. I remember how hysterical Geree' was when Gerry and I got back after the attack on you, and she realized George was dead. She left the camp and I never saw her again. I'm sorry. I wish I could tell you more. She seemed nice, and she was very pretty. She had a 'lucky band' on her back."

"A 'lucky band?'"

"A dark brown stripe on her thorax. It's not a common thing for anyone, so those who have it are said to be lucky. I guess it wasn't true for her."

The next day, Renae' helped Antony construct a safety cage. It was like a larva coop, but it had a lid, since roach nymphs had legs and could climb and run from the moment they hatched. They built it with thin, new, grassfrond stems. Renae' said that nymphs tended to chew on everything. Grassfrond stems tasted bitter and would discourage the nymph from chewing its way out. Nymphs tried to eat everything and many died of accidental poisoning.

"Most roaches leave the nymph in the cage until after they molt the second time. By then they're big enough to understand and stay out of danger," Renae' explained.

Henrietta was horrified. "You mean they never hold, cuddle, or stroke them?"

"Not that I ever remember."

"My young one will know all the care and attention I can give. It will not spend all its time in some cage. All young need to be held and cuddled for whole health."

*   *   *   *

Fourteen days later the egg hatched. Henrietta named him Rodger, to honor the memory of Antony's mentor. He was the third newly hatched young in the colony. They were amazed at the perfection of his tiny body. He had a "lucky band" like Geree'.

Unlike a larva, he ate adult food from the start and devoured plastic. He regularly jumped out of their pods. Sometimes it took an h-unit to catch him as he scurried around their domicile. They made a sign, warning others when he was out, so they would not open the portal. Henrietta had to be very sure to keep the portal to her work chamber closed.

Like a larva, he responded to their stroking and cuddling, squeaking for it, even during the night, and they never refused him. Antony took care of him most of the time, since Henrietta had two archaeologists visiting to learn the Duo Pod symbols. By the time Rodger was a season cycle old, they felt confident enough to take him to the larva nursery for half of each day.

*   *   *   *

Renae' often came to visit in the evening, always interested in Rodger's growth and progress.

One night as they watched Rodger, Antony asked, "What would you do if you had your freedom?"

"I would ask if I could stay here forever, because I like living your ways. It's better than anything I ever had or hoped to have in Roacheria. Yet, I am lonely sometimes. I don't like talking with Rex or Gerry. I like coming here, seeing little Rodger. It satisfies a longing I can't explain. I wish that somehow I could have a mate. But I know that's impossible."

"Was there some female you knew once?"

"Yes, but she probably ended up with someone else by now."

"What was her name? Tell me about her."

"Rita. We knew each other when we were nymphs. After my third molt, I ran about as I pleased. We did a lot of scrounging around the refuse piles together. Her family was about like mine. We used to pretend we found a fortune in the refuse and bought ourselves a huge, fancy domicile to live in forever... Silly nymph talk."

"Did you ever see her after you reached adulthood?"

Renae' sighed. "Yes, we planned to mate, but I told her that I wanted to give her a better life. I saved some of the extra credit I got from Sir Rex that I didn't send home. Well, no more. I saw her crying at the edge of the path the day we came back to you."

*   *   *   *

A few days later, without Renae's knowledge, Antony discussed their conversation with the other ant families. He wrote to Master Roland and asked him if he could make inquiries about a female named Rita who lived near the refuse piles. If he found her, she had permission to visit New South Dairy 50. He sent travel parchments with the letter and hoped that Master Roland would understand his message, since he could not mention Renae's name.

Three time frames later he received a reply. "My dear friend, Master Antony, I located the female you enquired about and convinced her she would be very foolish not to accept your invitation. I told her you had work for her, as I knew she was in a desperate state. She will be at the communications box waiting for an escort the first day of the sixth time frame."

To guard against Renae's disappointment in case something went wrong, Antony didn't tell him why they were going to the communications box that day. "Wait here in this grove of wood plants," he said, "since you can't be seen at the border crossing."

The two ant guards on duty greeted Antony. He sat down to watch for Rita's arrival. As she came into sight, he could see her holding out the travel parchment to two border warriors. They tried to restrain her. Antony whistled to get their attention. They pulled her roughly toward the communications box.

"Can't you see she has her travel documents?" Antony said when they reached him. "She is my guest and I don't appreciate your harassing her."

The one in charge recognized Antony and stammered, "Sorry, Master Antony. I was only trying to do my job. Parchments can be forged, and she's such a nobody."

"It's not your place to judge who is important." Antony took the parchment and pointed out the official New South Dairy 50 seal and his own signature at the bottom. "Even if you can't read, you should be able to recognize that. If you have questions, ask. Don't harass innocent creatures."

"Yes, Sir!"

Antony turned to the frightened young female. "Rita?"

She nodded.

"No one will harm you." He nodded to the ant guards and led Rita down the path toward the wood plants. "I'm glad you decided to come. I couldn't be specific in my letter. It's Renae' who wants to be with you. Do you still have fond feelings for him?"

"He's still alive? I was afraid to hope."

"He is not only alive and well, but has made important changes in his life. He may earn his freedom soon and hopes you will want to stay with him, but he doesn't know you're here. I was afraid we wouldn't find you, or you wouldn't come."

If Renae' had still had his mandibles, they would have opened wide in shock. "Rita?" Renae' wrapped himself around her, stroking her antennae. Antony moved a little way off, saying he needed to rest. He didn't intend to listen, but he couldn't help it.

"I can't believe he found you. I was daydreaming when I told him about you. Some things do turn out for the best. Say you'll stay with me. It's much better here than in Roacheria. When ants take a mate, it's forever. That's how I want to take you."

Rita touched Renae's scarred face. "Was it as horrible as they say?"

"It was worse, but it doesn't matter now."

She turned away and began to cry.

"Rita, I'm sorry. I had no way to let you know anything. What's wrong?"

She looked at him sadly. "I would like very much to stay, but I can't be your mate. I've been had."

"Who?"

She looked at the ground. "I don't even know. I was hungry. He promised me credit, but afterward, he left, and there I was, still hungry. I had a nymph, but it died."

"It doesn't matter. You can still be mine, because I will say it is so. We have a chance to make it better now. Any young you have will be mine because I'll say they're mine, like little Rodger is Master Antony's."

"I don't understand, but there's nothing for me back there but starvation and more nymphs who will die. If you'll have me, I'll stay."

Half a time frame later, Antony stood with Renae' beside his family's marker and they consumed his contract.

The first mating ceremony in New South Dairy 50 joined Renae' and Rita. Renae' gave Rita a blossom seed, and said they would grow into something beautiful together. Rita gave Renae' a butterfly's wing, saying he gave her new life.

*   *   *   *

Before Antony and Henrietta knew it, Rodger was three and ready to molt the first time.

Renae' tried to reassure Henrietta. "We've been molting for eons. It's painful, but we get through it. Leave him alone and protect him until the new layer hardens."

"I'm going to ask Allie for some pain potion," she insisted.

Allie contacted a physician in South Harvester 45. He suggested the potion used to treat carrier strain syndrome, but didn't know how much to prescribe.

Antony refused. "What if we give the wrong dose and he goes into a coma like Henrietta did? I'll contact the science facility in Roacheria."

Their reply was, "Quit worrying. We all live through it."

Henrietta laid Rodger on his thistledown mattress, stroked his antennae and cried. "He's too little and innocent to suffer this way."

"Here, try this," said Antony. "I put a tiny bit of my pain herbs in some honey."

It seemed to help. They adjusted the dosage carefully over the next several days with Allie making careful measurements and taking notes for future reference. When Rodger finally thrashed his way out of his first exoskeleton, he had expanded to three f-units in length.

*   *   *   *

When Rodger reached his sixth season cycle and molted the second time, he was almost as large as Henrietta, and enjoyed sitting near her as she worked on the Duo Pod manuscripts. She would let him stay for an h-unit or so each morning.

"What's that, Mum?" he asked constantly.

"Ancient writings. We learn a lot from them."

"What's writing?"

"Words on parchment. Here." Henrietta put his name on a scrap. "That says, 'Rodger.'" She stroked him fondly. "Now run along. Rita is here. It's time for you to go to the nursery."

"Rodger, Rodger, Rodger," he repeated, following Rita as she carried her daughter, Antonette.

Each day, Rodger snuggled up and asked for more writing. Henrietta jotted down a word or a few symbols in Ant and he'd scamper off repeating it. If he remembered it the next day, she praised him. If not, she wrote it down again.

Arthur, her new archaeology trainee, said, "Isn't he a bit young for formal training?"

Henrietta laughed. "I suppose so. Antony says they begin after the third molt in Roacheria, but I don't think of this as training. It's more like a game for him."

They enjoyed Rodger's middle season cycles. He was eager, curious, and affectionate. He talked constantly, switching easily from Ant to Roach. Antony made sure he learned Roach properly from the start.

*   *   *   *

When Rodger was nine and a half, and molted the third time, he needed a lot more of the pain herbs. As he thrashed his way out of his exoskeleton, he accidentally kicked Antony and re-cracked one of his smaller scars. Antony spent ten days confined in bed and had it plastered for two time frames. Rodger was now larger than Antony.

"I didn't mean to hurt you, Dad," Rodger apologized as Antony lay in bed.

"I know. I'll be all right."

"Why am I with you and Mum? Did you borrow me from Renae' and Rita?"

"Of course not. Where did you get that idea? You were ours long before Renae' and Rita mated."

"But I can't be yours and Mum's. I'm not an ant."

Antony sighed. "Factually speaking, no, your mum and I didn't create you."

"Who did?"

"The two roaches who created you died. Your mum and I found a female named Geree' mortally wounded. She begged us to give you a chance. So we took you as our own. Her mate's name was George. He was a warrior who died in a battle two season cycles before your egg was laid."

"That's all?"

"The rest doesn't matter any more."

*   *   *   *

Rodger began his formal training a time frame later. New South Dairy 50's training center at that time consisted of one chamber, one trainer, five young adult ants and Rodger.

Not long afterward, Rodger stomped into Henrietta's work chamber, slammed down his manuscripts and demanded, "Am I suffering from Plastic Deprivation?"

Henrietta gave him an odd look. "Of course not. You're very intelligent. You learned your reading symbols long before anyone thought you could. Remember?"

"Then why does it take me so long to learn anything? They're all way ahead of me. What's wrong with me?" He swept his front pod across the surface, scattering a pile of parchments.

Henrietta reached up and put her pods around him.

He pushed away. "I'm too big for that!"

"No one is ever too big for affection. There's nothing wrong with you. Sometimes we forget you're still a nymph. The others are adults and have been training longer. You'll catch up. By the time you reach their age, you'll probably be way ahead. Remember the letter from Master Roland? He said you needed a slower pace until after your last molt. Have some tea with me. You'll feel better."

This time he allowed her to cuddle him.

*   *   *   *

Rodger's changing moods grew worse as he approached his final molt. One minute he longed to be a little nymph and hide behind his mum. An h-unit later he would reject both parents and wander off alone. Confused and frightened, he turned to Renae'.

"What's wrong with me?"

"Lots of us get a little confused before our last molt. Maybe it's because it's more than growth. Your mind and your body are changing in many ways. Pretty soon you'll see Antonette with different eyes and I won't let you be alone with her any more. Be glad your father gives you herbs for the pain."

"Stop calling him my father. He didn't create me."

"So what? Any creature can pro-create. That doesn't make someone a father."

"You knew them, didn't you? My roach parents. What were they like?"

Renae' turned away. "Where are your manners, Rodger? What I do know, I told your father long ago. I'll tell you about anything else, but that part of my life I would rather forget."

"I'm sorry, Renae'. Don't turn away from me. You're the only one I can talk to. Sometimes I wonder who I am, that's all."

"Promise me you'll stay away from your parents during this last molt. You could injure them seriously. Remember last time?"

"Can I come to you?"

Renae' nodded.

*   *   *   *

Rodger's final molt happened a time frame later in the middle of the afternoon. He had taken a huge dose of pain herbs that morning, but it had worn off. While the others worked on a technical problem, Rodger was supposed to read his Antstory book, but he couldn't concentrate. He clenched his mandibles to keep from screaming as a wave of pain swept over him. The manuscript fell from his pods.

The training ant approached. "Rodger, are you all right? You can go home if you need to."

"I'm fine!" he snapped. "Don't touch me!" He picked up the manuscript, flipped the pages at random and began reading again.

There before Rodger's eyes was the published account of the events leading up to the establishment of his colony. In blunt, factual form, he read about his mum's early work, the murder of his father's family, subsequent battles, his mum's speech, Renae's confession, and his father's request for Renae', Rex, and Gerry.

It wasn't that Rodger was unaware of these things, but the fact that he combined them with his own beginning. Blinded by pain and fury, he threw the manuscript and fled from everything. He headed for the meadow where he knew Antony was tending the bee hives with Renae'.

"The rest doesn't matter! That's what you said. Matter to whom? Don't you think it mattered to me?" Rodger had never been so angry in his life and it frightened him, but it was nothing compared to the look of sheer terror he saw in his father's eyes as he towered over him flailing his front pods. "I'm tired of being your experiment. I'm not an ant. I'm not a roach. I don't know what I am!"

Renae' jumped between them. Rodger felt the sting of Renae's pod on his face. He turned and fled from both of them. The grassfronds were about ten f-units tall at that stage of their growth. Rodger grabbed one and tore it out by the roots. He grabbed a second and then more and more, shouting all the while. "What am I? Who am I? Who were they, anyway?" By the time his exoskeleton split down the back, he'd torn up quite a section. He thrashed his way out, lay limp, and slept.

He awoke to find Renae' beside him. Renae' had woven several grass fronds into a crude mat. Then he propped it up with stiffer stems to shade them. Renae' reached out and stroked Rodger's antennae. "It's over. You'll never have to go through it again."

"What have I done? Did I kill him? Are we both banished?"

"No, your father is fine."

"Did I hurt you?"

"No. You say you want to know who you are. I'll tell you. You are Rodger, a roach raised as an ant. You and I are lucky. We will always remember our parents. When ants emerge from pupation, they don't remember things. They take it on faith when someone says, 'I'm your mother.' But we remember. If you want to know who your real parents are, go back in your memory to the faces you saw when you hatched. Remember who stroked you at any h-unit, eased your pain. Those are your parents. Anyone else is only an organic science fact."

Renae' handed Rodger a water flask. Rodger accepted it and drank.

Renae' continued. "I have nothing good to remember but being stuck in a safety cage until I was past six. I remember hurting and starving and watching my mother cry because she had nothing. But I'm not bitter about it and I don't blame her. She did her best. I decided to do something about it. I picked the wrong way, and by all rights I should have been extinguished for it. But when I was offered the chance to start over, I did. What you do with yourself is up to you."

*   *   *   *

The following morning, Renae' and Rodger returned home. Antony took Rodger out to the glen and showed him Sir Rodger's and

Geree's markers. He explained how Sir Rodger taught him, his work as an interpreter, his feelings before, during, and after the battle, and everything he knew about Geree' and George.

"As for George, I'm not sure. Maybe I'm the one who killed him. That warrior I fought didn't exactly introduce himself before he tried to sever my leg. One thing I do know. When you came at me the other day, I saw his face in yours."

Rodger sat, lost in thought, for a long time. Then he turned to Antony and embraced him. "Renae' was right. You and Mum are my real parents. You always will be. You were right, too. The rest doesn't matter any more."

19.

*R*odger completed his basics at fourteen—the age at which most ants emerged from pupation and began their training. Job exploration in New South Dairy 50 was still limited, so Henrietta suggested that he go to South Harvester 45. Antony thought he should also spend a season cycle in Roacheria.

"Why would I want to go there?" Rodger asked.

"For one thing, you might want a mate someday," Henrietta said.

"I don't need to go there for a mate. I'll wait for Antonette."

Antony stifled a laugh. "Antonette might have something to say about that."

"We get along fine. She'll be pleasant again after she molts."

"Aside from that, you have many talents and should explore a wide variety of possibilities before you choose your life's work," Antony said.

Rodger's voice was firm. "I'm not going anywhere, so don't try to make me."

They discussed it many times, loudly, before Antony caught himself and remembered being on the other side of this argument. He stopped insisting. "Rodger, don't shut me out. Tell me honestly. Why don't you want to go?"

"Dad ... here I'm accepted ... but anywhere else I'm different. I may not fit in either South Harvester 45 or Roacheria. I'm part of both worlds, and yet part of neither, and I still have a temper. I wouldn't have Renae' around to get between someone else and me. I'm afraid of what I might do."

*   *   *   *

It took a tragedy to change Rodger's mind. One summer day, Antonette scampered off carelessly after her little brother. They got further from the bee hives than they intended and ran into a mantis. Little Antony squealed and ran for help. Antonette defended herself well, and the mantis fared no better than she. Although she was still alive when Art carried her to Allie, there was little the under-trained physician's assistant could do. Rodger and two other young adults were in the clinic at the time, learning basic emergency care.

"Allie," Rodger pleaded, "you've got to do something. Contact South Harvester 45. Let them direct you."

Allie did her best and Rodger helped, handing her the things she needed. The surgeon in South Harvester 45 tried to guide her over video wall, but conceded, "I'm afraid I don't know roach anatomy."

Antonette died two h-units later. Rodger's grief was two fold. He had intended to ask her to make a mating promise. He was also shaken by the fact that medical care for any of them was inadequate. When his grief eased, he knew what he wanted to do with his life.

At supper one night later that fall, he announced, "I'm ready to leave for more training and I know what I want to do. Even before Antonette died, I enjoyed working with Allie. I want to study medicine, ant and roach. We need both. I asked Allie to give me more to read, and wrote to one of the medical facilities in South Harvester 45."

"What about Roacheria?" asked Antony.

"I've thought about that, too. Will you find out what I need to do to train there?"

A time frame later, Rodger received a letter of acceptance from his mentor in South Harvester 45. He handed it to his father and asked, "What does she mean? 'Say hello to your father. We're old friends.'"

Antony looked at it and grinned. "You won't have to worry about feeling lonely or out of place. You mentor, Master Amy, is the one who invented my brace."

*   *   *   *

Amy had Rodger live with her in the clinic. She took advantage of every case available. If she heard about something different outside the military medical facility, she sent him there. She wanted to condense the normally five season cycle mentorship so he could begin his training in Roacheria sooner. The pile of manuscripts he had to read never seemed to shrink. Some nights he dreamed the pages were attacking him, but each day confirmed his determination to continue.

Near the end of the fourth season cycle, he received a packet from the Advanced Training Center for the Sciences in Roacheria. It contained a lengthy, highly technical exam and forms for witnesses to verify that he completed it alone in a specified length of time. All of it was written in Roach.

Two time frames later, Amy interrupted him as he attended a young male with mild carrier strain syndrome. "This came in a few minutes ago. I knew you'd want it right away." He'd been accepted at the Center For the Sciences in Roacheria.

Amy came with him to New South Dairy 50 to celebrate his certification as an ant physician. She stood before the whole colony and wrote, "Most Favorably Completed," across his training contract. Rodger accepted everyone's praise, but he knew he had a long way to go.

*   *   *   *

Five days later, Master Roland arrived to take him to Roacheria. Rodger remembered the archaeologist's frequent visits and letters over the season cycles and was glad he would be living with someone he knew. Rodger, his parents, and Master Roland sat in the parlor after dinner.

"How are things outside the world of archaeology?" Antony asked.

"Many things are better," Master Roland replied. "I don't think it will ever be possible for someone like Rex to gain control again. It's good not to need border warriors any more, but societies change slowly. Beneath the surface, greed, jealousy, and hatred are very much alive."

"How do they feel about me now, and how could it affect Rodger?"

"In the beginning, there were many who would have enjoyed seeing you fail here, but as time went on, they either respected you or simply forgot. Rodger's problems won't all be related to you."

He turned to Rodger. "I want you to know that your parents are the most wonderful creatures I ever hope to know, but it would be a good idea if you kept your identity to yourself. When asked, say you are from a country community and that your father is the Supreme Executor of the local board. Casually mention that he is well acquainted with Sir Reginald, the elder, and Master Surgeon Rufus."

He paused. "Remember him, Antony? He worked himself up to directing all the medical trainees, but he's a good creature and trustworthy."

Antony handed Master Roland a mug of warm honey dew. Master Roland sipped and then continued. "Rodger, your connections to these roaches of importance will discourage most trainees from bothering you, but many will be jealous of your abilities. You are the youngest ever admitted to this level of training. Others will insult you and try to goad you into a fight because of your size, and then condemn you if you touch them. Walk away and ignore them. Outside of training, females will flock to you hoping for a mate, because a physician in Roacheria earns a lot of credit. Don't go anywhere alone with one. She might try to seduce you and then demand a mating contract."

Rodger sat quietly, absorbing this advice from his mother's friend and colleague.

"Even the trainers will make things difficult. It's not like here, where your mentors strive to help you succeed. Put aside all your ant values and keep to yourself. Don't ask any trainee for help and never offer it. Some envious trainee will accuse you of cheating or bribery and try to have you expelled."

A look of dismay came over Rodger's face.

"If you have problems, go right to Master Rufus. He'll help because he feels indebted to your father. Refer to me as your uncle and I will introduce you to those you can trust."

"Rodger," Antony said, "even though we won't be able to visit like we did when you were in South Harvester 45, we will write constantly. I know you will do well in spite of all that Master Roland said. Maturity has softened your temperament and you will have Master Roland to guide you."

*   *   *   *

The first half season cycle was the most difficult. Rodger was lonely, frustrated and overworked. Without Master Roland's and his mate, Raylin's constant encouragement, he would have given in to despair. One trainee named Robert harassed him constantly. "Country Master Know-it-all," was his most frequent taunt, whenever Rodger answered correctly, along with insults Rodger would not repeat to anyone.

Rodger carried the latest letter from his parents in his satchel and would slip in his middle pod and touch it to control his emotions as he turned his back and walked away from his tormentor. Time passed and Robert saw that Rodger could not be provoked.

Rodger asked to take several exams and move ahead to clinical work. He never got used to the large number of trainees in each unit. He missed the intimate training groups of his colony and the personal attention of his mentor.

At the end of his sixth time frame Master Rufus called him in for a conference. "You've proven yourself. You're not as soft-hearted as I had feared."

Rodger knew he could speak freely with Master Rufus. "That's where you're wrong. I detest everything about this place and your ways. I manage to cover it in front of the others. Many are counting on me and I don't intend to give up."

"Master Amy prepared you well. You passed all those exams and I'm changing your training plan. You'll spend the mornings in advanced Roach medicine and your afternoons in the clinic with ten others, including your favorite, Robert, under my supervision. If you continue as you have, you'll complete your training in two and a half more season cycles."

"Thank you, Sir. Do you have any suggestions regarding Robert?"

"Keep doing as you have been. Ignore that spoiled pain-in-the-abdomen. I can't stand him either. Whatever you do, don't tell him who you are. I should not say his name, but Rex is Robert's great uncle. That clan still hates your father."

*   *   *   *

Rodger's first clinic patient was Sir Ronald, who came in every other day for joint therapy. Rodger had observed as each of the others took their turn with the surly old Board Member. He noticed that Sir Ronald wore a brace similar to his father's.

"How did you get this injury?" he asked as he began massaging the main support joint of Sir Ronald's back-right leg.

"Where did you come from that you don't know? Idiot."

"I beg your pardon, Sir. I'm from a small country community."

"I own the Number 2 Plastic mine. Many season cycles ago, I had to settle an argument between a supervisor and some workers. A fight broke out and I ended up in the middle of it. Hmmmm, that feels marvelous. Master Rufus, I want this one every time I come. He does a better job than you do. What's your name?"

"Rodger, Sir."

"I have an even better idea. What do you do with your evenings?"

"Study, Sir."

"How'd you like to earn some credit? Master Rufus, may I have this trainee come to my domicile and do this every first, third and fifth day?"

"What trainees do on their own time is not my concern," answered Master Rufus.

Sir Ronald looked at Rodger. "Well?"

"I'd be happy to, Sir."

*   *   *   *

Rodger gawked at the impressive domicile before him. Roach homes were another thing he couldn't comprehend. His mother had helped him establish some perspective.

"Primitive ants," she'd written in her letter, "lived underground and took care of each other. We continued to do that as we evolved in size and intelligence. Ancient roaches crawled out of the wood plants and grasses, and into the walls of the Duo Pod dwellings, where they lived on and fought over the leavings. Why is it a surprise that their domiciles resemble re-built ruins?"

Each time he looked at one of these elaborate homes, and thought of the squalor of reed mats and metal plates near the refuse piles, it reconfirmed his belief in ant ways.

He tapped at the portal. An attractive, young female opened it. "Excuse me," he said. "I must have the wrong location."

"Who are you looking for?"

"Sir Ronald."

"You're in the right place. He's my grandfather. You must be the medical trainee." She opened the portal wider. "Come in. I'm Ronda."

He followed her into an entry chamber. The walls were decorated with curious designs in various shades of green and blue. They proceeded down a passage lined with images of important-looking roaches and up a ramp to another level. The floor was covered with the softest mats of woven thistledown his pods had ever touched.

Tapping an elaborately carved portal, Ronda said, "Grandfather, the medical trainee is here."

"Send him in."

Ronda gestured toward the portal.

"Good evening, Rodger," Sir Ronald said when Rodger entered. "I'm glad to see you. I slipped on the ramp earlier and I can barely move. Don't ever get old. I see you two met, but I'll be formal anyway. Ronda, this is Rodger. Rodger, may I present my granddaughter, Ronda."

Rodger nodded respectfully. Ronda smiled, twitched one antenna and left. Rodger lifted Sir Ronald onto a padded table and went to work on the old roach's joint.

"You're too good for a beginning trainee," Sir Ronald said. "Where did you learn to do this?"

Rodger paused, guarding his words. "My father has a joint injury. I used to watch my mother massage it."

Small talk continued. Rodger used Master Roland's suggestions regarding his background and changed the subject, asking about the many unique objects he saw in the chamber. When he finished, Sir Ronald handed him a credit note.

"Sir, this is more than the agreed amount."

"Keep it. You're worth it. Perhaps you can come a little earlier next time and join us for dinner. I'm sure it would please Ronda."

Dinner with Sir Ronald became a habit. Rodger realized that Sir Ronald viewed him as a prospective mate for Ronda. It was a compliment, since he'd heard that Sir Ronald was very protective when it came to his granddaughter. He'd lost his mate and Ronda's mother in an epidemic five season cycles earlier. Ronda was very attractive, but liked her luxurious life, constantly talking about the things she wanted.

Rodger took a chance after a therapy session. "Sir Ronald, may I speak to you in confidence? There are some trainees who, if they knew what I am about to say, would try to end my training and I can't risk that."

"Of course. What's on your mind?"

"Please, don't be offended. Ronda is attracted to me and I enjoy her friendship, but I can never give her the life she wants and I don't want to hurt her feelings. I won't be staying in Roacheria when I finish my training. I have not been completely honest about myself. I am the adopted son of Master Antony and Master Henrietta, and New South Dairy Colony 50 is my home."

Sir Ronald stared at him.

"Sir, I hope you won't hold this against me. I really need this extra credit. Every family in my colony is working hard so I can be here. This job helps a lot."

Sir Ronald finally found his voice. "Well I'll be... No offense taken. I certainly don't want to lose the best therapist I've ever had. I'll keep your little secret." He began to laugh. "You're absolutely right about Ronda. I'll think of something to tell her. I'm dying of curiosity. How did you come to be adopted?"

Rodger told him the story.

"Absolutely incredible. Have you ever thought of looking for their families here?"

"No."

"Why not?"

"Their names are fairly common and I know very little. Geree's family abandoned her because George was a renegade. Who here would admit to being related to them? Besides, I have a family."

Sir Ronald grew sober. "Good reasons. I would never care to live like an ant, but I've always respected Master Antony. He's quite a creature."

"Thank you," Rodger said, turning to leave.

"One thing more, if you don't mind ... I've often noticed your 'lucky band.' Did your roach mother have one?"

"Yes, my father said she did."

*   *   *   *

"You might have told me," Ronda snapped on his next visit.

"Told you what?"

"That you already had a legal mate." She left in a huff.

Rodger went on up to Sir Ronald's chamber. "Why did you tell her I already had a mate?"

"It seemed like the easiest way to get her to leave you alone. That's what you wanted, wasn't it?"

"Yes, but now she's hurt and angry."

"She'll get over it."

The rumor got around quickly and other females left Rodger alone, too. Not that he minded. They were all like Ronda in their desire for luxuries. An unusual friendship formed between the elderly Board Member and the young medical trainee. They often talked about ant culture. Rodger now had two places where he could be himself, and it relieved the tension he felt every day in training.

After hearing about Rex, Renae' and Gerry, Sir Ronald's comment was, "Ha, ha, ha. Rex living like an ant. Now that's justice! Good for your father. What a fitting end to that greedy old rouge. He's the one responsible for this." He pointed to his disabled joint and laughed for several minutes.

During the second winter, Rodger opened up enough to tell him about Antonette and why he had decided to study medicine. "Antonette would have been a good mate. I thought I would find someone like her here. Sometimes I wonder if I'll ever find a female who is willing to live an ant's life."

"Let me give you a piece of advice. You're looking in the wrong places. I must be crazy to be saying this. Take a close look at the ones Master Roland is always picking up from the shanties to do domicile work for his mate."

*   *   *   *

Having someone clean up after him was another thing Rodger disliked. In the beginning he'd protested, saying he would take care of himself. He had been told to accept it and use all his time to study. The current employee was always gone by the time he got home, so he made a point to come home early the next day. He heard voices in Raylin's chamber.

"Try it again, Ginny. You can do it."

"Set the... heat box at mmm... med.... medi... medium. Roast seeds... half an h-unit."

"Very good. Now go do it."

Ginny ran into Rodger as she left Raylin's chamber. She backed away, antennae twitching. "I'm sorry ... I ..."

"No, I'm sorry," Rodger said.

Raylin came out. "Rodger, you're home early. It's all right, Ginny. I never realized it, but you two haven't met. Ginny, this is Master Roland's nephew, Rodger."

"So you're the one who keeps my things so tidy. Thank you."

"You're welcome," she said and headed for the kitchen.

"May I talk to you, Raylin?"

"I always have time for you."

They stepped into Raylin's parlor. "Tell me about her."

"Ginny has been with us half a season cycle. She's learning quickly. She has an older sister with a nymph. Roland is always sending extra plastic home with her."

"What happened to the one you had when I first came?"

"Racine? She left for formal training. Let me back up. I've always had help, like others of our rank. When Roland came back from that first season cycle with your mother, he was a changed creature. He said we were doing everything wrong and if he couldn't fix the system, he could certainly do something on his own."

Raylin paused and took a sip from a mug she had left sitting on her writing surface. "Roland went down to the shanties and came back with the most pathetic young female he could find. We cleaned her up, fed her well, and paid her more than the average. I spent two or three h-units each day teaching her to read. After three season cycles, he sponsored her for training and made sure she got a decent job. Roland says that every female he helps saves twice as many in the next generation."

Rodger slid his abdomen into an open-backed chair opposite her. "I never realized ... How many has he helped this way?"

"Ginny is the seventh he's brought home. Of our four sons, the youngest is the only one who understands, but he hatched late in our lives, right before Roland returned from South Harvester 45. The others accuse him of spending their inheritance. Roland tells them he can do what he likes with his credit."

Rodger went back to his chamber with more than medicine on his mind. After that, he came home early at least twice a quarter time frame and went straight to the kitchen for a snack. It took a while for Ginny to feel comfortable talking to him, but he enjoyed her company.

When spring came, he left a note on his work surface one day. "There is a grove of wood plants in the meadow near the shanties. Please, meet me there seventhday at noon. Rodger."

Arriving before noon, he laid out roasted seeds and honey dew. She approached timidly. When they had finished eating, she lay back and said, "I suppose you want me now."

He stared at her. "No, Ginny, I wanted to talk to you somewhere besides Master Roland's kitchen and for more than a few minutes."

"Why? You could spend time with any of those fancy, rich females. Someone from your station doesn't mix with a nobody like me unless he wants something else."

"You aren't a nobody. I'm not like the others, and I'm not really Master Roland's nephew."

*   *   *   *

Rodger's third and final season cycle began that fall. He handed the clerk his father's transfer of credit letter. She pushed it back. "It's been paid, Rodger. Like last season cycle."

"But who?"

"I would tell you, if I knew. It came in a plain packet, marked for you. Several important roaches sponsor trainees. They don't want others to know, like you don't want some to know who you are."

Rodger thought about Master Roland sponsoring so many and hoped it was not he. Master Roland was doing enough giving him a home. Sir Reginald from The Board? It had to be. Sir Reginald had helped arrange his studies and protect his identity.

*   *   *   *

Rodger and Ginny had met in the grove of wood plants every seventhday for several time frames. Like two playful nymphs, they tossed fallen leaves at each other and scampered about the thinning branches before settling down to rest in a pile of dry foliage.

"How do you feel when you're with me?" Rodger asked.

"Like someone wonderful. I feel so much joy it makes everything terrible go away."

"That's what I feel, too. Remember when I explained that ants mate forever, because they cherish each other? Will you make a promise to be my mate, even though we'd have to wait one more season cycle before we could be together?"

"Oh, yes! ... But what about my sister? Rayann needs me to help provide for her nymph."

"My father would let her come to New South Dairy 50."

"How do you know?"

"Because he's my father. He understands about families."

*   *   *   *

Later that winter, Rayann's nymph got very sick. Ginny convinced her to bring him to Master Roland's home late at night. Rodger examined him and left immediately to see Master Rufus.

"I need seven measures of variety twenty mold."

"For whom?"

"I told you about making a promise with Ginny. It's for her sister's nymph."

"You know that anti-infection agent is reserved for those of large variety."

"I'll pay for it myself. I can't let Rayann's nymph die."

"Nymphs die in the shanties every day. You can't save them all."

"But I can save this one. If you won't do it for me, authorize it for my father's sake."

Reluctantly, Master Rufus gave him the mold. "It's both our mandibles if we're found out."

When the nymph recovered, Rodger arranged for Ginny, Rayann, and her nymph to leave for his parent's home immediately.

Master Roland was away working in the ruins, so Raylin escorted the three to the trade center to meet the carriers from New South Dairy 50 on their regular plastic trip. Rodger wanted to go, but Raylin wouldn't allow it. She had heard a rumor that Robert had friends watching Rodger. She didn't want to take any chances with the end of Rodger's training only seven time frames away.

*   *   *   *

"Why the sad face?" asked Sir Ronald as Rodger worked on his joint.

"I miss Ginny. Did I ever thank you for the advice?"

"Many times. You did the right thing. A male has to protect his intended mate. You never know what might happen in the shanties. I hope I find Ronda someone who's half the creature you are. How many days left?"

"Fifty-six."

Sir Ronald groaned. "Then I'm stuck with Master Rufus again. Will your parents be coming to the Completion Ceremony? I'd like to meet them. It won't matter who knows then."

"Yes, they've changed the date of the next plastic shipment to coincide with it."

*   *   *   *

Rodger sat in the research center finishing his final project. He crossed another day off his calendar. One time frame left. He felt a pod on his back and turned to see Master Rufus. "We have a problem. Follow me."

Rodger left the research center with him. Master Rufus said nothing until they entered his private work chamber.

"Tomorrow is the day I take you and the others in clinic work to the Center for the Condemned. You are expected to observe and participate."

Rodger shook his head. "I didn't come here to learn to give pain. That's a procedure I'll never use, Sir. I won't do it."

"Yes you will. This time you've got to see it from our side. When you crossed our border, you became subject to our laws, whether you agreed with them or not. Remember the mold you needed last winter? Somehow, that stinking piece of fly bait, Robert, found out about it, and he knows who you are. He's been waiting for his chance. He told me this morning that if you aren't there tomorrow, he'll expose us."

Rodger's antennae drooped. "I understand. I'll pack and leave tonight."

Master Rufus shook his head. "It's not that simple. He can still expose the rest of us. You either do it tomorrow, or risk getting it done to you, and all of us with you—myself, Master Roland, Raylin, everyone who knows. But if you fulfill this duty, you'll buy his silence. If he exposes us then, he puts himself in jeopardy as well. I'll put you last. It won't matter what you do when you've finished."

Rodger rose slowly and headed home. Master Roland had not returned from work and Raylin was out with friends. He left again and headed for Sir Ronald's. Before he could tap on the portal, it opened and a distinguished young male came out with Ronda.

"Excuse me, Ronda. Is your grandfather in?"

She grinned and said absently, "Sure, go on up."

Sir Ronald listened as Rodger explained his predicament.

"I really don't know how I'm going to do it."

"Are you going to throw away everything you've worked for during the last three season cycles? This isn't New South Dairy 50. Sometimes, here, you are forced to do things you would rather not do. They're all condemned anyway. You can't save them, so don't think about them. Remember Antonette, and think about Ginny, that nymph you healed, and everyone you care about. Do it for all those you can and will save. When it's over, come back here and destroy anything you want in your anger."

*   *   *   *

Rodger walked at the very back of the group, afraid to look anyone in the eyes. Each criminal was brought in and strapped down. Their offenses were stated: murder, assault, treason ... The victims' families watched from a small gallery. He forced himself to watch closely as Master Rufus performed the first, so he would know what to do. Then he shut his eyes.

His turn came. His "victim" was brought in. He whispered to Master Rufus, "She's only a nymph. What could a nymph possibly do to deserve this?"

"You heard it. She assaulted an Enforcer," Master Rufus whispered back.

Rodger's whisper was louder. "What was he trying to do to her?"

"It doesn't matter. Please, don't let me down." Rodger had never heard a more desperate voice.

A whisper came from behind. "My, my. Master Soft Heart's losing it. Someone might mistake you for a stupid ant."

Rodger turned and glared at Robert. "Shut up."

Rodger stepped forward and looked at the condemned female. There was a small crack in the side of her thorax. She was molting. He took several deep breaths, bent down, as if looking at the angle of her mandibles and whispered, "Forgive me for what I have to do."

She twitched one antenna. He turned away from her terror, picked up the tool from its sterile tray, and cut off her mandibles as quickly as he could. His eyes filled with tears as he closed the wounds and branded her. He threw the tray across the chamber and ran.

*   *   *   *

If the day at the Center for the Condemned had been the lowest of his life, the Completion Ceremony ranked among the highest. Those who had completed their training were lined up by career group with the medical trainees last. Master Rufus had arranged it that way because he didn't want the possible uproar from Rodger's parting words to end the ceremony prematurely. Rodger didn't mind. This was his victory and no one would take it from him. He watched heads turn and heard murmuring as his parents entered the assembly hall with Ginny beside them.

Ginny had never looked better. Away from the constant fears that accompanied life in the shanties, she had gained weight and her delicate brown exoskeleton glistened. Confident and proud of herself, she was a match for any female present. Rodger's thorax swelled with pride and devotion.

He listened half-heartedly as one trainee after another stood in front, had a medal of knowledge placed over his head and told those assembled what important work he had accepted. Once in a while, one would mention how hard he had worked to reach that day.

Master Rufus called Rodger's name. He saw his father nod as he began to speak. "I would like to thank all those whose sacrifices and care helped me achieve this goal: Master Surgeon Rufus, Master Roland and his mate, Raylin, Sir Ronald, who employed me, and every family in my colony." He paused and turned. "Even you, Robert, in your own way."

Robert's mandibles opened wide. He glared at Rodger with pure hatred, but said nothing.

Rodger continued. "Most of all, I'd like to thank my parents, Master Antony and Master Henrietta, whose compassion toward my mortally injured roach mother, gave me the chance to live in the first place. When I leave tomorrow, it will be to return to my home, New South Dairy Colony 50, to provide medical care to every creature there."

The stunned assembly stared, mandibles opened, first at Rodger, then at his parents. Sir Ronald rose in a silent gesture of respect. About half the assembly joined him.

The reception afterwards was a typically stiff, formal, Roacherian affair of fancy foods and polite conversation, most of it insincere. Antony detested such things but knew it was important. He listened to the comments of those around him and treasured a few moments long afterward.

Sir Ronald approached first, greeted Ginny as if she were the daughter of the Supreme Executor and said with complete honesty, "Ginny, I'm honored to meet you. You're even more charming than Rodger described. I'm sorry I won't be able to join you for your ceremony. My granddaughter will join her prospective mate in ten days and we have so many things to prepare."

He pointed to Antony's brace. "It seems you and I have something in common. I'm proud of your son and I know you are, too. Rodger, I shall miss you terribly. Please, accept this parting gift, for your mating and for the completion of your studies. Promise me you will not open it until you get home." He handed Rodger a sealed parcel.

"Thank you, Sir, for everything."

"It's I who should thank you," Sir Ronald replied and turned to leave.

A large young roach wearing a Board Medal came up to them. "Excuse me, Master Antony, I am Sir Reginald, the younger. My father would have greeted you himself but he is very ill. He won't be able to travel for Rodger's ceremony. He said to tell you an ant mating ceremony was something he always wanted to see."

"Then you and your mate and family should come in his place and tell him about it."

"Thank you, we will."

Antony knew Robert would not approach them, so he went to the young male's group and offered his greetings, tipping his antennae graciously. "Robert, I'm pleased to meet you. I've been told you have many talents. I hope you choose a good path in this world. It would be a tragedy if you chose foolishly and followed the way of another." Antony searched the speechless young roach's eyes. "I see we understand each other. Some things are best left behind. Good luck to you." With that, he left.

*   *   *   *

When they returned to New South Dairy 50, Rodger sought out the privacy of his sleep chamber and opened the packet from Sir Ronald. Inside, he found several sizable credit exchange notes and a letter:

"To my grandson, Rodger,

"Yes, you are, could only be, hers. I had two daughters, Ronda's mother and Geree'. While you were correct in saying that Geree' and George are common names, there was only one at that time with a 'lucky band', my daughter. I knew you had to be hers from the day you told me about yourself, but you didn't want to know and I respected that.

"I am telling you now so that you will understand why I could not take her back. It may not matter to you, but it does to me, and someday your young may want to know. I had a good mating contract arranged for Geree' when she ran off with George, so I was very angry. It wasn't so much that George was a warrior, but that he was one of Rex's renegades. That was why I told her she could not come home. When Rex fell from power, everyone associated with him in any way had to prove absolute loyalty to the legitimate Board. The day she came back, half starved, pleading, carrying your egg, accepting her would have meant all of us being banished. I had no more choice than you did the day you removed the mandibles from that female nymph. Now, I think it's better that it happened that way. You would not be the wonderful, caring, compassionate creature you are if you had grown up here.

"I am the one who paid your training fees the second and third season cycles. If you want to call that guilt, you may, but I prefer to think of it as an investment in a better future. The enclosed gift is for some piece of equipment I'm sure your clinic needs.

"Although I will treasure every moment I had with you, I will not continue our relationship. You have your family and that is as it should be. Ronda will read a letter like this upon my death, at which time your portion of my assets will be placed in a fund to provide training for those who cannot afford it. I think that will please you most.

"Like your father, you are an instrument of change, and I am, most humbly, your grandfather, Sir Ronald."

Rodger read it through twice and then handed it to his father. "Order the internal imager. I'm going out to meditate for a while."

20.

*A*ntony's mind was full as he gathered the grassfrond seeds. In two more days the harvest would be complete and the day after that, the colony would celebrate Rodger's and Ginny's mating. It pleased him that Rodger had asked if the ceremony and celebration could take place outside in the yard near Antony's old home. The more he thought about it, the happier he was that this celebration of a cherishing commitment to life would take place there.

He looked up at the tall, golden grassfrond and recalled the first time he had climbed one and jumped. He turned and swung the tool, stepping back as the grassfrond toppled and fell, and then walked over to gather the seed. Others would pick up the stem later.

A voice in Roach came from behind. "Excuse me, Master Antony, I brought your lunch and a flask of water."

He turned. "Thank you, Gerry."

Gerry hesitated. "You're ... welcome," he said in poorly pronounced Ant. Before Antony could reply, Gerry turned and went back to Rex. Those were the first words Gerry had ever said in Ant. Out of habit, Antony listened to their conversation. Was it his imagination, or was Rex talking louder than usual?

"Did you ask him?" Rex asked.

"No, I got scared." Gerry untwisted the hemp lines that tied his back four pods to each other, crossed his back legs and sat down.

"Speak up. I don't hear as well as I used to. Scared of what?"

"That he'd say, 'no'. That he's still angry and hurt because of my words that day. I won't be forgiven, Rex. I didn't stand there like Renae', you know. At the time, I actually enjoyed it, and when I confessed, I wanted my words to hurt. Now I feel differently."

"You're such an idiot. In twenty-four season cycles you haven't learned a thing." Rex mocked him. "I feel differently," he laughed. "You've gone soft and turned into one of them and you don't even know it. Don't you realize he's waiting for you to say something? Don't keep telling me about it. How many times has he asked if you wanted to talk, or if there was anything you needed before he locked us in for the night?"

"I don't know. A lot, I guess."

"You've lived four and a half decades. How much more time are you going to waste?"

"What about you?"

"Forget about me. Ask him tonight, or I won't talk to you again."

That evening, Antony hesitated a moment as he returned the two of them to their chamber. He wanted to give Gerry the opportunity to ask whatever it was without revealing what he had overheard. Rex went immediately to his mattress and gave Gerry a you-better-do-it-now look before he turned his back.

Gerry stuttered. "Master Antony, could we ... talk ... for a minute?"

Antony nodded, stepped inside the chamber and sat down.

"I've acted pretty ... decent lately, haven't I?"

"Yes, you have."

"I was wondering if ... you wouldn't mind very much if ... I came to Rodger's ceremony like everybody else. I mean ... without these restraints." He tugged at the hemp lines. "I promise, I'll be polite and everything. I've watched other times from a distance. I know what to do."

"How will you feel, standing there in the yard, celebrating life with us?"

Gerry's antennae drooped. "I don't know for sure. I've been feeling mixed up lately. Is it too late for me to start over?"

"It's never too late."

"Then, can I go, and maybe talk to Ginny's sister? That is if she wouldn't mind."

"You may come. I'll be by early that morning and remove your restraints. If you're polite, I'm sure Rayann will talk to you. I have one condition, though. Sir Reginald, the younger, will be here with his mate and nymphs. Stay away and don't look toward them. Out of respect, make it easy for him to ignore you."

"I can do that. Thank you, Master Antony."

Antony switched to Ant, emphasizing the pronunciation of his words, and said, "You're welcome."

       *   *   *   *

It was nearly noon. Antony and Henrietta had rubbed oil onto Rodger's exoskeleton, and he was ready. Any minute, Renae' and Rita would help Rayann carry Ginny's basket.

"We can't put off asking someone any longer. Nearly everyone has offered to help. I know it means a lot to you, and it does to me, too, but you know I can't carry his basket, and if you slipped and fell ..." Henrietta's voice trailed off.

Antony knew she was right. It reminded him of the day he wanted to climb the conifer. Before he could respond, there was a light tap on their portal. Antony opened it to find Gerry standing there.

Gerry stooped low and spoke in Ant. "Master Antony, I came. I help carry Rodger's basket." He gave up on the Ant. "It's what I'm supposed to do, isn't it? The things you long to do and can't do for yourselves. You and Master Henrietta can stand on either side of me. It will look like you are carrying him, but I'll hold his weight. After Rodger climbs out, I'll stand aside and go in last, away from Sir Reginald."

Antony and Henrietta looked at each other, amazed. "Thank you, Gerry," Henrietta finally managed.

"You're welcome," said Gerry in Ant, pronouncing it correctly.

       *   *   *   *

Antony looked at his son, standing with Ginny as everyone moved into place. He turned to Henrietta and looked into her eyes, took her pods in his and whispered, "You are still my Queen."

"And you're still my Sun Spirit," she whispered back. "Maybe you should explain things to Sir Reginald."

Antony leaned toward Sir Reginald and whispered a brief explanation of the four parts of an ant mating ceremony.

Rodger spoke in Roach because he cherished Ginny. "When I was young, my father taught me that the best berries aren't always the easiest ones to reach. Sometimes the sweetest ones are among the briars. Later, another taught me a similar lesson about where to look for someone to share my life. I come to you now to give you myself and begin to fulfill our promise because you are the sweetest of all." He handed her a bright red berry.

Ginny handed him the delicate blossom from a thorn bush and spoke in Ant. Antony could not begin to count the number of times she had asked to practice with him because she wanted to say it perfectly. "All my life I knew thorns and wondered where the blossoms were. Then I ran into you and found a bud. I come to you now to give you myself and begin to fulfill our promise because you are the blossom in my life."

A few minutes later, Sir Reginald whispered, "What do I do with the seed?"

"I'm sorry," Antony said. "I forgot to tell you. Break it and share it with your mate and nymphs as a symbol of your care for each other."

Sir Reginald, unsure of himself, fumbled and the seed flew from his pods.

"It's all right," Antony reassured him, breaking his and Henrietta's into smaller pieces and passing them around. At the back of the assembly, he saw Axel move over toward Gerry and offer him a seed. Gerry accepted it.

After their mating dance, Rodger drew Rayann into the slow, swaying music. When the next pause came, she approached Gerry.

"I've never done this before," he said.

"Neither have I."

Rodger and Ginny also drew in Sir Reginald and his mate. "Don't worry about what to do. Relax and enjoy it," Rodger told them.

By the time the procession formed to carry Ginny and Rodger to their newly excavated domicile next to the expanded clinic, Sir Reginald was completely at ease and joined in the laughter. Once again, Gerry helped carry the basket.

"I really had a good time today, Master Antony," Gerry said as he helped put away the last of the banquet surfaces.

"Maybe you should have a good time more often."

"It felt good not to be in restraints. I don't suppose we could leave them off?"

"I appreciated your help today, because it was offered without my asking. I think we can do without the hemp lines from now on."

*   *   *   *

During the next half a time frame, Antony noticed that Rex spent more and more time resting, and Gerry took over the work assigned to him. Rex moved slowly, often leaning on Gerry. Antony asked Rex if he was ill.

Rex snapped, "I'm fine. I'm old and tired."

At the end of the following workday, Gerry ran to Antony. "Master Antony, come quickly! Rex can't get up and he's having trouble breathing. I think he's really sick."

Two dairiers arrived. Rex lay in the shade of a wood plant near the wild berry patch. Antony turned him over and raised his head and thorax.

"Gerry, go tell my son he has another patient."

"No," said Rex. "I don't want anything. Leave me here."

At Antony's nod, the other ants picked him up.

Antony waited while Rodger examined Rex. An h-unit passed before Rodger came out and spoke to his father. "He's suffering from disintegrating breathing organs."

"Can you treat it?"

"A season cycle ago, yes, but not now. This disease affects both ants and roaches in their advanced years. Creatures with it can live quite long, with the proper herbs, if it's diagnosed early. But eventually it's fatal. He's been hiding this a long time, and is at the end of the final stage. To be honest, I doubt he'll make it to morning. I can give him something to ease his suffering, but that's about all. He insists he won't take anything and keeps saying something about 'the natural end.'"

Antony sighed. "I guess I'll ask him if he has any final requests."

The two of them returned to the examination chamber. Rex looked at Antony. "The natural end of my life, Master Antony. If I had no right to shorten it, what right have you to prolong my misery? In all these season cycles, I only asked you for two things, a lamp and someone to talk to. Now I'm asking you for one thing more; let me die with dignity. Please, remove my restraints and let me crawl off somewhere and be food for fly larvae."

"That's not dignity."

"Neither is this underground chamber, not for me."

"Then I'll still give you a lamp and someone to talk to, and I'll make sure you're decently covered." He removed the hemp cords from Rex's pods.

"Rodger, I'll explain later. Bring me a basket, two coverlets, supplies for a fire, a pot for tea, some bread and seeds, and my pain herbs. Find Captain Alexander and ask him to help me. I'm taking Rex out into the meadow somewhere and I'll stay with him alone. Tell your mum not to worry. Tell Gerry it's all right, and tell the guards there's no need to lock Gerry's chamber any more."

He turned back to Rex. "I'm doing this for one reason. I appreciate what you told Gerry before Rodger's mating, even if this was your motive."

"Do you always have to listen to other creatures' conversations?"

"Do you always speak so loudly a creature can't help but overhear?"

*   *   *   *

Antony stirred the fire, put on the pot of tea, and nibbled a seed. When the tea was ready, he poured two mugs, put his pain herbs in one and drank it. He propped Rex up against the wood plant near them and handed him the other mug. "It's only tea. No sense being totally miserable."

"Do you always use so much pain potion?"

"Only when there's going to be sky water."

Rex took the mug and sipped. "You know, I only wanted you dead and her for our side. That stupid Raul. I never intended that. The truth is, I admired your father's courage. I should have hired better trained warriors."

"If they'd had better training, they wouldn't have been working for you."

"That's true enough."

"Any other regrets?"

"I regret I got caught. I should have taken care of Master Gerald personally much sooner, and I should never have sent Renae' and Gerry as a peace offering. Oh, well," he laughed weakly. "You were the least of my crimes. Do you want to know the first one? Right after I got myself appointed to The Board, I hatched that plot to get those ant engineers to do that tunnel into my main plastic mine. I got rid of my father and took control of everything. Master Henrietta's father was one of them. Did he ever tell you about that?"

"Yes."

"He never saw me or knew my name, but I watched him almost every day. He was some engineer. I was angry because they didn't bring tunnel liquid. That's what I really wanted. When I first realized that Master Henrietta was his daughter, I thought, 'Gifted father, gifted young.' That was part of why I wanted her—revenge for his escape."

Rex sipped more tea and rested. "I had the evidence against Sir Rodger planted, too. Another mistake. It wasn't enough to send him to the mantis compound. Then he had to find you." He went on to tell many other plots. Most of the names Antony didn't recognize, but he listened and did not judge.

"I did a lot of thinking during that time frame you left me in the dark. I decided your punishment was just. That's why I signed your parchment and why I never asked for anything else, until tonight." He laughed and coughed. "That piece of fly bait, Sir Rodger! He was right. Everything does come back to us. I had creatures killed, and I died a thousand deaths in that dark chamber. I dreamed of every one of them. I stole from others and everything was taken from me. I enslaved those ants and ended up working half my life for you. I never wanted to change. I tried to stop it in every way, but change happened in spite of me, rolled over me. It's time I got out of the way."

"What do you want me to put on your marker?"

"No marker, please. I couldn't stand the thought of a bunch of creatures standing around saying, 'Here's where that old renegade feeds the earth.' Master Antony, let my covering place be unknown."

"I'll make a deal with you. I have to send an official communication concerning your death. If you will let me quote what you said a moment ago concerning change, I promise no one but me will know where you are covered, and I'll make a point to forget it."

"Do you always have to win?"

"Do you always have to make things win or lose?"

Rex was too weak to argue. "All right. I agree to it."

The night grew colder and more damp. Antony wrapped the coverlet more tightly around Rex, added fuel to the fire, and wrapped himself. His joint ached in spite of the herbs. He knew sky water would be falling before morning. Rex began wheezing. Antony tried to make him more comfortable. Rex's eyes expressed gratitude and he accepted more tea.

"I've always been curious about one thing," Rex rasped. "The first day I saw you, you were nervous. You were afraid of Master Diandra, weren't you? What power did she have over you? It had to do with Master Henrietta, didn't it? I know, because in the beginning you looked at Master Diandra with fear, at Master Henrietta with sadness, and she looked at you with anger. Satisfy my curiosity before I leave this world. What fate worse than death did she hold over you?"

"You know better than to get personal."

"I'll be dead soon. What harm can it do?"

Antony was surprised at how much Rex had figured out on his own. He knew more about ant ways than he had ever indicated. It didn't matter any more. Why not tell him?

"I plagiarized Henrietta's archaeology report. Master Diandra held my contract. I faced permanent underground work in North Carpenter 5. When I had changed and everyone I had offended had forgiven me, I was released from it."

"Now it all makes sense. Will I ... ever be ... forgiven?"

"I can't speak for others, but I forgave you a long time ago. Your problem has always been with yourself."

Rex did not reply. Antony supported the old renegade, stroked his antennae and lifted up his thoughts silently. "This is the comfort I could not give you, Sir Rodger. Was this your illness, too? Receive the gift of my comfort now, through him."

Rex relaxed. His eyes had never expressed sorrow before.

"I must be insane," Antony said. "But there is a part of me that will actually miss you, you miserable, deceitful, selfish old roach."

Rex twitched one antenna and was gone. Antony left the circle of fire light, went several paces in no particular direction, dug a hollow, and dragged Rex into it. "Sorry to be so rough, but it's the best I can do. It's what you wanted."

He pressed the earth over Rex's body and scattered some grass from nearby on top. He thought about planting some grassfrond seeds, but there were no others in the area. They would stand as a marker and he had promised not to leave one. Without making any note of the place, he returned to the wood plant, loaded the basket, and covered the fire. The nearly empty basket was light enough for him to carry without tripping.

He headed home to the comfort of Henrietta's pods and thought of all the good that had grown from the tragedy of South Dairy Colony 50. If he grieved at all, it was because Rex had been too stubborn to admit that even he had begun to change.

Epilogue:
Henry Roach-Dairier

*T*he wind rustling through the boughs of the wood plants in the glen was the only sound when my grandfather finished telling me the story of his life. The glen—that place where he'd learned to speak Roach from Old Rodger and covered him; the same place he and my grandmother had found Geree' and carried home her egg—my father; the place I had used as an escape from my responsibilities. My brain was as stubborn to absorb the lesson as my exoskeleton was to molt.

I wanted to die. My muscles pressed outward painfully in every part of my body, yet I was unable to thrash my way free. "Please, Grandfather, I need more herbs for the pain."

"I'm sorry, Henry. You've used them all. I thought it would be over by now, so I gave you the last of them this morning."

"What's that you've got?"

"It's a different potion your father insists I take every day. He knows his job, so I do what he says."

"Then talk to me some more. It gives me something else to think about."

"Your father's mating and Rex's death had a great impact on Gerry. He started spending all his evenings with Rayann and her nymph. A few time frames later, they made a promise to mate for companionship. He told me he wanted to care for her and her nymph to make up for two females he had taken and deserted in the shanties long before. He was probably old enough to be her father, but she didn't mind. The night before their ceremony, I took him down to the yard. We stood beside my family's marker and consumed his contract."

My grandfather talked about how all of his grandnymphs hatched. First David, then Arthur, Dorothy, Drew, and finally me. I was hoping he would tell me more about my grandmother but he didn't. I suppose it was still too painful for him to talk about. All I knew was that she died of an infection that swept through the colony around the time I hatched. She did not respond to the mold treatment my father used to save everyone else. Grandfather lived with us after that and turned their domicile over to other archaeologists who carried on her work.

All the time he talked, he stroked me. He had always comforted me like no one else could. Only long afterward did I realize that he had suffered more pain in his many emotional molts than I ever would physically.

I felt the back of my thorax begin to split and cried out in agony, "Grandfather, get away from me! I don't want to hurt you!"

He scrambled out of my way as I thrashed free of my last youthful exoskeleton. Then I slept.

When I awoke, I found he had covered me. I stretched, feeling marvelous.

"Good morning. You've expanded one and a half f-units. Are you hungry?"

I nodded and accepted the seeds and honeydew he held out. When I finished eating he handed me a piece of parchment and an ink pot.

"What's this?"

"It's your contract with me. After all I told you, did you think you were going to leave here without one?"

"No, I suppose not."

I read it carefully. I had to return to training and never be absent unless my father verified that I was ill. I couldn't enter the clinic or the dispensary unless supervised. I was not to use any word in Roach that didn't have a polite equivalent in Ant. In some way of my own choosing, I had to seek pardon of everyone I had ever offended. I groaned. I had offended about half the colony. If I did all of that and spent my first season cycle of job exploration in New South Dairy 50, I would be able to spend the second in South Harvester 45. If that went well, I would be permitted to spend a season cycle at the training center of my choice in Roacheria at colony expense. If I wanted to stay there longer, I would be expected to make my own way. The contract stated clearly that if I got into trouble there, no one from New South Dairy 50 would be able to defend me. If I broke the contract, I faced banishment underground in North Carpenter 5. I looked at my grandfather, gave him a sarcastic smile, and signed it.

"A good start," he said. "If something happens to me, who do you want to hold this in my place?"

"What do you mean?"

"I've lived over seven decades. I don't take a single day for granted."

I thought for a while and finally said, "My brother, David."

He nodded his approval. "Are you ready to go home?"

"Grandfather, does my father know all of this?" I asked as we started back.

"Not in such detail. You're the first creature I've ever told about that last night with Rex."

"Why don't you write all this down? I think it's important for creatures to know."

"I detest parchment work, but if you think it might help even one other creature, I give you permission to write it down for me, but not until I've left this world."

*   *   *   *

I won't say I was perfect after that, but I never did anything serious enough to violate my contract. Three season cycles later we consumed it and I left for Roacheria. Unlike my father and brothers, who had hated every minute they spent there in training, I liked living there. I stayed, taking a job at the training center. It offered little credit by their standards, but I knew how to live simply.

In the middle of trying to explain the difference between needs and wants to a group one day, one of the clerks came in. "Excuse me, Trainer Henry, but your brother, David, is in the central work chamber. He says he must see you immediately. I'll stay with your group."

David didn't give me a chance to greet him. "You've got to come home. Grandfather is dying and he's asking for you."

The facility director was standing near by. "Henry, go on. Someone will dismiss your group. Take all the time you need."

We scurried down the trail. I asked David, "What's wrong with him?"

"The same thing he's been fighting for the last six season cycles, disintegrating breathing organs, not that you'd have noticed."

"David, that's not fair. I know I used to be an inconsiderate louse, but I'm not that way any more."

"Sure. That's why you stay there and don't even bother to write."

There wasn't any point in continuing the conversation. I hadn't written in several time frames.

I don't know why, but I was nervous as I entered my grandfather's sleep chamber. When I had left, he didn't look old, even though he was. Now, he looked ancient.

"Henry," he rasped. "I knew you'd come."

I embraced him, choking back tears. I should have been stroking him. Instead, I found once more that special comfort only he could give.

"Grandfather, I've found my life's work."

"Oh?"

"I'm working as a trainer, teaching Ant language and culture, and something more. Two time frames ago, I was accidentally assaulted by a nymph about to molt. I convinced the director to allow me to write a contract instead of having him sent to the mantis compound."

A spark came into my grandfather's eyes.

"Your father keeps asking me what I want on my marker. I told him you knew. How's your memory?"

"Excellent."

"When Henrietta was sick, we spent some precious moments together. As usual, she ended up comforting me. She told me she never regretted one moment of our life together. She was at peace because she had done what she set out to do and there were others to carry on her work. She told me there must be something left I was meant to do, and she'd be waiting for me when I finished it. Now, I know I'm finished, so I won't keep her waiting any longer."

After we covered him, I turned to my father and offered him a seed. "I know I haven't always been the most considerate creature in the world, but I know what I'm doing now. I promise I'll come back and visit more often, and I'll write more. If I ever find a female I want to share my life with, we'll come back here for a proper ceremony. Right now, I need time and privacy to write down everything he told me during my final molt. When I'm finished, please see that it's published. I'm going back to Roacheria to take what he taught me beyond the limits of New South Dairy 50. Grandfather's marker should say, 'Change is a choice.'"

Looking Ahead:

The Re-Creation of Roacheria, the final book of the trilogy, tells Henry's own story. The adult Henry is an enigma. Most members of New South Dairy 50 consider him too roach-like, even after he grows beyond the high jinx of his youth. Influential roaches consider his ways of Antism, and the fact that he is of mixed variety, dangerous to their power structure. Hatreds dating back to the days of Henry's great-grandfather rise again in an attempt to destroy him and the experimental community he attempts to build in order to carry on Antony's mission.

ISBN 0-9753410-3-0

Time Line of Major Events

SEASON CYCLE

Roach (O.R.)	Combined Colonies f Insectia (C.C.I.)	
1		Enslavement of border colonies by Roacheria
33	1	Beginning of the Combined Colonies, violent conflict to free enslaved colonies
177	144	Rex Hatches in Roacheria
198	165	Death of South Dairy 50; Antony Dairier hatches
201	168	Rex enslaves Henry, Howard and Herbert
212	179	Antony emerges from pupation as an adult
213	180	Sir Rodger banished from Roacheria
219	186	Beginning of Ant/Roach Archeological project, Henrietta's mentorship, Murder of Antony's family, Violent conflict with Roacheria
221	188	Peace with Roacheria, Henrietta and Antony mate
222	189	Establishment of New South Dairy 50
245	212	Death of Rex
257	224	Death or Henrietta, hatching of Henry Roach-Dairier
275	242	Death of Anthony
279	246	Henry establishes Meadow Commonwealth

Genealogy Charts
The Ant Families

Gen.1 Howard

Gen. 2   David/Dorothy   **Henry/Adeline**   Herbert/Corina   Cort

Gen.3 Arthur, **Antony**,   **Henrietta,** Hilda, Annie   Corin   Art/Allie
    Drew, Arlene, Allen,   Andrew

Gen 4. **Rodger** /Genny Roach (sister of Rayanne)   Corina/Al
    (adopted by Antony and Henrietta)

Gen.5 David, Dorothy, Arthur, Drew,
        Henry/Regina   Adeline-**Dell**/Donald

Gen. 6   Gabrielle and sibblings

The Roach Families

Gen. 1 **Sir Rudy**/mate (brothers) Sir Royal/mate
           (numerous descendents not specifically mentioned)
Gen.2 **SirRex**, Rolinda   **Gabriel**/mate (brothers)   Griffin/mate
        Regina/mate
Gen. 3   Rudy/mate   Gabrielle-Genette, Rochelle-Riley   Gallo

Gen.4.   **Robert/**   Rebecca   Richard/Ginger
        (not aware of her relationship to Rochelle)
Gen. 5 **Regina**-mate of **Henry Roach-Dairier**   Ruth (mate of **Rundell)**
                          Gallo, Griffen

Gen. 6   Gabrielle

Gen. 1 **Sir Rodger**

Gen.   4 daughters of Sir Rodger, youngest mates Sir reginald
         Sir Reginald   Mater Roland/Ralyn   Sir Ronald/mate

Gen. 3 Sir Reginald   three sons,   daughter, **Geree'/George**
       (the Younger)   late life son, **Rick/Genelle   Rodger/Ginny**
Gen. 4 various descendants
        not specifically mentioned

Gen. 5   Ray/Ramona   **Henry Roach-Dairier**
                                                    And sibblings

Other Characters
not necessarily related to each other
included so the reader may relate to approximate age of contemporaries

Gen. 1   **Master Gerard**/mate   **Sir Rolo/Rachael**

Gen. 2.   **Master/Sir Raphael**   son   **Master Diandra**

Gen. 3   **Renee**/ Rita   **Gerry**/ Rayanne Gen.4 (Ginny's sister)

Gen. 4 3 nymphs   **Sir Reese**   son   Master Riedel   Trainer Renard

Gen 5.   **Reese** (book 3)   **Gatlin**   **Rusty**

Printed in the United States
116581LV00002B/136/A